In A Young LifeTime

A Story Based In N. Charleston

Stacey D. Gibbs

For the tragedy of life is not death but
what dies in a man while he is still alive

Acknowledgements

Dreams do come true. It's so many people I want to thank for the progress of this project and I don't even know where to start. But first I would like to thank my mother Joyce Williams, the only one who was driving from SC to VA to come visit me while I was incarcerated. I love you and just give me a little time and I promise you I'm going to get you that house. To my brothers and sister Junnie, Sharika, and Shawn, love y'all and to my brother Kemone you my motivation just please don't stop, keep on succeeding, just know that I'm on you. To all the real stand up brothers in the penal system I'm representing for y'all (only the real stand up brothers). To my dude Shook, I got you fam just a lil busy, this taking a little longer than I thought but that's my word I got you, just do that time and keep allowing your mind to elevate. They can't take that away from you. To all my cousins I can't name all y'all but Danny, D, C.J., E.J., Andre, Karseam, Melanie, Josh and Tony(r.i.p.) just to name a few I love all y'all, all I'm trying to do is lay the foundation so we all can build. To both of my grandmothers Grennie Mitchell and Mary Brown I'm so bless to have the both of y'all still with me love y'all. Evonne, Suzie, Tasha, Debbie, Pearl, Lillian, Rosa and all my family in Sheldon, SC all the way to New York love all y'all. To all my dudes at Greensville Correction who I bothered day in and out to read my book, I appreciate y'all. To my second home town North Charleston, SC thanks for the inspiration. To my hometown Beaufort "I Will Not Lose" my second novel is which takes place in Bft is coming soon. And to everybody else out there who got at me on facebook, Instagram, in the grocery store, at gas station and everywhere else you saw me and kept asking about my book I appreciate all y'all. This book is not to glamorize selling drugs or all the derogatory things that happens in the urban communities all over the world, I'm just telling my story to my people who I feel can relate and hopefully we all can learn something and take a different course in life. PEACE.

Ch A p t e r 1

North Charleston, South Carolina 1982

J ennifer walked around in a trance. She couldn't believe that the man she made plans to be with for the rest of her life just walked out on her like it was nothing. The news spread through North Charleston that Damien denied her baby. She'd been trying to get in contact with him but Damien's mother Mrs. Scott always told her that he was at work or out with his friends. Later on she learned that he moved to Maryland with his aunt. As she sat in the bed with her face buried in her hands, tears started to fall down her face as she visualized her, perfectly planned future crumbling down. Her thoughts were interrupted when she heard the cry of her baby. She quickly ran over to his crib to pick him up and gently rocked him in her arms. The mutual love she had for her child was developed through the nine month bonding process she spent carrying him. But every time she looked at the child she was reminded of the day she got raped. As she held her baby, she looked into his eyes and saw pure innocence. There was no reason that this beautiful child should suffer. She continued to gaze in his eyes. He looked more and more like a dark skin version of her baby pictures. He was so clean and smelled so fresh and was so cute. As these thoughts came to her she suddenly pictured Jim Beans, "Why did he have to rape," she managed to say out loud. She remembered when she first met Jim Beans when she was in the second grade. Even when they were younger he had a reputation for fighting. She then recalled when she was in the fourth grade a boy by the name of Ricky Taylor who along with

1

Jim Beans was in her class, came up behind her and took her ice cream cone off the tray.

"Gimme my ice cream back Ricky!"

"Alright give me a cup and about forty-five minutes and I'll have it right up for you."

Then out of nowhere Jim Beans punched Ricky in his face causing him to fall on the floor. She remembered how Jim Beans always tried to get her to go out with him. The first time he built up enough confidence to ask her out was when they were in the sixth grade. The Average White Band had a song called "Play That Funky Music White Boy" which had everybody in the party dancing. Damien was the new student and Jennifer wanted to get his attention badly. Up until this point she hadn't had an interest in any boy besides Jackie Jackson from the Jackson 5. As she stood next to the table watching everybody have the time of their life her thought chamber was interrupted, "Hey Jennifer," the young Jim Beans said.

"Oh hey Jimmy," Jennifer glanced at him then looked back at Damien trying not to lose him in the crowd.

"You sound like one of my teachers. In case you ain't heard I go by Jim Beans now."

"Yeah that's right. I keep forgetting."

"So how come you came to the dance by yourself."

Because I wanted to," was the answer she gave him but the truth was because Damien didn't ask her.

"Well I didn't come with nobody because the person I wanted to come with I didn't ask her."

"Why not," she said with her attention still in the crowd.

"Case she would of said no."

"You don't know that she could of said yes." Jennifer looked at him then back at the crowd unaware that the girl he was talking about was her.

"So you would of said yeah if I asked you out?"

"Huh!" she said her attention now on him.

"If I would asked you out you would of said yeah?"

The first thing that wanted to come out Jennifer's mouth was "hell no" but she didn't want to hurt his feelings. He wasn't the cutest guy in the world however, he was real generous to her so for that she at least felt like she was obligated to talk to him every once in a while. But while her brain, was searching for an answer she said the first thing that came to her mind.

"I-I don't know," she said uncomfortably hoping he would drop the subject but not knowing indirectly she was leading him on.

Taking what she said the wrong way, "So you wanna dance," he said without thinking.

"I think my mother's on the way to come pick me up but maybe at the next dance."

Jennifer walked over to the closet to get her jacket. She was happy to get away from that conversation. While Jim Beans walked away counting down the days to the next school dance.

"Jennifer," Mrs. Willis said in a calm tone trying not to disturb her from feeding the baby.

"Yes."

"Did you check the temperature of that milk before giving it to that baby like I showed you."

"Yes Mama, what you think that I'll intentionally cause my baby harm."

Mrs. Willis studied her daughter for a moment then sat down in the chair across from her.

"Before you even ask Mama, yes I'm still going to college."

"How are you going to college right now when you have a new born baby."

"I'll manage. Didn't you manage when daddy died and you had to take care of me and Tereesa by yourself."

"Me and Louis were already established, having our home and a car and I already had a job. You mean to tell me you're going all the way to California with no house, no job and on top of that you're going by yourself."

"Well I was going to ask would you mine looking after Rasheid until I get situated."

Mrs. Willis looked at her daughter then exited the room. A couple of minutes later she returned with an envelope in her hand and gave it to Jennifer.

"What's this?" Jennifer positioned the baby face down across her knees and opened the envelope.

"Some money I saved up for you to go to college."

"Seven thousand dollars!" she looked at the check in disbelief.

"Yeah I got seven for your sister too whenever she decide to get her act right."

"Mama, where you get all this from."

"Saving it through the years. Plus your daddy insurance helped out a lot too."

"Thank you Mama," a tear formed in Jennifer eye. She was happy to know that her mother still supported her.

"You know education is a must in this house." Mrs. Willis bent over to kiss her on her forehead like she did when she was younger. She wanted to ask about the baby's father but decided against it. She looked down at her baby and wondered if she would ever come close to being the type of mother to her child as her mother is to her and her sister. Then Damien flashed in her mind. This was supposed to be their baby she was holding. His name was supposed to be Rasheid Scott not Rasheid Willis. It could have been Damien Seth Scott Jr. "I am not supposed to be the mother of Jim Beans child!" she said as the tears fell from her face. "Oh my God what am I going to do!" she buried her hands in her face.

***

Mrs. Willis gently closed the door being careful that her daughter didn't hear the latch close. She overheard everything that her daughter had just said to herself then went into deep thought.

"Jim Beans. I heard that name before," she said to herself before she entered her bedroom and made a phone call. "Hey Ida."

"Hey Gertrude, what you doing?" "Ain't nothing is James Jr. home?"

"Yeah he's right here why?"

"Ask him do he know a Jim Beans?"

"James do you know a Jim Beans," the woman yelled out. "He said the only Jim Beans he knows live in Liberty Hill... What you say? He said he's the one who got shot and is in the wheel chair for trying to break into that drug dealing boy house from Dorchester... what's his name? His name is Jason."

"The same Jason Tereesa messing with," Mrs. Willis said to herself.

"Why, everything alright," Ida asked concern.

"I'm going to talk to you later okay?" Mrs. Willis said.

"Alright then talk to you later."

As the weeks went by, Jennifer tried to come to a conclusion of what was going on in her life. She watched everything that mattered to her the most fall apart in just the matter of months. Her boyfriend who she was supposed to be married to and have children with, was nowhere to be found. She came to the conclusion that the child she's grown to love is the child she doesn't want. The more she looks at her baby the more she realizes she wouldn't fit the standards of being a good mother to him. All because she was raped by Jim Beans. He didn't know she had his child and she hoped it stayed like that. She stood over his baby cradle and stared at him as he slept. She knew that he didn't deserve this and felt guilty for bringing him into this world. He's never going to have a father and she'll never be able to be the mother to him that he deserves. She just hoped that God protects her baby and that he doesn't grow up to be anything like Jim Beans. "Please Lord watch over my son," she said in softly.

"I see it didn't take you long to get ready," Mrs. Willis indicated how fast her daughter got packed.

"Yeah I guess this is it huh," Jennifer looked down at the luaguage. "The start of a new life."

"I wish Tereesa was here to see this."

"Don't worry Mama, Tereesa is going to come around. But tell her I said I love her and I love you too Mama," she gave her mother a big hug.

"You know baby, no matter how old you get I'm going to always be your mother and you can come and talk to me about anything. I mean anything and don't you ever forget it," Mrs. Willis emphasized as she hugged her daughter back. "How long is the plane ride going to be again?"

"I think it's like twelve hours or something," she looked around her mother's house as if she was trying to memorize everything the way it was.

"That's a long way from here to California. You sure you don't want me to take you to the airport. I could put something warm on the baby real quick and drop you off. This way you wouldn't have to worry about cab fare."

"It's alright Mama. I'll be okay but thanks anyway," she looked at her mother knowing that it would be a while before they see each other again. "Just make sure you take care of my little man."

"You forgot that I'm the one who took care of you."

"Okay," Jennifer walked over and gently kissed the sleeping child on his cheek. They both looked at the window as they heard a car horn blow. "That's my cab."

"I'll get the door," Mrs. Willis walked towards the door.

"I love you Rasheid," Jennifer whispered into her child's ear when her mother left the room. She kissed him once more on his cheek and rubbed his hair softly. "Be a good boy for me and always remember Mommy loves you," she said as a tear involuntary came down her cheek.

"Make sure you get my baby there safely because she has a long trip to California," Mrs. Willis said to the taxi driver as he took her suitcases to the trunk of his cab.

"Take care Mama, see you in a few months," she hugged her mother one last time.

"You take care to baby. Rasheid's going to be just fine. You just go and get yourself straightened out and maybe me and the baby will fly out there once you get your apartment," she hugged her then lead her into the back seat of the cab. Although she didn't know this would be the last time she would see her daughter, something indeed felt strange about her departure.

"Bye-bye Mama," Jennifer took the seat in the back of the cab.

"Bye," Mrs. Willis waved to her daughter. She pressed the issue all of her daughter's life how important it was for them to go to college. Now that the time has finally come it actually hurt her to watch her baby girl leave the house. After watching the taxi drive off, she went back into the house and thought about how fast the years went by. Now all she had to do is get Tereesa on the right track then she could really take a load off. Mrs. Willis checked on Rasheid and saw that the he was still asleep, and then decided that she'll eat a fruit salad for dinner since there's nobody in the house to cook for.

Jennifer sat in the backseat of the cab and tried not to cry. Her mother had done such a good job raising her, and providing for her and her sister a warm bed to sleep every night. Neither she nor her sister ever went to bed hungry. They weren't rich but they had everything they needed. And after everything her mother done for her she just told her a lie about going to California. What will her baby think of her when he gets old enough to understand what happened. Will her mother forgive her after she realizes what she done? Even worse, what if something was to happen to her baby, "Oh God," she couldn't help the outburst.

"You alright ma'am," the cab driver looked in the rearview mirror then back at the highway.

"I'm just excited," she uttered with her hand on her forehead.

"I imagine you would be. Going off to college and all."

Jennifer wasn't interested in the small talk. She then massaged her temple as a conversation her and Jim Beans had at their last school dance popped into her mind. It was their last conversation before he raped her.

"Mama went over to Ms. Ida's to play bingo... wanna finish this at my house," Jennifer said as she kissed Damien again.

"Where your sister?" Damien asked.

"With her boyfriend. We'll have the house to ourselves."

"So why are we still sitting here," he jumped up to get their jackets.

Jim Beans swallowed long and hard as he passed the bottle back to his friend, "That's it right there Ronny."

"Hey Beans," a short light skinned girl said who had a reputation for not being the hardest girl to have sex with.

Jim Beans looked down at her then his attention went back into the crowd.

"Hey Rhonda."

"I thought you said you were coming to Macon last week?" she looked at his chocolate skin from his neck down to his masculine arms. She wanted to suck on him right there in the middle of the party.

"I think my Mama had something for me to do that day," he reached for his drink. Then he spotted Jennifer in the crowd with Damien nowhere in sight. He put his drink down and headed in her direction, leaving the girl standing alone.

"What's going on Jennifer?" he asked.

She rolled her eyes at his approach, "Hey Jim Beans."

"I saw you and Damien together."

"He's still here," she looked around the party.

"So you thought about what I told you."

"Have you been drinking!" she frowned at him.

"Never mind that," he held his hand up to her. "Just know that I'm still here and my feelings for you is real. And if you give me a chance I' ll treat you like you deserve to be treated," he tried to convince her.

Jennifer looked at him for a moment then burst out into laughter.

"What's so funny?" Damien walked up behind Jim Beans.

"Nothing" she continued to smile as she reached out for Damien's hand. "Yeah nothing," Jim Beans added. "Ain't a motherfucking thing funny," he walked off as he gave Jennifer a look that could kill.

She quickly lost her smile as she saw how serious he looked.

"What the hell is going on?" Damien looked puzzled.

"He don't mean no harm," she looked on as Jim Beans disappeared in the crowd. " He just had a crush on me since we were younger and I think I just hurt his feelings."

"Well you need to let him know I'm your man and I ain't going nowhere."

"That'll be four dollars and thirty-two cents," the cab driver said as he put the car in park and pressed the button on the meter.

"Oh," Jennifer snapped back to reality. "You got here kind of quick didn't you," she handed the driver the five dollar bill. "Keep the change."

"Thank you. You need some help with your luaguage."

"No thanks. I'll manage."

"Well you have a safe trip to California," the driver opened the trunk and put the suitcases on the ground for her.

"Thank you," she looked up at the airport. Her dream was to go to UCLA. But Hampton University doesn't sound too bad. She grabbed her bags and entered the airport. "Hopefully I'll have a better life in Virginia."

ChApter 2

~~~~~~

Mrs. Willis jumped out of bed traumatized as the sound of the doorbell echoed throughout the house. She looked at the clock that read 2:42 a.m. "Who could this be this time of the morning," she put on her robe and slippers. "Hold on a minute. I'm comin!" she looked in Rasheid's crib and saw that he was undisturbed then went downstairs to answer the door. Mrs. Willis turned on the porch light, looked through the peep hole and when she saw who was on the other side of the door she quickly opened the door.

"Hey Mama," her oldest daughter Tereesa stood in the doorway.

Mrs. Willis looked her oldest child up and down as if she was a total stranger.

"Girl where the hell you been!" she noticed the weight lost since the last time they saw each other.

"I found a job Mama. I've been working twelve hour shifts," she said as if her mother was supposed to be proud of her.

"You found a job where?"

"At this motor company in West Ashley," Tereesa held her hand on her waist as if she was talking to one of her girlfriends. "So are you going to let me in or am I unwelcomed," Mrs. Willis stepped to the side as her daughter walked in the house. She never took her eyes off her as she closed and locked the door.

"So you heard from Jennifer yet?" Tereesa picked up a picture of Jennifer and Damien on graduation night.

"No not yet. And lower your voice, that child's upstairs sleeping."

"I can't believe that punk Damien ditched out on Jennifer like that and denied their baby just because the boy is dark skin," she put the picture down. "Got my little sister looking like a hoe out here in these streets."

"Girl watch your mouth!"

"But Ma, you know that wasn't right. Jennifer use to go to sleep and wake up in the morning talking about Damien. And he just out the blue left her stranded with a baby just because he don't want no extra baggage on him when he got to college and play ball."

"So who is Jim Beans," Tereesa looked at her mother as if she knew something she wasn't supposed to know. Her mind suddenly went back to the night in Allen's apartment when Jason shot Jim Beans and left him lying in a pool of blood.

"He's from Liberty Hill. About the same age as Jennifer. Why you ask?"

"Was Jennifer messing with him?"

"No!" Tereesa said with a frown on her face. "I think he used to like her but Jennifer
never paid that boy no mind."

"Oh really," Mrs. Willis said with no facial expression.

"Why you ask that?" Tereesa wondered how her mother knew Jim Beans.

"No reason. So I haven't seen or heard from you in the past three months and now you just pop up at three in the morning," she quickly changed the subject.

"I came to see if I can borrow ten dollars until Friday. I'm trying to have some lunch money for the week."

"Tereesa, where are you staying?"

"I'm staying with my girlfriend Carmen and she said that she wouldn't charge me rent as long as I help watch her kids when she's at work."

"So what happened to that drug dealing boy you was messing with."

"He wasn't dealing drugs Ma," she lied." And we're not seeing each other no more."

Mrs. Willis gave her daughter a suspicious look then exited the room. She came back with a twenty dollar bill in hand.

"Tereesa, this is your home too and you're welcome back whenever you want," she placed the twenty dollars in her hand.

"Thank you Mama," she put the money in her back pocket.

"So I guess college is out the question."

"No Mama, I'm just not ready to go right now. Anyway let me see my nephew before I leave," she walked up the steps with Mrs. Willis behind her.

"Ahhh… he's getting so big," she was astonished at the sight of her nephew. "How old is he now Mama?"

"Eight months old."

"Eight months old already. It seems like the other day Jennifer was walking around here pregnant." She pulled the blanket down pass his face to get a better look at him. "He is so cute. He looked just like those baby pictures of Jennifer."

"It's her child, how is he supposed to look."

"Well I have to go now," Tereesa didn't want to take her eyes off the baby. She had to admit that she was proud to be an aunt.

"When you coming back," Mrs. Willis followed her daughter downstairs.

"I'll be back Friday to pay your money back," she opened the door and made her way out.

"Just take care of yourself Tereesa," her voice sounded nervous.

"Alright Mama. Thanks," she waved to her mother as she got in on the passenger side of a car which Mrs. Willis didn't see at first. As she got in the car the driver started the ignition and within seconds the car disappeared down the streets. Between wondering why Jennifer was pulling a disappearing act and hoping she doesn't lose Tereesa to the streets, she knew her daughters would send her to her grave early.

"Thank you for calling University of California Los Angeles main office Classification, this is Cindy Porter how can I help you sir or ma'am?"

"Yes my name is Gertrude Willis and I'm the mother of Jennifer Renee Willis who was enrolled in your school approximately three months ago and I was wondering how can I get in contact with her?"

"Yes ma'am, give me one moment to pull her files up to see what dormitory she's enlisted in and I'll just give you the extension to the building."

"Okay, thank you," Mrs. Willis lightly patted Rasheid on his back as she waited for him to burp.

"Wait one moment please….Ms. Willis."

"I'm still here."

"I'm sorry but I don't have a Jennifer Willis. I have a Jennifer Wilson and a Jeanine Willis but Jennifer Willis is not enrolled in this school."

Mrs. Willis looked puzzled. "Are you sure?"

"Yes ma'am I am."

"That's spelled Willis W-I-L-L-I-S."

"Yes ma'am that name is not showing up on my computer."

"Okay," Mrs. Willis still looked puzzled.

"Is there anything else I can help you with?"

"Uhh, no ma'am, thank you," Mrs. Willis paused then hung up the phone. She held the baby in her arms as she stared at a spot on the wall. She slowly put the pieces together in her mind. *Jennifer didn't let anyone know she got raped because she didn't want to face the humiliation but it did more harm and now she has run away from her problem thinking she could just start a new life.* Mrs. Willis looked down at Rasheid as he smiled at her. She smiled back though deep down she really wanted to breakdown. She didn't know where her baby girl was in this world and felt like she had lost Tereesa to the streets. The only thing she could do was leave it in God's hand and not doubt her faith in the Lord. She just prayed that they would come to their senses before it was too late. "Louis always wanted a son," she looked at Rasheid. "I just wish he was here to see his grandson." She put Rasheid in his playpen as he stood up using both of his hands to hold on to the rail continuing to watch her. She knew that he was her full responsibility now so the only thing left for her to do was to turn Rasheid into an intelligent and responsible young man. "Don't worry baby, Grandma got you now," she playfully touched his nose. Rasheid smiled at her as she walked in the kitchen to start dinner. She said a silent prayer for her daughters. She had faith that they both would come back home and she would help them both resolve their issues. She just hoped that it'll be sooner than later.

ChApter 3

12 Years Later

"You know you shocked me when you spelled that word sipa, sepa, how you pronounce it?" Mrs. Willis asked Rasheid as she drove down the interstate.

"Septuagesima," Rasheid corrected her.

"Oh well excuse me," Mrs. Willis said proudly. "Now do you know what it means?"

"It means the third Sunday before lent," Rasheid sat in the passenger seat of his grandmother's Volkswagen in his Sunday's best. "I didn't know it was going to be that many people there. I've never been that nervous in my life."

"But you did so good and I'm proud of you," she rubbed the back of his head with her free hand. "Now the only problem is finding some space for that trophy back there," she said as they both laughed. "So where you want to eat at, Red Lobsters or Old Country Buffet?"

"Old Country Buffet," he smiled as he looked out the window.

"Well Old Country Buffet it is."

"I couldn't believe that I beat out Johnathan for the third time. He was bragging for the last two months on how he was going to win the spelling bee this year and he misspelled pomegranate."

"Listen Rasheid, I don't want you to get caught up in competing with the other kids. Be concern about you," she said seriously. "As long as you do your best that's all that matters. Don't let this get you big headed, and don't you ever let me hear about you looking down on anyone else. We are all God's children. In life people are going to dislike you for any reason they could find but don't you ever let that hinder you. And don't ever take on any of those negative characteristics because that's only going to stagnate, your growth and development. You can never hold a person down without staying down with them. So the next time Johnathan or anyone else say anything like that to you, just tell them I wish you the best and keep on moving. You understand?"

"Yes ma'am," Rasheid digested everything his grandmother just said to him.

"Alright then. Let's go eat," she put the car in park and they both got out. As they walked towards the entrance of the restaurant she noticed for the first time that he was at least a half inch taller than her. "Boy you're getting taller by the hour," he blushed.

"Yeah when I'm standing next to you but compared to some of these eighth graders I still feel like a midget," he opened the door for his grandmother.

"Don't worry, you'll catch up," she said as they both entered the restaurant. Mrs. Willis opened her pocketbook and grabbed her wallet.

"I hope so. You know how hard it'll be to convince a girl to go out with somebody shorter than her," she couldn't help but laugh at his comment. Through the years Mrs. Willis had developed a relationship with Rasheid that she never had with both of her daughters. To her it seemed like it was a whole lot easier to raise a boy than a girl. Rasheid never gave her any problems. Not that her daughters did when they were that age, he was just a little more content. Mrs. Willis never understood where he got that confidence from. Especially, since he was the only child. Taking on his mother features in a masculine way with a smooth dark brown skin complexion. Rasheid continued making straight A's. When he was in the fifth grade, he was reading at a ninth grade level. He won all kinds of trophies and awards in spelling bees, math bees and science fair's. He was living proof that God works in mysterious ways. He was like a sun shine to the gray clouds Mrs. Willis had in her life. Though every once in a while things would get a little rocky, but not to the point where it'll get out of hand. For instance, it was this one case when he was in the fourth grade he got into a fight with this other kid in the cafeteria because the boy called his mother a whore. The principal who had a personal relationship with Mrs. Willis, told her the only reason he didn't suspended Rasheid was because of what his academic skills reflected on the school and the fact that the other student was a trouble maker. Therefore he sent the other student home for the rest of the day and had a talk with his parents and sent Rasheid back to class. It was times like that when Rasheid asked about his mother and father. Mrs. Willis never lied to him. Though she never told him the whole truth. She explained to him the reason she left was because she wasn't strong enough to take on the responsibilities of motherhood. Not that she didn't want him, it's just that she didn't felt like she was strong enough to carry all her weight and still be successful in life. So basically she didn't think she was fit to be his mother and the same with his father. The good thing was that he didn't dwell to long on these topics. Still there is not a day that goes by that she doesn't ask God to watch over her daughters. It's been twelve and a half years since Jennifer left. About ten years ago she got a letter from her stating that she was alright and how much she loved and missed them but that she just couldn't come back right then. The letter had no return address and she had never heard from her since. She never brought up the fact that Jennifer was rape to Rasheid or anyone else. Even though Mrs. Willis knew about it, she didn't want to touch that subject unless it was with Jennifer and only her. As far as Tereesa, her condition went from bad to worse. She moved back to North Charleston and lived in Airport Projects off of Dorchester road. Every week she would show up at her mother's house to talk with her and play with Rasheid. She would always end her visit by asking to borrow ten or twenty dollars but never paying it back. She wasn't as attractive as she used to be but she still might be able to turn a couple of necks if she was to clean herself up. But that was out of the question to her. She always said if a man really wants her he'll take her as she is. That's probably why she never kept one for more than a night or two. She tried to hide her condition from Rasheid being that he was the only one who was not judgemental towards her. She was proud of her nephew and she always bragged about him to the other boys and girls in her neighborhood. After a few years she stopped asking her mother about Jennifer. She missed her sister but never quite understood why she ran away from problems just because Damien didn't want to be in her or Rasheid's life. She tried to play her part in raising her nephew.

She wasn't a bad aunt, however what she did in her personal life didn't allow her to exceed in her abilities to her full potential. So life for her was a bit unbalanced.

Mrs. Willis sat down at her kitchen table and thought about what her doctor had told her the past week about her blood pressure and diabetes, which she discovered she had about four years ago. Since then it seems like the heart pain had gotten worse. As she sat at her kitchen table thinking about what would be more healthy between stewed chicken or sliced okra and tomatoes, Rasheid opened the door with his book bag on one shoulder and reading a paper he had in his hand.

"Hey Grandma," he closed the door still looking at the paper.

"Hey baby, what you reading," she got up and opened the cabinet.

"This riddle that Mr. Arnold gave out to the class. He said whoever answers it correctly would get a homework pass.

"Well what's the riddle?" Mrs. Willis poured some rice in a pot.

"What's bigger than the universe but smaller than an atom? Dead people eat it and if you eat it you'll die too."

"Umph that's a good one," she poured water into the pot. "Well what do dead people eat," she put the pot on the stove then turned it on.

Rasheid looked at her dumbfounded, "Dead people don't eat nothing." She smiled as she looked at him from the corner of her eye, "Still haven't figured it out yet."

Rasheid shook his head.

"You will," she dried her hands with the towel. "I need to talk to you for a minute, sit down," she directed him to the chair and sat beside him. Do you remember when you were younger and I always used to tell you that you're special."

"Yes"

"Well do you actually believe that you're special."

Rasheid thought on it for a moment, "Yes, I know I'm special."

"I'm going to need you to promise me that no matter what happens in your life that you'll graduate from high school and do something productive with yourself," he looked at his grandmother confused.

"Okay," he still didn't understand where the conversation was headed.

"Rasheid listen. We as black people really don't have much as a whole. So we can't afford not to accumulate as much knowledge as we can and more importantly that knowledge we accumalate must be transferred to its physical equivalent. We also have our word. And once people find out that your word is stronger than oak, that's as good as gold and it could also take you a far was in life. So what I want you to do is promise me no matter what happens you'll graduate from school and make something of your life," she looked directly in his eyes.

Mrs. Willis' words frightened Rasheid a little as he thought about why she would be saying this.

"I'm going to graduate and make something of myself."

As the words left his mouth, he came to the realization that this was just one of her usual lectures.

Mrs. Willis stared at him for a second.

"I know you will," she got up from her seat and kissed him on his forehead. "So what you want for dinner, stew chicken or okra and tomatoes."

"Stew chicken," he washed his hands.

"So you figured out the answer to that riddle yet?"

"No not yet."

As Rasheid sat in class waiting patiently for the bell to ring he pulled out the riddle that Mr. Arnold gave the class the day prior. He hated when he couldn't solve a problem and he was determined to keep at it until he figured the answer out. As he thought about the question his grandmother voice popped into his head. *What do dead people eat? What do dead people eat? But dead people don't eat nothing,"* he continued to rack his brain on the riddle. Then it hit him. Dead people eat nothing and nothing that science proves is bigger than the universe or smaller than an atom. And if you eat nothing you'll die. After Rasheid thought about how simple the riddle actually was he smiled to himself. Then the bell rung and he quickly grabbed his belongings and hurried on his way.

It's only been two years since Mrs. Willis retired from North Charleston and since then she had been trying to find a way to occupy her time instead of eating so much. Since she retired she put on an extra twenty-three pounds in areas she definitely didn't need it. Mrs. Willis walked downstairs to get started on dinner then stopped in her tracks to rub her chest. The pain was so sharp in her chest that it took her breath for a few seconds. As she grabbed the little rail a little harder, the pain eased up and a few seconds later it was gone like it had never happened. With a look of pain on her face she continued on her way to the kitchen.

Tereesa walked up the steps in some faded jeans with a hole in it exposing her whole knee, and a wrinkled shirt with Michael Jackson on it. She inhaled the cigarette one last time then flicked the butt before she entered her mother's house.

"Hey Mama," she walked through the living room into the kitchen. "What you doing?"

"Hey," the tone of her voice was weak.

"What's wrong Mama?" she looked at her mother from head to toe. "You sick or something."

Mrs. Willis nodded her head to indicate that she was alright but that's when the sharp pain struck her chest again this time harder than before. The pain sent a chill through her body as if an ice pick went through her heart. It was so painful it caused her to reach for the chair to have a seat.

"Mama!" Tereesa reached for her mother's arm to aid her. "Are you alright? You starting to scare me!"

Just as Mrs. Willis tried to speak the pain struck even harder causing her to slide out of her chair onto the floor.

"OH MY GOD!" Tereesa panicked as she ran for the phone and dialed 9-1-1. "HOLD ON MAMA!" she held her mother's arm as the tears build up in her eyes. "HELLO OPERATOR….. YES I THINK MY MOTHER'S HAVING A HEART ATTACK. I DON'T KNOW. SHE CAN'T TALK. YES. CAN YOU PLEASE HURRY UP!" She was on her knees over her mother as the tears fell helplessly from her face.

Mrs. Willis felt the pain with every breath she took. But the pain didn't interfere with her thoughts. She knew she was having a heart attack but she could think clearly. Matter of fact it was the clearest thoughts she had ever had in her life. Then suddenly her whole body went numb and her mind shifted to her daughters. For some reason she knew Jennifer was okay where ever she was in this world. She only wished that she could have shown her that it was easier to run to your problems than to run from it. Deep down inside she knew that Jennifer would come back and take care of responsibilities. Even though she had her eyes closed, she could see Tereesa very clearly over her. Her oldest child got caught up in the wicked ways of the world. She never once confronted her about the rumors she heard. Some of them she wished she hadn't heard. The only thing she wanted to stress to Tereesa was that no matter what kind of cards life dealt her, she still had a mother who loved her and wanted to see her succeed in life. And as for Rasheid, he was the purest thing she had in her life. He was definitely going to be somebody and make a difference in this world. She was so proud of him. She just wished that she could be there to read about him in the newspaper or see him on the news. Some big time lawyer or doctor of some sort. As Mrs. Willis opened her eyes, she saw a bunch of people around her strapping her down to this little mattress with an oxygen mask on her face.

Rasheid got off the school bus and took a good look at his shoes, a pair of K-Swiss. They were in good condition but his mind went back to a conversation he eavesdropped on by these two females a grade higher than him. They were talking about the kind of sneakers their boyfriends would and wouldn't wear. All the popular kids in the school wore name brand clothes and shoes. So now he was contemplating on how to ask his grandmother for a pair sneakers that cost a hundred and twenty dollars. While he was figuring out how he was going to ask her during dinner he noticed an ambulance truck in the front of his house. *Mrs. Ida must have had another asthma attack.* He wondered why the ambulance truck was closer to his yard than Mrs. Ida's. As he observed the scene a little harder he saw that there were people standing in his front yard. Then he saw the stretcher come through the front door with someone laying on it and his Aunt Tereesa along the side holding on to the rail. That's when he walked faster, and noticed that all the people were his neighbors.

"Rasheid!" Mrs. Ida yelled out trying to prevent him from seeing his grandmother in the condition she was in. She knew Mrs. Willis wouldn't want that. Rasheid kept in the direction of the truck only to get a glimpse of the paramedics putting his grandmother into the back of the ambulance.

"Grandma!" he yelled helplessly. Tereesa ran quickly to her nephew holding him tightly in her arms. "What happened to Grandma?" the tears fell down his face.

"I don't know baby," Tereesa held him close to her as the tears came down her cheeks as well. "I think, I think she had a heart attack."

As those words left his aunt's mouth, Rasheid could feel his heart beating through his whole body. He couldn't even fathom the idea of his grandmother having a heart attack yet he was witnessing it firsthand.

"Come on Tereesa," Ms. Ida was truly hurt for her friend and tried to do something to help out. "I'll give y'all a ride to the hospital."

Ch A p t e r 4

Exactly one week later a funeral was held for Gertrude Eva Willis at Lovely Hill Missionary Baptist Church. A lot of the staff who worked at North Charleston High throughout the years showed up to pay their respects. Mrs. Willis had a lot of distant family. Some of them Tereesa had heard of and some of them she hadn't. Mrs. Ida prepared a big meal for the family and played hostess. That was the least she could do for a friendship of more than twenty years. Besides all of the work she was doing helped kept her mind off of how lonely she was going to be. Not having her around to play cards with, or sit up late nights drinking coffee, and reminiscing on the good old days. As she left out of the kitchen with a plate of fried chicken, rice and collard greens, she noticed Rasheid sitting in a corner by himself staring at the floor. She handed the elderly woman the plate who thanked her as she smiled in return. Ms. Ida then walked through the living room, saying hi and smiling at every other person she passed then stopped in front of Rasheid and took a seat next to him.

"You alright Darling," she put her arm around his shoulders.

Rasheid nodded his head without removing his eyes from the floor.

"Everything is going to be okay. But always remember that your grandma is looking down at you. So the important thing to do now is make her proud."

Rasheid nodded his head again. She then gently hugged him.

"You hungry yet?" he shook his head.

"You should eat something baby. You haven't ate all day. I'll just fix

you some macaroni and cheese and a piece of sweet potato pie," she then
went back into the kitchen.

Tereesa sat outside on her mother's porch watching the sunset. She tried to
figure out how she was going to take care of her situation. Mrs. Willis left
her will to Rasheid but being that he wasn't eighteen yet, he couldn't touch it.
Now since it looked like she was going to be Rasheid's new guardian she
wouldn't be able to get any money either. Mrs. Willis didn't legally adopted
Rasheid therefore she wouldn't be able to either without the say so of Jennifer.
On top of that, Mrs. Willis taxes for the house were due in another six
weeks which was eleven hundred dollars. Tereesa didn't even have eleven
dollars. She sat on her mother's front porch and lit a second cigarette as she
looked down at her dress. It was the second time she wore it. The first was
five years ago at one of her friend's wedding. She never would of thought
the next time would be at her mother's funeral. She didn't have no idea how
to get in touch with Jennifer and at this point she really didn't care. If her
sister didn't want to be a part of her family's life then the hell with her. Now
the biggest issue she had to deal with was to find a way to take care of
Rasheid. She had just started working at Wendy's about two months ago. So
it was too early to ask her boss for a raise. As she inhaled her cigarette one
last time and flicked the butt in the yard, she looked at her mother's all white
1989 Volkswagen. "Well at least I got a new car," she stood up and straightened
out her dress. She honestly dreaded going back inside. She noticed how
some of the people looked her up and down as if she was the bad apple,
but she really didn't have a choice. So she swallowed her pride, opened the
screen door and headed back in the house.

As the days went by, Rasheid didn't talk or eat much. He didn't even get a
chance to get over his grandmother's death before he made a transition
from one environment to another, which meant he had to switch
schools. He never would of expected his Aunt Tereesa's apartment to be so
small and unorganized. The room she gave him was used for storage but

she got one of her male friends to help her clean it out. He also brought Rasheid's bed from Mrs. Willis house in his pickup truck, which the three of them rode in. Rasheid could tell that the man was a bit older than his aunt but he couldn't stop staring at his teeth. It looked as if every single one of them was rotten. After they got back to Tereesa's apartment and finished setting up Rasheid's room, Tereesa looked around the room then put her arm around his shoulder,"I know it doesn't seem like much now but just give me a little time. Then I can get a better apartment with a bigger room for you okay," she said as she kissed the side of his head.

"Alright," Rasheid hoped the time would be sooner rather than later.

"You hungry?"

"No I'm alright," he sat down on his bed.

"Well I'll be in the next room if you need something okay."

"Okay," he said as she exited the room. Rasheid took a look around his new room that had a smell of cigarette smoke and the sweet fragrance that Tereesa sprayed throughout the apartment. He laid back on the bed wishing that this was just a bad dream but it all felt too real. And then for the first time since his grandmother's funeral, he broke down and cried.

"Listen to me Rasheid, don't you let any of these kids around here punk you. If any of them bad asses hit you, you hit they ass back. And if they're bigger than you, you pick up anything you can find and knock they ass upside their head. You hear me?" Tereesa was a little concernedthat he may be a little on the soft side.

"Yes, I hear you," Rasheid said.

"You don't have nothing to worry about," Tereesa male friend said to Rasheid. "All you have to do is carry yourself like a man. Don't take no mess from nobody and you'll be okay," Rasheid still couldn't help looking at the man's teeth as he sat in the backseat of his grandmother's Volkswagen waiting to arrive at his new school. As they pulled into the driveway of River Oaks Middle School, the three got out of the car and headed towards the entrance. Rasheid looked the man up and down then suddenly felt embarrassed. He hoped that nobody would think that this dark man dressed in a faded black pair of jeans and a shirt with speckled of paint on it with a wrinkled Chicago Bulls hat on backwards was his father. His Aunt Tereesa wasn't looking too hot either. She wore a pair of skin tight jeans and a t-shirt almost down to her knees, with a hole on the side. Her almost shoulder length hair looked as if she had brushed it with her hand. As they entered the school, it looked as if they had entered a new world through Rasheid's eyes. The hallways seemed a little wider than his last school and it was a lot more lockers. This meant that there were a lot more students. When they entered the main office, the secretaries and clerks stopped and looked at Tereesa and her friend like they were about to raise hell about a teacher mistreating their child.

"Hi my name is Ms. Graham and this is the administration office. How can I help you?" the elderly white woman said nervously.

"Yes, my name is Tereesa Willis and I'm here to enroll my child Rasheid Willis. I called yesterday and you said you were waiting from Garrett." She said in her most professional tone.

"Oh yes ma'am, we were expecting Rasheid," the elder woman said relieved that she weren't one of the angry parents. "The other school already sent the transfer papers so I need you to sign a few papers, fill out this in case of an emergency form and I'll take it from there."

Tereesa did as she was asked and handed the woman back her ink pen.

"Yes ma'am," the woman took the ink pen from Tereesa and looked at her friend examining the potraits on the wall. "Would you like a copy of Rasheid's schedule?"

"Yes. Thank you," Tereesa took the schedule, folded it and put it in her back pocket. "Okay Rasheid, you take care and I'll see you when you get home from school. Alright."

"Alright."

Tereesa kissed him on his forehead.

"Let's go George," she signaled to her male friend as he took his attention away from the potrait and walked towards the door.

"Hang in there champ," the man playfully punched Rasheid on his shoulder then left through the double doors.

"Alright let's see… this is second period, so that means you have Mr. Woods class," Ms. Graham said in a more authorative tone. "Grab your things and follow me," she opened the door then held it for him. "Here at Berkley all you have to do is follow the golden rule and you shouldn't have no trouble," she walked briskly down the hall as Rasheid tried to keep up. "Do you know what the golden rule is?"

"No ma'am," Rasheid said. Ms. Graham turned around and really looked at him for the first time. "One with manners. You don't see that too often," she said to herself. "Well the golden rule is be where you're supposed to be, when you're supposed to be there and doing what you're supposed to be doing. And you shouldn't have nothing to worry about," she said as if that was her thousandth time quoting it. "This is your class," she stopped in front of a classroom and signaled for the teacher to step out.

"Hey, Ms. Graham, who do we have here?" the middle age light complexion man said as he observed Rasheid.

"This is your new student. His name is Rasheid Willis. You think you can do something with him," she said in a joking manner.

"I guess I'll try," Mr. Woods shot back as he put his hand on Rasheid's shoulder.

"Be good," she said to Mr. Woods as she playfully tapped him on his arm then walked off.

"Where you from man?" Mr.Woods said in an energetic voice.

"Right here in North Charleston, just a different school," Rasheid looked him in his eyes like his grandmother taught him.

"Well it's the same thing. Just a different school," Mr. Woods opened the door and walked Rasheid into the class. "Alright class, I'll like you all to meet your new classmate, Rasheid Willis," Rasheid tried to get a good look at everyone. It looked as if they got their dressing tips from Soul Train and BET. The girls dressed like adult women with real short skirts on and skin tights pants with weaves in their hair either braided or fixed very fancy. The boys dressed lively in oversized pants and shirts. Their haircuts had designs on the sides and in the backs of their heads. "You can take that seat right over there." Mr. Woods instructed Rasheid as he pointed to a seat in the back of the class.

"Hey man," one boy said as Rasheid made his way to the back of the class. "I like that outfit," he said causing all the other students to laugh. "You thought you was coming to church or something," he added as they continued to laugh.

"Josh!" Mr. Woods said in a serious tone. " Since you have so much to say. What's the answer to number eight."

The boy sat up in the seat then looked down at the question. "Mercury," he said with a look of doubt on his face.

"Are you sure?" said Mr. Woods.

"Venus," he said with more confidence.

"Well I guess I'll be seeing you again next year. Anybody else?"

"Ooooh," the whole class uttered at their classmate then burst out in laughter, causing the boy to have a look of humiliation on his face.

━━━━━━━━━━

Rasheid felt awkward as he sat in the back of the class. For the first time he was ashamed of the clothes he had on. While everyone else wore Tommy Hilfiger, Polo and Nautica, he had on a khaki Bugle Boy pants and a blue collar shirt with his all white K-Swiss. He took another look around the class and noticed that there were no white students. At his other school the white students outnumbered the blacks. He also took notice to the females. They didn't look twelve and thirteen. They looked more like sixteen and seventeen. They had their nails done and wore makeup. Some of them even had the shape of grown women. He then studied the teacher. He couldn't been no more than thirty-five years old. He wore black slacks with a white shirt and a black tie. The more he observed his new classmates the more out of place he felt and he had a lot to learn.

━━━━━━━━━━

Tereesa got out of the car with her Wendy's uniform still on and walked up to a crowd of young boys. One of the young boys out the crew who was about eighteen or nineteen stepped off to do business with her.

"You got that," he asked.

"Look. I just got paid and all I have is a hundred and eighty-nine dollars to last me till another two weeks," she avoided eye contact with him as she searched through her purse.

"Look Tereesa, I don't have nuttin to do with that. I let you credit a hundred and fifty dollars worth and I need my money."

"I know Dre but this was just bad timing. I just had my nephew move in with me," she begged. "And I just buried my mother so money just been tight."

"Tereesa, what the hell that got to do with me?"

"Dre don't act like that now," she knew she had the advantage once she started to plea to him. "After all that money I done spent with you, you can't spare me this one time."

Dre looked around with hopes that no one would notice him getting suckered by a crackhead and that's when he spotted the car. Tereesa got out. "Who's car is that," he checked the car out.

Tereesa looked back at the car he was checking out. "That's my car. Why?" she said as if it was out of the question for him to get it.

"Well let me borrow the car for a little while and I'll kill fifty dollars," he said as he thought of the more money he'll make if he had a car.

"Uh-uh. No!" she said determined. "That's my mother's car."

"Ain't nobody gone mess up your car. I just need to make a few runs real quick. I'll probably be a couple of hours. The most."

"No Dre. I'm sorry baby but I can't give you my car," she said as she watched him pulled out a Ziploc bag with about an ounce of crack cut up and ready to be smoked out of his pocket. He opened the Ziploc bag and pulled out an individual wrap with three blocks of crack in it and held it in his hand.

"How about if I give you this and you owe me fifty," he knew that he would soon be driving her car by how big her eyes got from watching the package in his hand.

"How long you said you was going to be," she didn't take her eyes off the package.

"A couple hours. I'll be back by dark," he knew that he gain more than he lost.

"Make sure you put some gas in it," she took the package from him and handed him the keys. She then cuffed the small package in her hand, put her pocketbook under her arm and walked upstairs to her apartment as if she had a long day at work.

School was over with and Rasheid looked for bus number seven, which would be the bus to take him home. As he stepped out of the building, he observed hundreds of students mingling with each other. He seen a few boyfriend and girlfriend couples kissing. He saw some taking pictures while throwing up gang signs and others just carrying on conversations. It wasn't hard finding his bus, being that all the buses were in order according to the number. As he got on the bus, he saw that it was just as wild there as in the parking lot. The bus driver was a dark skin lady about in her early forties. She was short and plump with long breast that reached all the way to the steering wheel. He walked down the aisle and tried to find a seat. It was hard for him to see which seats were taken from the ones that weren't. The students were moving from seat to seat talking and playing with each other. Two guys were in the middle of the aisle play boxing with a small crowd around them. He walked passed this boy sucking on this girl neck with his hand up her skirt. She had her eyes closed with her hand gripped tightly around his forearm. When he finally saw a seat that wasn't being occupied, he got to it, sat by the window with his bookbag in lap and observed everybody. He then noticed the boy that was in his math class got on the bus. It was the only kid that he knew by the name and that was because he heard people calling his name all day. The boy came and sat next to Rasheid only looking at him once as his attention quickly went to a wad of money he pulled out of his pocket as a tall Asian looking girl whom to Rasheid favored Pocahontas sat in his lap. She had light smooth skin and her hair was long and jet black. She sat in his lap as she gave him a seductive look.

"Hey Baby," she said.

"Whassup," he looked directly in her eyes.

"I've been thinking bout you all day," she said in a sexy tone as she placed his hands on the top of her thighs. Rasheid looked at them both. The boy who everyone called Rookie, was light skinned, about his size with real curly hair. From what he seen so far, a lot of girls really liked him. He was dressed in some jeans about three size too big for him, with a white t-shirt and an Orlando Magic basketball jersey on over it. Rasheid looked down at his sneakers. He wore a pair of Penny Hardaway's which was in commercials and in the magazines for the past couple of months. He studied the boy and wondered where he could have gotten all that money from and took a second look at the hundred and fifty dollars sneakers he had on.

"What you chewing on?" Rookie said aggressively as she chewed even harder exposing her pearly white teeth.

"Some bubble gum. You want some?" she stuck half of the gum out of her mouth leaning down to put it to his lips. He opened his mouth and before you knew it their lips were smacking against each other. A few females in the back cheered them on, who must have been friends of the girl. As she stood up still kissing Rookie, they finally managed to snatch away from each other, then she headed to the back of the bus hi-fiving her friends. Rookie sat there with a blush on his face as he wiped his mouth off and started chewing the gum. He then looked over at Rasheid.

"Ain't you that new nigga?" Rasheid

nodded his head.

"What you can't talk."

"Yeah I'm new," Rasheid sensed he was testing him.

"Where you from?"

"I'm from Glenn Terrace but I stay in Macon."

"Oh you stay in Money Macon. I got a lot of niggas that stay out there. What's your name?"

"Rasheid."

"Who?" he tried to hear him over all the noise.

"Rasheid!" he said louder.

"Alright Rasheid, my name Rookie," he extended his hand to shake Rasheid's. Then the bus came to a stop. "Alright dog, this my spot. I'ma catch up wit you later." Rookie hoped that he realed in another nerd friend to be doing his homework.

"I'ma call you Rookie!" the Asian looking girl yelled out as Rookie threw his hand in the air and exited the bus. As the bus did its frequent stops, the noise started to decline a little bit which gave Rasheid time to clear his thoughts. He felt his stomach growled as the reality settled in on him again that he will not be going home to eat any of his grandmother's cooking. He then looked out the window imagining that she was on vacation and would be coming back soon. The bus stopped again which is where he got off. Rasheid stepped off the bus and saw his grandmother's car coming in his direction full speed. When he saw that it was older boys in it with the music blasting and blowing smoke out the window he was about to brush it off until he saw the North Charleston High School Cougars sticker on the bumper of the car. The driver barely stopped at the stop sign, then mashed the gas pedal down to the floor. Rasheid hurried home to tell

Tereesa that the car got stolen. There were crowds of people just walking around his building. It was a lot of people out, a few were his age but most of them were older than him. Some of them had on jewelry, pagers and cell phones. Females younger and older were running around half naked, some screaming from one building to the other. Babies looked like they were having the time of their lives, running around wearing nothing but pampers with some of them having on socks. As Rasheid ran upstairs, he used his key that Tereesa gave him, unlocked the door and entered the apartment, dropping his bookbag on the floor.

"Aunt Tereesa!" he ran to her room door. "Aunt Tereesa, somebody stole Grandma's!" he said excitedly as he opened Tereesa's door. Rasheid then stopped in his tracks as he saw his aunt on the floor wearing nothing but her panties and bra with a clear tube in her mouth lighting the end of it.

"Oh shit!" she took the tube from her mouth and tried to hide it behind her back which was obviously too late. "Close my damn door Rasheid! Don't you know how to fucking knock!" she screamed at the top of her lungs shocking even herself at how she went off.

Rasheid closed the door and stood in the hallway horrified. He wasn't exactly sure what he saw his aunt doing but whatever it was he knew it wasn't good. Tereesa stood up and quickly got dressed as a feeling of embarrassment came over her. She looked in the mirror at herself. She was high. She turned on the cold water splashed some in her face, dried it off with the towel then opened the door.

"Rasheid," she stepped out of the room.

"Yes," he sat on the couch just as embarrassed as her.

"Baby, you just can't be running around here opening doors like that. I know Mama taught you better than that," she said in a calm voice assuring him that she loves him no less.

"I was trying to tell you that somebody stole Grandma's car. I seen four boys driving off in it."

Tereesa covered her face with her hands shaking her head, "No Rasheid. Nobody stole the car. I let one of my friends borrow it for a little while. That's it," she said as he really sensed something wrong. "Um…I bought you some Frosted Flakes, which I know is your favorite. Some hot dogs and some Krispy Kreme donuts," she said politely trying to stay on good terms with him.

"Thank you," Rasheid got up grabbed his bookbag and headed to his room not having an appetite. She wanted to stop him but decided against it. Not wanting to humiliate herself no more than she already did, she went back into her room.

———————

As the days went by, it didn't get easier for Rasheid at home or at school. The kids in his class comment on his attire on a daily basis. It was like a greeting to him. He only had three different types of clothing which was Bugle Boy, The Hunt Club and Levis. No matter how many times he tried to switch his pants and shirts up, it wasn't enough to stop him from getting teased at school. As he closed his locker and headed to his third period class, he saw a crowd of students ahead of him surrounding two boys and a girl. All the commotion being made sparked his curiosity. As he got closer, he observed a bigger boy getting punk by a kid much smaller than him. Standing next to the smaller boy was a girl with her arms across her chest with a look of revenge on her face. Then suddenly the smaller boy smack the bigger one so loud, that the sound echoed in the hallway causing the whole crowd to go off in oooh's.

"Now I'm going to ask you one more time. Do you know this girl?" the smaller boy said as he pointed at the girl. The bigger one looked confused. Of course he knew her but he didn't know that touching her butt would lead to this. **SMACKKK** was the sound that echoed in the hallway again as the smaller boy caught him off guard. "Dog, this the last time I'm gonna ask you this, now do you know this girl?" he said as the crowd went off again with a few people laughing. The incident had everyone's attention as if they were watching an Al Pacino flick. The bigger boy rubbed his face for a quick second, swallowed every ounce of pride he had and uttered, "No." The smaller boy smacked him a third time as the crowd really went off enjoying every second of it. "And let it stay like that," he said as he walked off with the girl behind him with pure satisfaction on her face and leaving everyone something to talk about for the rest of the week. That was just one of the many conflicts Rasheid saw in his short time at his new school.

It seems as if he was invisible at school, if he weren't being made fun of. The bus ride home went as usual and the only person who talked to him on a consistent basis was Rookie. He couldn't really tell if Rookie was all black or mixed with Puerto Rican as he looked at his all black Jordan's. Rasheid understood that to his peers your status was classified according to how you dress who you hung out with, who your boyfriend or girlfriend were and how well you fight.

"Yo man," Rookie said as he sat next to Rasheid. "You have any brothers or sisters," he slightly brushed the side of his sneakers with his hand.

"No," Rasheid looked down at his sneakers then back at him. "I'm the only child," he wondered for the first time if he really was the only child or not.

"Damn. I bet you spoiled as hell," Rasheid didn't comment, instead he looked out the window. "Well I'ma get at you tomorrow," Rookie exited the bus as he threw his hands up to the females in the back of the bus who was yelling his name.

Rasheid walked down the street with his bookbag on his back as he took notice of his new neighborhood. He was now becoming aware of all the drug addicts and drug dealers where he lived and suspected his aunt and Rookie to be a part of what he saw took place. As he entered his aunt's apartment, he took a look around the living room which had sofas with clothes that he couldn't tell were clean or dirty all over them. Then he looked in the kitchen that had dishes in the sink from two day ago. Since he couldn't stand living in filth and remembered what his grandmother told him about keeping a clean household, he decided to clean up his aunt's apartment. After about a hour and a half of cleaning, which consisted of folding clothes, vacuuming, washing dishes, cleaning the bathroom and the kitchen Rasheid worked up an appetite. He opened up the cabinet and reached for the box of Frosted Flakes, opened it and saw that there was nothing but crumbs at the bottom of the box. He then opened the refrigerator and saw nothing but a half jar of mayonnaise, a box of baking soda and a quarter of gallon of milk, which was on the verge of being spoiled. He then closed the refrigerator just as Tereesa walked through the door. With her work uniform on, grease stains all over it and a look of exhaustion. Tereesa face brightened when she stepped in her apartment. She looked around like she didn't know where she was for a moment.

"Gosh Rasheid, you got the place looking real nice."

"Aunt Tereesa, there's no food here," he said unmoved by her compliment.

After Tereesa realized that she spent her last twenty dollars on drugs instead of putting groceries in her house she had a feeling of guilt in her heart.

"Are you sure?" she walked in the kitchen and looked through the cabinets hoping that some food would just magically appear.

"Yes I'm sure," he said disappointed.

Unable to look at her nephew she said, "Well I'll just have to go to the grocery store," As if it wasn't a big deal. "I'll be back in a few minutes okay."

"Alright," Rasheid felt relieved.

Tereesa went downstairs got into the car and just sat in the driver seat. Not knowing where she was going to get the money from to buy some groceries, she started pulling her hair knowing she was really messing up. She knew if she continued this, it wouldn't be long before child services got into her business. Wrecking her brain as she buried her face in the steering wheel, she knew she couldn't go back in her place without some food. But more than anything she needed a hit worse than ever. She didn't know where she was going to get it from but she was determined that she was going to get it from somewhere. Hours later Rasheid laid in his bed and tried to get some sleep but couldn't manage because of how hard his stomach growled. He tried to think of something other than food to keep his mind off of being hungry but all he kept seeing when he closed his eyes was his grandmother cooking some fried chicken, collard greens, macaroni and cheese with some sweet potato pie. Unable to bear the pain of his stomach any longer, he got out of bed and head to Tereesa room. He peeked in and saw that she still wasn't back. He then went to the kitchen, opened up the cabinet and grabbed the cereal box hoping that there were more crumbs in the box than he remembered. But as he opened the box he saw that it wasn't. He poured the remainder of the crumbs in his hands then put it in his mouth. Nowhere near satisfied he then opened the refrigerator, reached for the half jar of mayonnaise, screwed the top off then started feeding himself the mayonnaise with his finger. After doing that a few times, he opened the draw and reached for a spoon to allow the mayonnaise to get in his mouth much quicker. When he was finished, he looked at the empty jar got up and threw it in the trash can. With nothing else at all to eat in the apartment, he realized that he had to find a way to make some money.

Rasheid woke up from a few miserable hours of sleep to get himself ready for school. It's been two months since he's been living with his aunt and out of that two months, he ate a decent meal twice. He took a bath with dish detergent when there wasn't no soap, and when that ran out he used washing powder, which had him scratching throughout the day. He hand washed his clothes and laid it around his room to let it dry, and then had to wear it to school wrinkled because there was no iron. And on top that, most of the time Tereesa wasn't home, so he was usually in the house by himself. It was amazing through this dramatic change in his life, he was able to maintain his high grades. His new school really wasn't a challenge to him academically but on the other hand he had to deal with a lot of pressure from peers. After he gathered his things and headed out the door, he was greeted with the fresh southern air that the city of North Charleston had to offer. He walked down the street to the bus stop and stood aside from the rest of the teenagers that totally ignored him. When he got on the bus the ride went like it usually do in the morning time. Not loud at all but it wasn't silent either. As the bus entered the school parking lot. Rasheid waited for everyone else to leave off so that he could be last. Not wanting no more attention than he had to have. Upon entering the building he noticed a lot of the students crowding the hallway waiting for the first bell to ring. As he got closer to the crowd, he also noticed there were a group of guys joking on anyone that walked pass who wasn't in accordance with the ghetto fabulous dress code. Right then he wanted to turn around, until he realized that it was the only entrance the students can use to the school. He sucked it up and tried to brace himself for whatever insults he was about to take in. Everyone was still laughing at the last comment one jokester made on another student and wasn't paying him any attention until he got in the middle of the crowd.

"Damn Homeboy, what you got dressed in the dark or something!" one of the jokester said causing everyone eyes to set on Rasheid and start laughing. Rasheid ignored him and kept walking, trying to hide the embarrassment. He was almost out of the crowd before he felt his left foot being kicked behind his right foot and from the result of not being able to think fast enough, he fell flat on his chest almost kissing the floor. This caused everyone standing in the hallway to really burst out in laughter. Filled with rage, Rasheid got up, turned around and threw off his bookbag only to see that the kid who tripped him up was almost twice his size.

"Oh so you wanna fight little nigga," the teenager threw up his fist and jumped around in a playful way. "Come on then. Bring it on."

Just then another teenage girl who Rasheid never saw before walked up and stood between them.

"Leave that boy alone and go mess with somebody your on size," she said as if she was sick and tired of seeing him pick on smaller kids. "How would you like it if somebody was to do that to you," the tone of her voice carried a bit of authority which caused the teenager to back down.

"Whatever," the boy walked off as the bell rung and everybody else started to move along.

"Yeah I know, that don't make no doggone sense," she bend over to pick up Rasheid's bookbag.

"It don't make no sense how much crack yo mama smoke either!" somebody shouted out from the crowd causing the teenagers another burst of laughter before they went to class.

"Yeah, well come and say it to my face!" she turned around with Rasheid bookbag in hand. Being satisfied that the coward who made the comment didn't step up to the plate. "That's what I thought," she turned around with Rasheid bookbag in hand. "Are you alright?" she said to him.

"Yeah," he still felt angry and embarrassed. He looked up at the girl who was a few inches taller than him. "Thank you," he took his bookbag from her and headed straight to the bathroom. Once he got in the bathroom, the smell of days old pee almost turned him around. He went straight to the mirror and looked at the streaks of red lines on his eyes. As he heard the second bell rung, he realized he was late for class, then wondered was it really worth going. That's when he remembered the promise that he made to his grandmother. "I'm going to graduate from high school and make something of myself," he recalled himself saying as he thought back to that day when him and his grandmother talked in the kitchen. It was hard to believe that six months passed that quick. He also remembered and quoted what his grandmother used to say to him, "What don't kill you can only make you stronger," and with that in mind, Rasheid went to class.

Ch A p t e r 5

R asheid woke up the morning of his fourteenth birthday not really
felling a difference the day before. He rolled over and looked at
the clock which read 9:18 a.m. He sat up in his bed reached under his
mattress and grabbed a roll of money from his new hiding spot. He knew
it wasn't a good idea to keep money lying around giving temptation to his
aunt Tereesa. He counted it to make sure it was all there which was
seven hundred and twenty-five dollars. His conscience ate him up stealing
clothes from the mall but the circumstances called for it. He knew the
idea alone of him being a thief was enough to make his grandmother turn
over in her grave. So he tried not to keep that thought buried in the back
of his mind.

"Happy birthday," Tereesa stood in his doorway fixing her work attire.

"Thank you and good morning," Rasheid got out of bed then looked
through his closet.

"Morning. I need to borrow twenty dollars if you can."

Rasheid knew it was coming, "Alright," he took a pair of jeans out the
closet and laid it across his bed.

"You need a ride anywhere before I got to work."

"I'm alright."

"You sure?"

"Yes," he laid a shirt on top of his jeans and walked pass his aunt to
the bathroom. He loved his aunt but her behavior embarrassed him to the
point that they hardly communicated with each other.

After he got himself together he walked out into the kitchen and looked in the refrigerator. Not being moved by what he saw, he closed it back, took a twenty dollar bill out of his pocket and walked out the door. Going down the steps, he heard Nas's hit song, "If I Ruled the World" from the trunk of a money green and gold 96' Cadillac Seville riding pass. He tried to make out the driver but was unsuccessful in doing so. As he started on his walk to the bus stop he noticed one of his neighbors seated on a crate chewing on sun flower seeds. "Whassup Dee," Rasheid spoke.

"Whassup," he spat out some shells.

"Who Lac was that, that just came through."

"That's Rino shit," Dee spat out some more seeds. "I think that was one of his bitches pushing it though."

Rasheid often heard people spoke on Rino but he never saw him. Dee then observed a car that drove up real slow then came to a stop. "Hold on Rasheid. Let me go make this sale real quick," he pulled a medicine bottle out of his pocket and walked up to the car. He returned back to his seat, put a roll of money in his pocket and then took a good look a Rasheid, " Boy you dressed up to day ain't chu," Dee looked him up and down.

"A little something," Rashid tried to hide the blush on his face.

"That's what I mean't to ask you. I need you to hook me up wit that Polo Jean outfit, like the one you got Rodney."

"I charged like a hundred dollars for that whole outfit," he looked at his watch.

"I got money nigga," Dee smiled admiring the potential he saw in him. "Little Rasheid, just the other day you was round this bitch scrambling. Now you got a little change in your pocket. I little that."

Rasheid smiled then shrugged his shoulders, "I gotta go."

"Alright little homey," Dee shook his hand. "Make sure you get that for me."

"I got you," he walked off.

<hr />

Rasheid walked up the block to the bus stop making a quick stop at the Starvin Marvin to get a hotdog and a bag of chips. As he left out of the store, he remembered just a little over a year ago was the first time he ever stolen anything. And it just so happen to out that very corner store. It was

nothing at home for him to eat and it was one of those days he went to bed
hungry and woke up even hungrier. As he walked to the school bus stop,
he stepped in the store to use the bathroom. On his way walking out, he
seen the aisle of cinnamon buns which he could taste just by looking at it.
He looked at the woman behind the cash register who didn't even notice
when he came in. She was too busy flirting with the guy who was filling
up the soda machine. He then carefully unzipped his bookbag, grabbed a
few of the cinnamon buns and dropped it in his bag without making any
noise. Then he walked out the store without being noticed by the lady who
was still occupied. After that he continued to steal food items until stealing
became a habit. Then he went from stealing food to stealing clothes being
that he had no one to buy it for him anyway. One day he stole a jacket he's
been eyeing for a while in which a drug dealer offered to buy it from him
for a hundred dollars. Those bad decisions created an idea. He stole
clothes and sold it to drug dealers. Anything they wanted he'll get it and sold
it to them half price. Tereesa never asked where he got the extra money
from but she never turned it down when he voluntarily gave her a couple
dollars here and there.

Rasheid stepped off of the bus into Northwoods Mall parking lot. He
entered the mall through the entrance of the food court. It was just a little
before noon on a Saturday morning and the mall was crowded the way he
liked it. The first store he entered, he purchased a couple pairs of Nautica
Jeans and t-shirts to go with it. The total came up to one hundred and
sixty-one dollars and sixty-one cents. He took out two hundred dollar bills,
got his changed and walked away from the counter. He then looked as if
he was about to walk out of the store but got his attention taken away from
him. He went to the corner of the store where he folded a few pair of jeans
when he first came in, before he purchased his items. He looked around
from the corner of his eyes to see if anyone watched him, put the jeans in
the bag in all of a split second and left out the store without being noticed.
He did the same in all the other stores he went into. Before he purchased
anything, he'll go into the corner of the store out of obvious eye sight, fold up
a few items and put it in a spot where it wouldn't be noticeable. After

he paid for his personals, he'll then make it look like he was exiting out of the store then made his way back to the corner and slip the clothes in the bag, leaving the store carefully without bringing any attention to himself. By the time he left the mall, he calculated three hundred and sixty dollars he should make within the next couple of hours. His customers were indeed happy to see him when he made his way back to his neighborhood. He made more money than he planned on. By the time he made it home he had a total of eleven hundred and fifty-six dollars. He took out two hundred dollars, put it on the counter for his aunt and left out to go get something to eat. He was starting to adapt to the projects more than he thought he would. He went from not even being noticed to making a name for himself in less than two years.

<hr />

Rasheid decided to eat at Bertha's. A new soul food restaurant that just opened up. He heard they had the best cooks in the city and wanted to see if it was true. When he walked in, he realized he was more hungrier than he thought, when he took in the aroma of the food that went straight to his stomach. He took a seat by the window and started to look through the menu.

"Good evening welcome to Bertha's my name is Tania. How may I help you?" the caramel complexion girl said with an unfamiliar accent that had Rasheid's full attention. He looked at the girl and was memorized by how beautiful she was. She had straight jet black hair that came a little pass her shoulder with light brown eyes the same complexion of her skin. She was about 5'2" with a perfectly hour glass figure.

"Are you planning on eating here?" she interrupted his thought chamber.

"Yes….umh," he tried to remember what he wanted to eat. "Oh yeah, can I get the barbecue dinner with a side of cheese cake."

"Would you like something to drink with that," she wrote down his order.

"Could I have some sweet tea please?"

"Would that be it?"

"For now yeah."

"Your order should be ready in about ten minutes," she said as she reached across him and grabbed his menu. He took in a whiff of her fragrance and the scent was so sweet and seductive he got an erection.

"Damn," he said to himself as he watched her walk off.

When she returned with his food and drink she left the receipt on the table, asked if he needed anything else since he couldn't think of anything, she left him with a smile and told him to have a nice evening. He enjoyed the food without realizing it because the whole time he ate, his thoughts were on her. He waited for her to come back but after seeing she was busy serving other customers, he left her a twenty dollar tip and left the restaurant.

Rasheid was still unable to get her off of his mind during his walk home. That was the first girl he ever had instant feelings for. As he walked down the dark streets of North Charleston, the gun shots he heard in the far distance bought him back to reality. He opened the door to the apartment and was welcomed by Dre in the kitchen standing in front of the stove.

"Lil Rasheid, what up nigga," he looked at Rasheid then put his attention back to the stove.

"What's up Dre?" he closed the door then locked it. "What you doing here?"

"I had to do a favor for your aunt. Oh yeah man, that's what I meant to tell you," Dre said while slightly shaking a mayonnaise jar inside a pot. "I'm trying to get my hands on that new Ralph Lauren, you think you can do something."

"Yeah. I might can do something tomorrow," Rasheid was more interested in what he was doing at the stove. "What you cooking?"

Dre looked up at him, "You mean to tell me that you never seen nobody cook up crack before."

"That's crack," he looked in the pot.

"What you know about cocaine?"

Rasheid looked dumbfounded for a moment. He knew that it had his aunt strung out. He knew that people who sold it got a lot of money and he knew it could get you sent to prison. But besides that he really couldn't tell him nothing about it.

"You see this right?" Dre showed him a Ziploc bag of individual bags of cocaine. If you handle this right she'll turn into this right here," he took two rolls of money and dropped it on the kitchen table which made a thump sound. Rasheid looked at the two rolls of money which was about ten times the amount he had. Just then he heard the bathroom door opened and Tereesa stumbled out. She grabbed hold of the wall to catch her balance, took a few more steps then entered her bedroom and closed the door. Rasheid wanted to see if she was alright but then thought against it. Dre's attention went back to what he was doing.

"I heard you suppose to be smart. You know how much grams in an ounce?"

"Twenty-eight."

"This is a gram," he cut the hardened cocaine. "This is an ounce. Better known as a O. Now if I sell each gram for fifty dollars and it's twenty-eight grams then how much money is this worth?"

"About fourteen hundred dollars," he watched Dre used a razor to slide the drugs into its individual wraps.

"Aiight now if I sell this three and a half o's how much money I made?" he sealed the plastic around the drugs then put it to the side. "You might need a calculator?"

Rasheid done the math in his head which couldn't have taken no more than ten seconds.

"fourty-nine hundred dollars."

Dre stopped and looked at Rasheid, "Damn boy, you really is smart."

Rasheid disregard his comment and went back into the conversation.

"So you mean to tell me that you can make fourty-nine hundred dollars off of three and a half of those?"

"Sometimes more sometimes less. It depends," he wrapped the drugs in the plastic and put it in his pocket. He then took the cigarette from behind his ear and gathered all his things. "But this ain't the game for everybody," he put the drugs in his pocket and poured the water out the pot while the cigarette dangled up and down in his mouth. "Look at me, I'm twenty-one years old. I gotta a few cars, a few bitches and shit made a little bit of money but I've been doing this for eight years. You can't just walk out of this shit like you walk into it. Just like how dem crackheads out dere fienn for this shit, we fien for the money and get addicted to the lifestyle. And then you gotta worry about the police and feds fucking wit chu every chance they get and I don't even wanna talk about the disloyal niggas that's in the game. Like the people say jealousy is a motherfucker," he was interrupted by his cellular phone. "What's up?... Yeah I just finished....Don't worry about that man I got chu...I'm sayin, you out on bond right now man you hot....Look man.....Look....Ric would you chill the fuck out and meet me at Bubba Zeek's.... Ric just meet at Bubba Zeek's I'm leaving right now," he hung up the phone. "You see what I mean, it's always gonna be some shit in the game. I'ma holla at chu man. You make sure you take care of that thing for me," he made sure he didn't leave anything behind then left out the door.

"Aiight man, I got you," Rasheid sat down and thought about all money he just saw. "That had to been at least seven thousand dollars," he said to himself. He was about to go check on Tereesa but quickly changed his mind, went to his room and closed the door. He laid down across the bed and thought how much easier life would be if he had the kind of money Dre had. He felt like Dre was trying to discourage him. He couldn't see how life could be so stressful when you was making thousands of dollars like it was nothing. Then out of nowhere Tania popped up in his mind. He could still smell her body fragrance as clear as he could see her face. He took off his shirt and tried to do some push-ups, losing all his strength after doing twenty-three. He looked over at the clock and saw that it was one o'clock in the morning, he grabbed a fresh pair of boxers and headed to the shower.

The next day Rasheid got on the bus with two bags of clothes and a paranoid feeling. He witnessed this pregnant booster who got caught stealing and being escorted out in hand cuffs by two police officers. That's when the reality settled in on him of what he was doing. He pictured himself being carried away in hand cuffs and wondered how would he get out of a situation like that. But what scared him more was that he knew if he kept this up it'll be a fact that he'll get caught. It'll just be the matter of time. The bus came to a stop and he got off with the bags in hand. He walked down the streets until he got to his neighborhood and saw Dee, who was still seated on the crate as he spat out sunflowers seeds.

"What's up Dee?"

"Ain't shit. What you got in the bag."

"Something for you," he pulled out an all black stonewash Polo jean with the jacket to match.

"God damn right!" Dee smiled as he reached for the outfit. "This bitch woulda cost me two and some change. What else you got in the bag?"

"Some personals for me and something for Dre."

"You coming to Dre's party tonight," Dee pulled out two fifty dollars bills and gave it to him.

"Naw what party?" he took the money and put it in his pocket.

"Well really he's throwing it for Ric. You know he got sentenced to five years the other day. He gotta turn hisself in Monday."

"Now I ain't knew," Rasheid recalled the conversation Ric and Dre had the night before over the phone.

"Well that's going to be the motherfucking party of the summer. Everybody gone be there. Its going to be at the Embassy."

"Alright, well I guess I'll see you there."

"Make sho you do that man. I'ma holla though," Dee pulled out his medicine bottle and walked over to the car that awaited him.

Rasheid wondered why Dre didn't ask him to come to the party. He thought it was because Dre looked at him as being too young. Whatever the case was it didn't matter because he was going to that party. Being that the summer was almost over and school was about to start back up made it an even better reason why he had to go. Plus it'll be his first official party he ever attended. He went home to drop his stuff off and came back out to get something to eat. As he walked down the street he heard some music coming from behind him and turned around to see a burgundy 89' box Caprice slowing down. As the car came to a hault the window rolled down slowly.

"What the fuck you looking at nigga," the driver said.

Rasheid tried to make out who was in the car. When he recognized who the driver was, a big smile covered his face.

"What up Rookie!" he was shocked to see his best friend driving.

"Man get in. Let's ride out."

Rasheid didn't hesitate. He hurried into the passenger seat as Rookie mashed the gas pedal.

"Man do you got yo license?"

"Where the hell I get it from," he laughed. "I got my permit though."

"When you get this," he looked around his car.

"About month ago. I told you that I'm not stepping one foot on the grounds of Naughty By without a whip."

"Yeah you did say that," Rasheid looked at how long Rookie's braids were. The last time he saw him his braids barely came down to his neck. Now they were down to his shoulders. He assumed it was because of the Puerto Rican in him that made his hair grow so fast. Him and Rookie came a long way from when they first met two years ago on the school bus. Its because of Rasheid that Rookie passed the seventh and eighth grade. At first Rookie's whole intentions were to take advantage of him and play it for what it was worth. But the more he hung around Rasheid, the more he took a liking to him. Then after Rasheid started boosting clothes and made a little money, he seen that he was a hustler and didn't even knew it. Another thing they had in common was neither of them knew their real parents. Rookie's mother got killed when he was four years old, leaving him and his seven year old sister to be taken care of by their grandmother, a Puerto Rican woman who spoke very little English. His father who was a blackman, went to prison right after he was born, so Rookie whose real name is Reginald Santez and his sister Eve both turned to the streets at a young age.

"So where you headed at?"

"I was about to go to get something to eat from Bertha's"

"Yeah I heard about that shit. Right up the street right," Rookie fired up his black and mild.

"Yeah right up here. You trying to go."

"Yeah we can do that."

"So where you was heading at."

"I was riding up here to see if I'll run into you. Shit was kinda slow for the last couple days. You know that nigga Ric caught five years, so nigga acting real antsy and shit. Ric running around talking about all these motherfuckers owe him money and shit. Dem niggas from the Ville and back round my way charging like a thousand fifty dollars for a O. I'm not about to pay them motherfuckers a extra hundred or two hundred dollars, you know what I'm sayin?" he looked over at Rasheid. "Shit, so I had to go cop some work from them niggas out West Ashley and I'm just about to sit for a minute until all this shit clear over. The niggas hot as a bitch, the police all over the motherfucking place," Rookie let out some of the frustration he's held on to for the last couple days as they arrived to their destination and he put the car in park," but besides that you know everthing is everthing," he put out his black and mild as they entered the restaurant, "So what's up wit you?"

"I'm chillin," Rasheid opened the door stepped in the restaurant. "I'm bout ready to stop messing around wit boosting these clothes. I'd seen a shorty got knocked off today. And she was pregnant."

"I'm sayin man," Rookie said as they sat down and looked through the menu. "It's chances at everything we do. You just gotta make sure you don't get caught," he said with all his attention on the menu. "Damn this motherfucking Philly Cheese look good as a bitch."

"I don't know," Rasheid looked through the menu. "I'm just sick of stealing period. I be feeling like my grandma be watching me every time I do that."

"Hmm-mm you be alright," Rookie said as the waitress stepped to the table.

"Hi welcome to Bertha's my name is Tania, how may I help you."

"Yeah let me get that Philly Cheese and that strawberry shortcake to," Rookie gave her his menu.

"Umm," Rasheid looked down at the menu hoping she didn't see him staring. "Let me get that double cheeseburger and fries with some sweet tea."

"Would that be all?"

"Yeah," Rasheid tried not to make eye contact with her.

"You sure?" she asked.

"Yeah I'm sure," Rasheid looked up at her then at Rookie and hoped he didn't see him blushing. But Rookie noticed the change in his behavior.

She turned away to walk off but turned back around.

"Oh yeah, thanks for that tip the other night to," she said and walked off.

Rookie and Rasheid both looked at her as she walked away.

"So you leaving big tips now huh?"

"Come on man," Rasheid said looking around the restaurant trying to avoid the conversation.

"That's alright dog. If you like to be the big tipper that's cool wit me," Rookie teased.

"Whatever," Rasheid got irritated then looked out the window.

"Ha ha ha," Rookie burst out laughing causing other customers to look over at him.

"Yo you blushing. You got a thing for Shorty."

"What you talkin bout man?"

"Nigga you don't gotta front for me, shit I ain't nobody! Plus Shorty bad as a motherfucker. If you pull her shit you'll be doing alright," just as Rookie got the words out of his mouth she was walking back to the table with their order.

"Thank you," Rasheid said still not making eye contact with her.

"You're welcome," she said politely.

"Yo check this out Shorty. My name is Rookie," Rookie said with his hand on his chest. "And this my homeboy Rasheid," Rasheid mumbled something then looked away as he sensed his friend about to make a fool of both of them. "Now my boy wanna holla at chu, he just don't know how to OUCH!" Rookie looked at Rasheid like he was crazy then rubbed his leg from where he just kicked him. Tania watched them both.

"How old are y'all? Like sixteen or something," she said. "You two look a little too young."

"Like my home girl Aaliyah said, age ain't nuttin but a number," Rookie bit into his sandwich.

"And she's right. Its nothing but a number that distinguish the difference between mature and immaturity. Here's your receipt thank you for doing business with Bertha's You gentlemen have a nice day," she gave Rasheid one last eye contact before she walked off.

"Damn that was a dis," Rookie took another bite out of his sandwich.

"That was a dis to you. Why you told her I like her for."

"Life is all about chances man, you need to try it sometimes," he said with a mouth full of food. "Why the hell you kick me with them hard ass sneakers fo?"

"That's what you get for talking so much."

"Anyway, what's up with the party tonight. You going or what."

"Yeah I'm going. I'm thinking about what I'm going to wear now," Rasheid took a sip of his drink.

"Oh you know it's the everyday uniform for me. White tees and Willy D's," Rookie showed his fresh pair of all white Air Forces. They continued to converse as they finished their meal. Tania came an picked up their plates and glasses on the table, told them to have a nice day and walked off without eye contact or saying another word. Rookie and Rasheid paid for their meal and left the restaurant.

"See that kind of broad right there want you to chase her," Rookie picked the food from between his teeth with the toothpick.

"I ain't tripping off that. Right now I gotta find a better way to get my hands on these clothes without stealing it."

"The only way you gone be able to do that is if you get your license. Other than that any type of dealings you have with it is going to be hot."

As they got inside the car Rookie went to light his black mild. Just as he flicked the lighter, he heard the tires screeched and in the blink of an eye there was blue and white North Charleston police cars surrounding him. Rookie got so scared when he heard the officer's voice on the bull horn telling them to get out the car with their hands up, he wasn't able to think clear enough to remember if he had drugs on him or not. As he contemplated for a second he remembered stashing the drugs away before he came to pick up Rasheid.

"What the hell is going on?" Rasheid looked around terrified.

"It ain't nothing," Rookie tried to stay calm. "Just get out the car. I'm clean so they can't do shit to us."

"STEP OUT THE CAR WITH YOUR HANDS UP!" the officer repeated on the bull horn. Rookie and Rasheid both stepped out the car the same time with their hands in the air. There was officers all around them aiming their guns. By the time they got out of the car, policeman had them lying face down on the ground with hand cuffs on. Some customers as well as employees watched what took place. For the past couple years, Rasheid was use to embarrassment but this was a different kind of humiliation he faced. He looked at some of the customers face as he sensed by their expression that they automatically categorized him as the derogatory image that society has placed upon the black man. As he looked around the faces he caught eye contact with Tania. Her eyes shown concern like the girl who helped out for him that day he was being picked on. The more he looked at her the more he felt a connection with her, like they had a relationship that was not yet developed. The police placed them both in separate cars as a few other officers searched Rookie's car. After they searched Rasheid and asked him a bunch of questions relating to Rookie's drug affairs, they let him go after doing a background check on him and seeing that he was clean. Rookie got indicted on four drug charges. They already had secret indictments on him, pictures of him making drug sales and some more. But it was all a part of their scheme. Catch the little fish and hopefully he'll lead the way to the bigger ones. Rasheid was about to walk off until he looked over at Rookie and tried to read his lips. Rookie said, "I'ma call you so be home."

Ch A p t e r 6

~~~~~~

R asheid walked around the house debating on should he go to the party tonight. Dee said that he could ride with him, which he should be arriving shortly. Rookie called a couple hours earlier and said that he needed him to pick up some money from his house. He told him to get it from Eve, she knows what he's talking about. Rasheid went to put on his black and white Air Jordans to match his all black Polo jeans and white and black Polo collar shirt. He took out a fourteen karat gold necklace which he only wore on special occasions and put it around his neck. Just as he looked in the mirror to double check himself he heard Dee car horn blow. He grabbed his house key, made sure his money was in his pocket and left out the door. Just as he got into the car and slammed the door, Dee pulled off. Dee drove a 1987 Buick Regal that definitely needed some work done on the inside.

"Hand me that cd right there," Dee put the fire to his blunt.

Rasheid handed him Master P's Ghetto Dope album. He put the cd in the player and turned up the volume. "Rookie a sturdy young nigga. All they gone do is try and shake him up and try to get him to tell on somebody," he inhaled the blunt.

"Nah my boy ain't going out like that," Rasheid looked out the window.

"That nigga betta not," Dee passed the blunt to Rasheid.

"Nah I'm good man," he turned it down. "Yo what time you leaving the party."

"Why man. What you got a curfew or something."

"Nah, I just gotta go pick something up for Rookie."

"Check this out," Dee exhaled the smoke. "Tonight is my night off. So I'm bout to drink, smoke and try to find some pussy," Dee turned up the volume singing in with Master P. "Pass me the weed I need some green wit my Hennessey /pass me the weed I need some green wit my Hennessey."

They rode with the music bumping down East Montague until they got to the Embassy Suites. When they pulled into the hotel there was already a section for the guests of Ric and Dre's party. Rasheid and Dee stepped out of the car and looked around the parking lot seeing nothing but Cadillac's, Acura's, Cutlass and a couple of Benz's. There wasn't one single car out there that didn't have any rims on it. Dee lead the way through the building into the elevator. The party was being held in the penthouse on the fifth floor. When they opened the door, Ric and Jason had the place looking like a small club. There were ladies everywhere. The music was so loud Rasheid couldn't hear himself think. Just about every guy at the party was a known drug dealer who at some time had some type of dealing with Ric or Dre. Some of the hustlers came to the party to show their respect but most of them came to hear the what's happening. See who's driving what, who's getting money, who snitching and who's hooked up with who. And whenever you got a lot of hustlers under the same roof at the same time the ladies are sure to follow. Rasheid followed behind Dee as he walked up to Ric and gave him a hug. Ric had a bottle of Moet in his hand as him and Dee made a quick pose for a picture, shook hands one last time and went their separate ways. Rasheid seen a lot of the faces before but knew none of them on a personal level. He walked around to see if he bumped into somebody he knew and that's when it dawn on him, there wasn't nobody at the party was his age. And the more he realized it, the more he felt out of place. Everybody else was having the time of their life, partying, dancing and drinking like it was New Year's Eve. As Rasheid was making his way back to the living room where the entrance was he ran into Dre.

"What the hell your young ass doing here," Dre playfully slapped him on the back of his neck.

"What's up man," Rasheid shook his hand.

"Ain't no what's up man I said what the hell yo young ass doing here," Dre took a sip from his cup.

"Just trying to show some love."

"Yo ass just trying to live fast," he said as a young lady walked up behind him and gave him a hug. "Oh what"s up Trice baby. How you been doing?"

"I'm good. What's been going on with you sexy?"

"Oh you know doing what I do. How's your brother doing?"

"He fine. He got eleven months left."

"That's what's up. You want something to drink?"

"Okay."

Dre escorted her where the drinks were.

"Yo Rasheid I'ma holla at you," he said as him and the young lady moved through the crowd.

Rasheid still felt out of place as he stood in the corner pretending as if he was enjoying himself. He wish Rookie was there with him as he wondered what he was doing. As the night went on, the crowd started to simmer down a bit. He grabbed a soda from out of the kitchen and looked around the party. He couldn't find Dre or Dee as he observed all the faces his eyes ran across. Then he saw a familiar face. It was a girl who he known he seen before but where he couldn't remember. Just then a guy came up and started talking to her and it looked as if she was telling him no. He said a couple more words to her, she smiled shook her head no again and the guy walked off. Then Rasheid remembered exactly who she was. It was Tania. And she looked even better out of her uniform. She had to be about 5'3" or 5'4" in the heels she wore. Her skin look like it had more of a glow to it. Her hair was back into a ponytail coming a little pass her shoulders. She wore a black skirt that came right above her knees with a tight short sleeve shirt tucked in and a black four inch wide belt around her waist. All the black she wore bought out her caramel complexion skin even better. Just as Rasheid was about to make his way over to her, he seen Dre walked up to her and gave her a hug. Then a big smile appeared on her face as she opened up to him as they laughed and talked with one another. Just then he seen the female who Dre was talking to earlier sitting on a guy lap drinking a beer as she moved her body to the beat of a Biggie Smalls song. Then everybody's attention went to Ric who was standing on the counter with a microphone in his hand rapping along with the song, "Cause I see some ladies tonight that should be *having my baby-baby*," he sung as the crowd cheered him on. Rasheid's attention then went to Tania and Dre who was now looking at the drunken Ric make a fool out himself. Tania looked at Ric with her arms folded across her chest shaking her head as if she was disappointed with his behavior. Dre smiled at him taking baby sips out of the beer bottle. Tania then took her eyes off of Ric and engaged into another conversation with Dre. She and Dre talked for a while as the party started to simmer down a bit. Dee finally came out of one of the bedroom with this female who was as drunk as him. They both crashed on the couch laughing and whispering in each other's ear. Dre disappeared and Tania was standing up with her purse on searching through it looking as if she was ready to go. Rasheid then decided to go talk to her. He figured it'll be now or never. As he walked up to her she was still searching through her purse then pulled out some keys in time to look right into his eyes. Out of the blue he just gained a whole lot of confidence.

"How you doing Tania?"

Tania just looked at him for a second as she closed her purse back and put it under her arms, "Hi. I didn't know you knew how to talk," Rasheid smiled. "So what you doing here. Being that you almost went to jail today I thought you'll probably be home counting your blessings."

"Well yeah, I'm doing that. That little situation today was just a little misunderstanding."

"Of course it was," she said sarcastically. "That's what it always is. A misunderstanding, breaking the law or committing a crime had nothing to do with it."

"So anyway," Rasheid started to feel like he was being scolded. "What you doing here."

"A going away party for my brother," she pointed at Ric.

"Ric your brother!" he said surprised.

"Yeah he's my brother, why you said it liked that," she got defensive.

"Nah. It's just that I was shock. I look up to Ric a whole lot."

"How do you know my brother?" Tania asked intrigued.

"Well I really don't know him but I see him all the time and I respect how he carry himself."

"If you don't mind me asking, how old are you?"

"Why? How old are you?"

"Didn't your mother ever told you it was rude to ask a lady's age."

"As a matter of fact no, she never told me that. But how can I be rude for me to ask your age when you're here giving me the third degree," Rasheid said serious.

"Ha ha ha," she laughed out loud. "That was cute," she tried to get her words in between laughing. "But you know what, I'm not going to take that the wrong way."

"You know what, my bad I apologize. I came over here to introduce myself not to get off on the wrong foot with you."

"You're not getting off on the wrong foot with me. I'm actually enjoying the conversation Ra-shawn."

"Rasheid."

"Rasheid that's right," she smiled at him. The truth was that she really was enjoying his company. He caught her attention when he first came into the restaurant and she saw how nervous he acted when she came around. She liked feeling superiority to a man but at the same time she also wanted a man to take his place. "So um...is your friend going to be alright? The one they took to jail today."

"Yeah, Rookie he'll be out in a minute."

"You know I just really think its sad how many young black males get locked up, thinking it's cool to go to jail and prison not knowing that that's taking valuable time out of your life and all the pain you cause your family to go through. I try to tell my thick head brother that all the time but you think he listen to me," she pointed at Ric who still acted a fool on top of the counter. "And now he's about to go to prison for five years and I'm going to be the one sending him letters, pictures and putting money on his books. You seem like your bright Rasheid but when I saw how those cops had you and your friend on the ground today in handcuffs that picture keeps playing back in my head when they took my father and I don't want to see that happen to nobody else. Especially somebody whose so full of potential like you," there was a long paused between them as Rasheid let the reality settled in on what she was saying.

"So your father still in prison."

"For life," Tania stared off at a distance.

They continued to talk for a while and found out a lot about each other. Tania was surprised at how smart Rasheid was but he didn't conceal his full history about himself or the fact that his grandmother passed away and made him promise her that he'll graduate from school and make something of himself. Tania told him how her father sold drugs and ran numbers back in the seventies and eighties. They lived a lifestyle above their means until her father caught a life sentence back in eighty-six. They lost their house and cars and was forced to move to Trailwood trailer park. Since then her mother fell to the streets and started smoking crack, leaving her and Ric in the house by themselves throughout the day and sometimes at night. So that forced Ric to start hustling at the young age of ten and that's when he met Dre. The money Ric was bringing in he was basically looking out for the needs of him and his sister. When Tania got old enough to understand how Ric was getting his money and couldn't get him to stop, she pushed herself to finish high school and get a college degree so that she can get a good paying job and then maybe help put Ric on the right track. Even though Ric was paying for her to go to school she still didn't agreed to the lifestyle that he lived. The more Rasheid revealed his thoughts the more potential she saw and she start to admire him even more.

"So is your mother and father still alive," Tania asked as they sat on the couch with all her attention focused on him.

"I don't know neither of them," Rasheid looked away. "They left me with my grandmother when I was a baby."

"So you don't even know if they're alive or not?" she felt sorry for him.

"Nah," Rasheid looked down. He started to feel a little emotional so he then looked around and noticed about half of the people already left. He then looked back at Dee and saw that him and his female friend was in the corner asleep leaning on each other.

"Yo but it's getting late," he looked at his watch and noticed for the first time the hour and a half that flew by.

"Ooh!" Tania looked at her watch and realized it was late too. "It's almost four o'clock in the morning. And Ric probably left here with one of those hoochies," she looked around for her brother. Rasheid smiled. "What you smiling at?" she stood up fixing her clothes.

"Nothing," he lied. "I'm just happy I got a chance to come over here and talk to you," he said as Tania tried to hide her blush.

"Well I'm glad I got the chance to talk to you too. You need to come by the restaurant and check me out sometimes," she really wanted to give him her number but felt desperate for falling for a boy who was only fourteen. Being that she was eighteen that four year gap made a big difference in her eyes.

"I will," Rasheid stood up beside her. They both felt the chemistry connecting between them as they stood face to face looking in each others eyes.

"Well I gotta go wake my ride up," Rasheid pointed at Dee asleep on the couch next to the girl.

"You want me to give you a ride," Tania said without thinking. Rasheid then remembered that Rookie wanted him to go over to his house and pick up some money or something and he then wanted to beat himself up for forgetting.

"Nah that's alright. I just remembered something I had to do tonight." "At four o'clock in the morning," she said suspiciously.

"I just gotta go pick something up for my friend."

"Okay," she knew it was more to what he was saying.

"Well I'ma definitely be coming through to check you out," he extended his hand to shake hers.

"Goodnight," Tania reached out to shake his hand.

"Goodnight," Rasheid walked away in the direction towards Dee.

"Dee. Yo Dee. Wake up," he tapped Dee on his shoulders.

"What's up man," Dee said half awoke with his eyes still closed.

"The party's over. It's time to roll out," Dee looked around the room seeing that most of the people left. He gave Rasheid his car keys woke up his female friend then the three headed outside. The cold morning air took the little bit of tiredness he had out of him. Dee and his friend hopped in the back seat and went back to sleep. Rasheid got in the driver's seat and started on his way. He learned to drive through Rookie from renting so many crack addicts cars. The first few times he had a little trouble but after a while driving became natural to him. He looked in the rearview mirror and saw that Dee and the girl was back asleep, so he headed to Rookie's house. When he got to Rookie's house he got out the car leaving it running and knocked on Rookie's grandmother door. After about two minutes of knocking, Eve opened the door.

"Hey Rasheid," her voice was just above a whisper. "Come in."

"What's up Eve," Rasheid tried not to look at her smooth legs and pretty manicured feet.

"You picked a fined time to come over," she closed the door behind him.

"Sorry bout that," Rasheid said.

"Hold on for a minute," she walked to Rookie's bedroom. The silk robe she had on displayed how perfectly round her butt was as she walked off with her hands across her chest and her hair in cornrows coming to the middle of her back. Rasheid always had a secret crush on Eve but he never acted on it. Eve came back within seconds with a key in her hand. "It's a little black bag in that car trunk right there," she pointed at an abandoned car. "Rookie said that he trust you know what to do with it, he need the money for a lawyer," Eve looked at Rasheid. Curiosity aroused in Rasheid as he headed towards the car trunk. He opened the trunk using the light from the bulb inside to see. He looked around the trunk then lifted up the spare tire and saw a little black pouch about the size of his hand, maybe a little bigger. He grabbed the pouch then opened it. It was crack cocaine. He opened the bag all the way up and counted the blocks. He held it out to the street light to get a better look at it and saw that it was nine ounces of crack, if he wasn't mistaking. He zipped the pouch back up and went back to the house.

"Tell him I'ma take care of it," Rasheid gave Eve back the keys.

"Alright, you want me to tell him to call you," Eve said as Rasheid headed back to the car.

"Yeah, tell him to do that," Rasheid opened the car door.

"Rasheid!" Eve yelled out. "Be careful," she looked at him with sincerity in her eyes.

"I got chu," Rasheid slammed the car door and drove off.

ChApter 7

T he first few weeks Rasheid was absolutely clueless to what he was doing. He knew how to measure it, cook it, and bag it. But when actually came to selling crack, he didn't have an idea of what to do. When he first went out on the corner with a couple of ounces cut up in his pocket, he felt uncomfortable asking people if they wanted to buy drugs from him. He would see junkies drive up and about six or seven people run to their car advertising that their product was the best. He tried to do what they were doing but was beat out through competition. The addicts that did gave him a chance made him feel as though they were doing him a favor for choosing him over the rest. They expected more than what their money was paying for. Rasheid started out losing more money than he was making and saw that it was useless for him to continue to sell drugs. That was until Dre took him under his wing and taught him the ins and outs of the drug game. He taught Rasheid that selling drugs was like a sport. "You must be very competitive," he told him there was a difference between drug dealers and hustlers. Drug dealers sold drugs in return for money that's it. Drug dealers are inpersistent, unbalanced and didn't appreciate the game for what it was. But hustlers were more discipline and focus. Hustlers sacrificed their time, money and life to get ahead in the game. Hustlers mastered the art of stacking money and was about the dollar bill by all means. Rasheid rode around with Dre for a few weeks. Seeing how he conducted business and managed drug deals throughout the city, in different towns and neighborhoods. Dre felt as though it was alright to introduce Rasheid to Roger to see what he thought of him. Roger

considered himself the type of person who was born to sell drugs. He was
in his early forties and carried himself very humbly, never flashy. Some
people say that he resembled the late Robin Harris, which in fact was the
truth. Rodger automatically took a liking to Rasheid. He mainly dealt
with people who he sensed had loyalty, honor and trust. And very few
of them had a direct relationship with him like Dre had. He taught Dre
about the drug game when he was young who in return taught Ric. Rodger
dealt with Dre like a son in law but saw Ric as a loose cannon and knew
that in time he'll either be dead or in jail. Rodger was mainly known for
supplying drugs throughout the city of Charleston, Mount Pleasant and
some parts of Walterboro and Beaufort. The people who bought drugs
from Rodger considered him to old school and narrow minded, because
he was always complaining about the young boys today who's in the drug
game didn't have a clue to what they were doing. "Y'all ain't being coached
properly and have no type of honor amongst each other. Then have the
nerve to get death before dishonor tattooed on your body but when the
people threaten you with a little bit of time you fucking snitch on the
whole neighborhood." After being groomed and instilled with principles
and morals for the past couple months through Dre and Rodger, Rasheid
saw the drug world for what it was rather than what it appeared to be. He
then equated selling drugs to selling clothes. It was all about having the
best brand for the most reasonable price. He still had to go through some
trial and error being that he was a new face and a lot younger than the rest
of the hustlers. But the advantage he had was that the quality of cocaine
he was selling came from some people out West Ashley who bought it
from Rodger who was connected directly to Rino. And everyone knew
that Rino supplied the city with nothing less than the best. And
everyone was trying to get a piece of it. Rookie just luckily happened to
stumble across the best batch, which in return ended up in Rasheid's hands.
After a while Rasheid's clients were constantly raising and before he
realized it, he was making hundreds and sometimes a couple thousand
dollars per day. On a day to day basis so much money was coming through
Rasheid's hands so quickly that he would find himself being nervous
sometimes for no reason. Drug addicts drove by specifically looking for
him putting the original people they were buying from secondary. Every
once in a while some junkies still tried to take advantage of him, being
that he was young and thinking he

was naïve but once he recognized it, he acknowledged it by standing firm and remembering what Dre said, "People only gonna try it if they think they can do it."

///////////////////////////////

As Rasheid sat in his room with his doors locked. He couldn't believe he saved over eleven thousand dollars within the matter of months. He then took eight thousand and put it to the side for Rookie's legal fees. It left him with thirty-four hundred dollars to himself. He had enough money to take him through the rough days to come. But for some reason he felt as though he bonded a relationship with the drug game. He looked around his room and saw that he came a long way from two years ago when he first moved in with his aunt. His closet was filled with clothes two thirds he haven't worn yet. He had over ten pairs of sneakers all of them still looked brand new. He had a thirty-six inch t.v. and a stereo system that crackheads gave him from around the way in return for drugs. He was amazed at some of the things people would trade just to get high. He had people bringing him their jewelry, ancient souvenirs, food stamps, lending him their cars and he always had drug addict females throwing themselves at him. The most disgusted suggestion he had approached him yet was this one time right after he made a sale he saw a white man who could have the played the part of Santa Claus in a movie rode up on a bicycle and said, "Excuse me son, you don't sell crack or anything like that do you."

"Nah man. I don't think you know me," Rasheid tried to walk away not trusting the man.

"No, no son. It's not like that. You see I love to get high. Its just so hard for me to get the drugs."

"Well I'm sorry man but I can't help-"

"Listen, I know you sell drugs," the old man cut Rasheid off. "And I know you like money too," Rasheid started to get nervous not knowing what the man intentions were but started to walk off again. "But how would you like some head."

"What!" Rasheid was caught totally off guard.

"How about I give you a little head and if you like it-," Rasheid walked off before the old man could even finish his sentence. He left the man with an embarrassing look on his face. He pictured himself beating the man down with a bat but quickly thought against it when his grandmother came to mind. He knew his grandmother would turn twice in her grave if he would have been in the middle of the street beating up an elderly man. So he figured he had done the right thing by walking away.

The next day Rasheid came home from what was actually a decent day at school. He wasn't the most popular kid in school but he was acknowledged by some who were. He'd only been in the ninth grade for two months and he already had a couple girls who were trying to be his girlfriend. He was flattered at the fact but wasn't interested in either of them. For some reason he couldn't get Tania out of his mind. He felt self-conscious about the age difference between them and wished he hadn't revealed it the day he was pouring his heart out to her, but he got caught up in the moment. He decided that this would be a nice day to go see her since the last few times he went to the restaurant he didn't really have a chance to speak to her, being that the restaurant was so busy and his time was limited. But now since he had a free day with nothing else to do but a little homework, he figured today would be perfect. He took his school work as a joke. Since he'd been in high school he hadn't had anything less than a B plus, which was a Spanish class. The only class that gave him a slight challenge. As he headed out the door, he turned around and went to his stash and took out two hundred dollars in twenties. He counted the money and made sure there was thirty-two hundred dollars left, put it in his empty Timberland shoe box then headed towards the door. Just as he opened the door, Tereesa was getting ready to insert her key.

"Hey Aunt Tereesa," Rasheid looked at how wide her eyes was open and her disorganized hair. 'She must be high.' He thought to himself.

"Hey Baby. How you doin?" Tereesa rubbed her nose. "How was school today?"

"It was fine," he tried to leave out the door.

"Rasheid," Tereesa blocked the entrance. Rasheid cursed himself as he looked his aunt in her eyes already knowing what she wanted. "Let me borrow twenty dollars till I get my paycheck on Friday," she used the same line she always used. They both knew that she knew he sold drugs but for some reason she never exposed it. And it was probably because he took care of the house and paid more bills than she did.

"Aunt Tereesa, I just gave you fifty dollars this morning."

"Boy I took the car today to get a tune up and I had to get a oil change and I had to get some new brake pads. Shit the way you drive we ain't gone have a car soon," Rasheid knew it was useless to try and argue with his aunt, so he took out a twenty dollar bill and gave it to her. A big smile appeared on her face as she took the money and put it in her bra. "Thanks nephew," she said as she poked his nose with her index finger like she use to when he was younger. Rasheid hated to see his only family member being sucked up by the streets like that but he was in a no win situation. He didn't want to give her the money because he knew she was getting high with it, but if he didn't give her the money he knew she'll get it the best way she can and he definitely didn't want to see her in that image. So the best way he could deal with it was by not dealing with it. As he stepped outside, he noticed the guys standing on the block and some walking back and forth to the drug addict's cars. He didn't want to be seen so he tried to avoid them by going the opposite direction. When he saw that he was out of sight, part of him was saying he needed to be out there getting as much money as possible. Then the other side of him said he completed the mission he set out for and he had enough money saved for himself. Yet he thought about what he was going to do when his money ran out. He still wasn't at the age where he could get a job yet and at the rate Tereesa was going, he knew the money wouldn't last but for so long. As he wrestled back and forth with the thoughts in his head, he tried to alleviate it by thinking about Rookie. He'll never admit it to Rookie but he missed him. He was the closet person to a brother that he had. He dropped eight thousand dollars off to Eve cash the day prior. She was grateful for the lawyer's money though she wondered what took him so long. They had a brief conversation about Rookie. His lawyer said for the most it looks like he'll be doing eighteen months. He could have gotten out days after his arrest but they wanted him to snitch on his supplier and since he refused to cooperate, they threaten him with prison time. The lawyer James Sterling had a little pull with the judges in circuit court, so he was able to make a plea agreement for eighteen months. Rookie was a first time felon and was really looking at five years. They were just waiting on the money to make it happen. Rasheid was glad he was able to help, he just wished he had less time. A lot can happen in eighteen months. By the time Rasheid looked up, he was walking in the entrance of the restaurant parking lot. His attention was quickly drawn to the nineteen ninety-two Honda Accord that was backing out of a parking spot then headed in his direction. As the car got closer he heard the clear stereo system blasting a song by Mary J. Blidge. As the car got even closer, he saw that it was Tania and she wasn't in her uniform. When she saw that it was him she slowed down then came to a complete stop and turned the music down.

"What's going on stranger," she looked him up and down.

"What's up," Rasheid stepped closer to her car. He saw that even on her average days she still looked good.

"I'm sayin," she was still checking him out. "Nautica jeans, Nautica shirt, Willy D's and a gold chain. I know you sell clothes and everything but can a sister get a hook up," she said as he tried to hide his blush.

"Anyway," he brushed off her complaint. "You got the day off or something."

"Why, you came up here to see me," she teased him with a big smile on her face.

"Well really I came to get something to eat and I figured I'll say hi to you since you do work here," Tania quickly erased her smile. "Nah I was just playing," Rasheid laughed.

"Oh!" she smiled with him. "Because I was about to say you must want to get cursed out trying to dis me like that."

"So what you came here to eat on your days off too."

"No silly. I came to pick up my paycheck."

"Okay! So you ballin out tonight huh," Rasheid rubbed his hand together.

"Shh. I'm barely making it," she pointed to her gas meter that was pointing at the E. "You see where my tank is at right."

"Yeah," Rasheid looked at the meter. " You need to hurry and put some gas in here, because you are to pretty too be walking out here in this hot sun."

"Shut up boy!" Tania laughed at him.

"I'm serious. And I don't got a car so I can't give you a ride," he said.

"Have anybody ever told you, you look like Rakim."

"Who?"

"Rakim. The rapper. You know Rakim and Eric B. They got the album Paid In Full."

"Nah I ain't never been told that before."

"Well you look like a young Rakim. And that's a good thing because he's my favorite rapper," she excluded the fact that she also had the biggest crush on him.

"Well thank you. I guess but um I'm not really feeling standing out here in this hot sun so uhh-"

"Come on and get in. I know a place where we can get some good food," she moved her pocketbook from the passenger seat to the back seat. "That's if you don't got no place else to be."

"I'm the one who should be asking you that. Today is your day off," Rasheid got in the car and closed the door behind him.

"So how you been doing?" she said as she drove off.

"Alright."

"No. I mean how you really been doing? Have you been holding up okay?"

"Yeah I'm alright. I don't have a choice but to be alright."

"You don't talk like your fourteen."

"How is a fourteen year old is supposed to talk?" She

thought before she answered, "Inexperience."

"Well everybody's inexperience to a degree. I can't be held accountable for tomorrow but I can be held accountable for today and the previous."

"What you mean?" she asked intrigued.

"I'm only liable for the circumstances I've already encountered. If I haven't been face to face with this certain situation then you can't hold that against me. For a child who's been in the suburbs his whole life and goes to a private school he'll be naïve to what goes on in the projects and vice versa. So they are inexperience to the challenges they haven't been face with yet."

"See that's what I mean!" Tania smiled and hit the steering wheel. "Listen to how you talk! You don't talk like your fourteen!" she was impressed. "I bet you make straight A's don't you."

"Nah. Not really," he said after he thought about it. "I make some B's here and there."

"You know what. You are just too much," she drove in the parking lot of the gas station and pulled to the nearest pump.

"You need me to pump gas for you."

"That's thankful of you. Pump ten dollars worth," she took up his offer. "I only said that to be courteous. I didn't think you was going to have me pump your gas for real," Rasheid teased.

"Well you can't tease a black woman like that. That's like sayin I'm pay your light bill then turn around and say nah I was just playin. We take things like that serious," she grabbed her pocketbook and stepped out of the car. As she got out of the car she turned around and stated, "Well that goes to show you are inexperience to somethings," she then smiled and walked into the store. Rasheid smiled to himself as he got out and pumped the gas. When he was finished he got back in the passenger seat and waited for Tania to return. As he sat back and looked at how backed up traffic was, he observed a white truck pulled up with five guys in it. All looking like they were in their late teens and early twenties. One in the driver seat, one in the passenger seat and three in the cab compartment. They all got out of the truck laughing and joking each other while entering the store. Tania exited out the same time they were coming in and she caught all five of their attention. They all turned around and stare in her direction whistling and shooting her cat calls. She noticed it but simply ignored them and kept walking towards the car. "A gurl," one of the guys yelled out. "I can't tell you nothing bout your future but yo past look mighty fine," he and all of his friends laughed and gave each other hi-fives. Tania turned around looked at them and kept walking. She got back in the car and closed the door behind her.

"I hope you don't end up like these types of niggas," she pointed at the group of guys. Rasheid smiled to himself hoping it'll take over that little bit of frustration he held inside. He realized that it wouldn't be a smart move being that he was out-numbered by four, "Its okay. I can take care of myself," she read his facial expressions and saw that he wasn't too happy about what took place.

"Nah. I ain't trippin. Just stuff like really irks me."

Tania drove off, "It's alright. I get that all the time. I just pay niggas like that no attention. So," she changed the subject. "You ever thought about what you wanna do when you get out of school," Rasheid was embarrass at the question. When he was younger he wanted to be a lawyer because he was always fascinated by watching them in the courtroom. But through the last couple years he lost that desire and haven't been putting much thought to it or his future lately.

"I wanted to be a lawyer when I was younger," he looked out the window.

"What. You don't want to be one now or something," Tania looked at him then back at the highway.

"I don't know," she stared at him for awhile.

"You know what. The problem with you is that you don't see the type of potential you possess. I can see that it's not hard for you to lose or gain a passion for something. You just don't have nobody pushing you."

"What you trying to be a psychic or something," Rasheid said sarcastically.

"No. But I am taking up psychology as a minor," she smiled at him.

"Ohh. So that explains."

"I guess. But seriously, you just don't have nobody pushing you. That's probably why you so smart now, because I can tell your grandmother use to push you."

"Yeah, so where are we going at to eat?" Rasheid tried to change the subject.

"Uh-uh. I know you ain't trying to get off the subject," she playfully pushed the side of his head with her two fingers.

"Why, you being so violent, I'm just trying to get something to eat," Rasheid grabbed her hand as they continued to flirt with each other. They ate at the Italian restaurant Vincent Chicco's, then drove downtown Charleston at the waterfront area as they talk and grew more intimate with each other. Rasheid opened up to her like he never opened up to nobody else. They told each other their most embarrassing moments. Tania told him about her past relationships. She told him about how her life use to be before her mother got hooked on drugs and her father went to jail for forty years. She also told him how she always had a crush on Dre through the years, but now she looked at him as if he was a brother. She spoke on her desire to teach and how much she wants to be a teacher. Rasheid told her the transition he made from living with his grandmother to his aunt. He told her about his aunt's condition and how it grew from bad to worse and how he basically had to take care of the bills and a lot of other money she owed out. They literally talked the night away until they both realized that it was after midnight and they had to get up it the morning. They rode and continued to talk to each other as Rasheid gave her directions to his house. He then remembered that he lived in the projects and he wasn't too comfortable with her seeing where he lived.

"Yo, you can drop me off at this corner store, I need to get a couple things before I go home," he pointed at the store.

Tania put on her signal light and turned into the gas station, "I'll wait for you."

"Nah that's alright. I can use the walk home anyway, to unwind a little bit."

Tania gave him a nonchalant look.

"Boy go get what you gotta get and hurry up so I can drop you off home."

"I'm alright. Seriously."

She put the car in park and cross her arms over her chest, "Rasheid!" she looked him in his eyes. "Go get whatever you got to get and come on so that I can drop you off where you live. Now I don't have all night," Rasheid leaned over and kiss her on the cheek. She was shock and impress but tried to contain herself because she knew he was using it as a way to get out.

" I had a good time tonight but I gotta go," Tania feeling the wetness arrive between her thighs tried to hold herself and show no sign of vulnerability.

"You think you gonna get off that easy," she said with their faces inches away from each other.

"Nah. But I think you're beautiful," Tania unhelplessly leaned over and open mouth kissed him as he returned the favor. They explored each others mouth as their tongues discovered parts of them that they didn't knew exist. When they pulled away, they were at a lost for words and couldn't give each other eye contact.

"Um how about I just give you a call tomorrow," Rasheid said still not capable of looking her in her eyes.

"Alright," Tania felt the same way. Rasheid got out of the car walking in the direction of the night as Tania stared at him until he disappeared.

"He didn't even go in the store," she said coming back to realization.

Rasheid walked home smiling to himself as he envisioned what just took place over again in his mind. As he stepped into his neighborhood he saw the usual. Dee and a couple other guys from the neighborhood standing around smoking and drinking waiting for drug sales to come through. It's been a few days since he sold any drugs and he could tell by the looks on some of the guys face that they weren't too happy about his presence. Since he was feeling himself, he decided to walk up and talk to Dee for a minute. As he walked up to the crowd, he noticed the chattering stopped once he appeared.

"What's up Dee?"

"Ain't shit. What's up with you?" Dee also sensed the tension.

"Chillin. What's up Marco? Bryan," Rasheid nodded his head at the other two guys.

"What's up," they said in unison. Then there was an awkward silence.

"Dre asked about chu yesterday," Dee broke the silence.

"Oh he came through?"

"Yeah I guess he was just checking on you or something."

"Im'a holla at him."

"Where you been at all day. I saw you sneakin off earlier," Dee puffed on a cigarette.

Rasheid put his hands in his pocket feeling the coolness of the night coming along," I was chillin with a friend."

"Who?"

"Why you all in my business man?"

"Nigga who the fuck you was wit?" Dee said in a tone as if he was the older brother.

"This girl name Tania."

"What Tania? I know you ain't talking bout Ric sister.

All eyes was on Rasheid, "Yeah that's her."

A bit of jealously came over Dee, "Stop lying. Yo young ass don't know what to do with that."

Rasheid blushed then looked around, "If you say so. But yo I gotta go. School in the morning," he shook Dee's hand and nodded at the other two as they did the same. As he walked off he turned around and looked back at Dee who was still looking at him smiling. He knew Dee wasn't a threat to him but he couldn't say the same about the other two. He knew that he took money out of their pockets which they weren't to happy about. But like Dee said, in this game it's competition and may the best player win. Rasheid headed up the steps, inserted his key and stepped into the apartment. He went to the kitchen and saw that Tereesa added nothing new to the refrigerator. He then went to his bedroom and was caught off guard when he saw that it wasn't the way he left it. His drawers was open his mattress was leaning halfway off his bed as if someone was looking under it and his closet door was wide open which he knew he closed it. As he got to his closet, he saw that his clothes and shoes was everywhere. On the top of the pile of clothes and shoes he saw the empty Timberland shoe box that he had all of his money in. Anger began to take over him as he punch the wall as hard as he could not even feeling the effect. Tereesa wasn't home but he knew she was the only one who could have done this. He sat on the bed and said to himself. "Intelligence over emotions," which is what Dre taught him. As he tried to figure out what he was going to do he looked up at the empty shoe box again. The thought hit him that there wasn't no food in the refrigerator, Tereesa's part time paycheck wasn't enough to last her let alone the both of them and the bills. All he had left to his name was one hundred and forty-seven dollars. Rasheid kicked the shoe box then started kicking the pile of clothes. He then flopped on top of the pile with his face buried in his hands thinking about how he's going to get out of this situation.

ChApter 8

R odger just looked at Rasheid as they both sat on the front porch. "So you mean to tell me your aunt hit you for your whole stash."

"Everything. And now I don't even know what to do. I mean we dead broke and she ain't even come home yet," he explained his whole story leaving nothing out. Roger sat there and studied him for a minute. He could see that the boy had no deceitful traits and he could definitely feel his pain because he remembered when he was young how hard it was. Especially when there was no one he could depend on at a time when you really needed them. So he understand exactly what Rasheid was going through. He just didn't want to feel to much sympathy for him because the world isn't. Besides if you want anthing in this world you're going to have to get it and he wanted to see if Rasheid had that drive and ambition.

"I tell you what. I'ma give you five ounces. Monday bring me me back thirty-five hundred dollars. And from there you should be set straight. " You should be able to get rid of it at least by Sunday," he got up and went into the backroom. A couple minutes later he returned with a Ziploc bag with five ounces of crack and gave it to Rasheid. He then got back into his seat, "You got a scale?"

"Nah," Rasheid observed the bag then put it in his pocket.

"Well you need to get one."

"That'll be on top of my list to do," he then stood up. "Yo Roger, I appreciate this man."

"Just make sure you be here to see me Monday."

"I got chu I'll see you Monday," he shook Rodger's hand and left out the door. Roger studied him as he walked down the streets. He honestly couldn't answer why he was giving this boy a chance. That was something that he usually don't do but it was something on the inside that was giving him a good feeling about Rasheid. Just then a red Camaro pulled up with two white girls looking like they were in their mid twenties. They got out both wearing halter tops and short pants exposing their narrow legs all the way up to their butt cheeks. The females stepped on the porch trying to look sexy, giving Rodger eye contact with hopes of seducing him.

"I thought I told y'all don't bring y'all skinny asses round here no mo," he said without moving a muscle.

"Well were glad to see you too," one of the females said as she made her way to him then sat on his lap and rubbed his chest. Rodger now looked at the girl still not moving.

"What yo daddy won't give yo no more money?"

"Don't act like that baby. We drove all the way down here just so we could make you feel good," the female said working her way into seducing him. One weakness Rodger definitely had was for white women.

Rasheid went straight home and went to his bedroom and start breaking down the ounces. After he was finished he individually bagged up his break downs then headed outside. He still had an uncomfortable feeling for a little while but within hours all of that was gone. As soon as the drug addicts got a whiff of the quality of cocaine Rasheid had, a lot of the other flat foot hustlers got bumped back to secondary. And again Rasheid was seeing hundreds of dollars coming through his hand by the hour. By the time midnight fell, he went into his bedroom to re-up on his product. He stepped on his bed and took the screw out of the ceiling light cover. He then took the remainder of the cocaine out of the cover and put it into his pocket and screwed the light cover back in place. Then he went to the socket, unscrewed it and stashed four thousand three hundred and forty-five dollars in it. He put the dresser back in front of the socket then made his way back outside. As he got into the living room, Tereesa opened the front door. She had the guilty expression on her face before any words could be passed.

"Hey Rasheid."

"Where you been at for the last four days?"

Tereesa rubbed the back of her neck as her eyes hit the floor, "I've been doing some thinking. Rasheid I took-"

"You don't got to explain," he cut her off and walked pass her.

"Rasheid."

"I gotta go," he walked off from her. Even though he was not as mad at her as he was days ago he still wasn't in the mood to hear any of her excuses. As he got back outside, he looked down from the balcony and saw that it was at least a hundred people outside. There were the local crackheads walking around looking for where they could get their next next hit from. There was all kind of hustlers out. Some selling weed, crack cocaine others selling powered cocaine. There were females advertising their bodies in return for money. Some was just hustling to use the money to get high on their drug of choice. There were about five different stereos blasting music as loud as the volume would go, with other people around conversing with each other passing blunts back and forth. Some were drinking beer and some drinking liquor but everybody mingling as if they were at the happy hour spot. Rasheid went and join the mist. As he went amongst the crowd seeing how most of them welcomed him. Not knowing that they would welcome anybody who was getting money. He finally felt like he was a part of something. Then he went back and thought about what Tania asked him a few days ago. About what he wanted to do when he get out of school. He then wondered what if this was his calling. He thought about what of he was meant to be a hustler. As that seed was planted in his thought it started to grow. He made a promise to his grandmother that he would graduate out of high school so that was a must. But he was making hundreds sometimes thousands of dollars each day just using it as a way to get some extra money. Then he thought what if he was to take this serious. What if he was to dedicate not only his time and knowledge he acquired from Dre and Rodger, but also his life to this game. As he continued to think about it the more he felt that this was meant for him to do. To be a hustler. So that night was the first time Rasheid ever made a vow to himself. And as he was doing that, a strange feeling overcame him in a good way. A feeling he never felt before. He didn't know exactly what it was, but he brushed it off as he seen one of his clients then headed in his direction to conduct business. He didn't know that the feeling he felt was confidence.

ChApter 9

Tania ran around her two bedroom apartment doing what she usually do at six o'clock in the morning. After she got her books together for her morning classes, she ate a plate of grits, eggs and two piece of toast and drunk a glass of orange juice. She started to regret staying out pass midnight as she grabbed her bookbag and headed out the apartment door, then second guessed it when the thought of Rasheid came to mind. She got in her car, turned on the engine and let the car run for a few minutes as she thought about her day to come. All the money Ric gave her was gone and the three hundred dollars she got paid per week at Bertha's was barely enough to take care of her bills, rent, tuition, and school books. On the first of the month when she's finish paying all her bills and college expensed and give her mother whatever she can spare, she never have no money left over for herself. She never had a financial problem when Ric was on the street. He paid for her rent, college expenses and kept money in her pocket. Even though she didn't agree with how Ric was getting his money, she didn't turn any of it down. Now she realizes just how much he carried her financially. As she drove down the street she heard her cellular phone ring which also reminded her that she needed to pay her phone bill.

"Hello."

"You already left out the house," a female voice said.

"Yeah. Why what's up."

"I was calling to remind you of that project we had to do for Professor Clemons class."

"Yeah I got it," she adjusted the volume on the radio. "I finished it up the other night."

"Oh. So what you did yesterday on your day off."

"I went out to Vincent Chicco's with a friend. And then we went downtown at the battery. Talked and chill and what not."

"Who is he?" the girl asked eagerly.

"None of your business."

"Bitch! I'll reach through this phone and choke your ass out," Tania laughed at her friend. "Now who the fuck is he."

"Kanesha, you know your ass can't hold water in a bucket."

"What the hell is it supposed to be, a big secret. And how is you gone front on me and we been friends since the sixth grade."

"Because you talk too damn much!"

"Whatever," she didn't deny it. "But who was it Memphis."

"Hell no it wasn't that broke ass wanna be hustler."

"Hell, he can't be that broke. You use to be talking bout his ass every other day."

"That was until I found out he was perpetrating. Country ass nigga with that fake ass New York accent."

"But don't front though, that nigga had you gone," she laughed at her friend.

"Yeah whatever," Tania tried not to think about that chapter in her life.

"But tell me who this nigga is so I can finish getting ready for class.

"You remember when we was at Ric's party and your fast ass left me to go chill with that boy from Liberty Hill."

"Yeah"

"Well you remember that boy I was talking to. He had on a black and white Polo shirt."

"Who Taheim?"

"No! The one I was talking to after him," they got quiet for a moment as Kanesha tried to retrace her memory.

"Girl I don't know who the hell you talking bout," she worked her brain trying to remember.

"Well anyway he's this little cutie I met at work-," Tania suddenly heard the sound as if her friend slammed a hard object down.

"I KNOW YOU AIN'T TALKIN BOUT THAT LITTLE BOY ASS!

BITCH YOU TRYING TO GO TO JAIL OR SOMETHING! I KNOW THAT BOY AIN'T NO MORE THAN SIXTEEN YEARS OLD!"

"Kanesha, if you was to talk to this boy you'll swear that he's twenty-four."

"But if you look at him you'll swear that he's about fifteen."

"Whatever, I gotta go!" she got upset.

"Don't get mad at me cause you robbing the cradle hahaha," Kanesha laughed in the phone as Tania hung up on her. She tried to dismissed those thoughts in her head but found that she was unable to. She knew her friend was right. She really didn't have no business being serious with Rasheid. But then she thought about the sparks that went flying through her body last night when they kissed and before she knew it her inner thigh got moist again. She tried to shift her thoughts to school.

Rasheid came home from school, went to his stash, took out a Ziploc bag full of hardened cocaine and went back outside. He already paid Roger the money he owed him and bought another five ounces on top of that. Roger wasn't in need of the money, but he wanted to see exactly where Rasheid head was at. In a way Rasheid reminded him of himself when he was younger. He seen that he had the type of potential that he could take him up under his wing. He did him a favor by giving him the connect of having the best quality of cocaine in the city of Charleston. Rasheid was the only one in his neighborhood who had a connect with Roger. So slowly but surely as the drug addicts got a taste of Rasheid's brand, they couldn't help but to keep coming back for more.

As the weeks went by, Rasheid became more consistent with selling drugs putting everything in his life secondary. The more he got into the game the more he started seeing some of the other guys in a different light. It was like some were hustling because it was the thing to do and some hustle because it's what they had to do. Dre came through every once in a while to check on him but he was really making an indirect statement of saying that Rasheid was his protégé. Dre looked at Rasheid as a little brother but deep down inside he knew this life wasn't for him and sooner or later trouble would be knocking at his door. He knew Rasheid was smart but he was still naïve to the game as a whole and didn't believe that he had what it takes to survive through war if it ever came down to that. Or better yet when it came down to it. But through all he was still proud of him because he was showing that he was focus and willing to learn more.

When Saturday came around, Rasheid was awaken by his aunt who had the phone in his face.

"I told her you was sleep, but she said it's important," Tereesa said half asleep herself.

Rasheid looked at the clock that read 8:13 a.m. then took the phone from his aunt talking with his eyes still closed.

"Hello."

"Wake up Rasheid."

"Who this?"

"This Eve."

"Oh what's up Eve," he started to wake up.

"Nothing. Look I was trying to call you for bout two days now. I'm bout to go visit Rookie and he said he wanted you to come with me. So you trying to ride or what?"

"Yeah. What time you leaving."

"Right now so you need to go ahead and get ready."

Rasheid hung up the phone, got in and out of the shower and was dressed and ready to go in less than ten minutes. He took a stack of cash with him, left twenty dollars on the counter and made his exit out the apartment.

"I'm leaving Aunt Tereesa!"

"Alright, you be careful," she said still half asleep.

As soon as he walked down the stairs, he saw Eve pulled up in an all-black Acura Legend. He went down the stairs and got into the passenger side.

"This you Eve," he checked out inside of the car.

"Shit I wish," she said as she drove off. "I had to beg this busted ass nigga all week to let me drive this car."

"Who, your boyfriend?"

"That's what he'll tell you."

Rasheid laughed at her as they openly conversed on their hour and thirty minute drive to Columbia. Rasheid noticed the whole aura Eve always seemed to set around herself. She's the type of woman you can see on the arm of a big time lawyer or doctor someone with high prestige or with the change of hair and attire, she could also be the wife of a hustler. Today she had the conservative look. She wore a casual blue turtle neck sweater with some slightly tight blue jeans showing out her thick thighs and perfectly round butt and some baby blue and grey Timberlands. She had her hair down about a quarter way to her back, which was all hers and she never wore make-up. Just lip gloss and sometimes lipstick. She wasn't the stuck up type or conceited, but she was a dime piece and she knew it, so she carried that confidence wherever she went.

"So how is Mrs. Santez doing?" Rasheid sparked another conversation.

"She aiight. She still a little depress about Rookie but she'll be okay. I took her last month to go see him and she damn near cried the whole way back. Saying she can't go see him no more cause she can't take the feeling of leaving her grandson in a place like that."

Rasheid then thought about his grandmother and wondered how would she feel if she was still alive and had to visit him in prison. He shook off the feeling realizing he was a little jealous that Rookie had someone who loved him that much.

As they pulled into the correctional center, it could have passed for a college campus if it weren't for the fences and barbwires surrounding it. There were correctional officers walking around in their uniforms and other men and women in their business attires as if this was a place of business rather than a prison, but in all actuality it was. They handed their id's to the correctional officer and was patted down firmly for drugs, weapons or any other contrabands that were prohibited from being on prison grounds. The correctional officers then escorted them into the visiting room as they waited patiently for Rookie. Within minutes Rookie was escorted in the room by a correctional officer. As soon as he saw Rasheid a big smile appeared on his face.

"What's up nigga," Rookie walked up to him and gave him a hug.

"What's up man!" Rasheid embraced him in return. On the streets they tried to be discreet about their feelings because it's not in a man's nature to show his emotional side too much, but this was one time that they couldn't hide their love for one another. Eve looked on with a smile seeing how happy the two looked for the moment. "What they made you cut your hair," Rasheid brushed his hand across the top of his head.

"Hell yeah," he turned to Eve. "What up sis?"

"What up Bro," she imitated him as she kissed him on the cheek and gave him a hug. When the two stood next to each other, they looked like twins. They had the masculine and feminine version of the same face. Eve and Rookie were a lot closer than most brothers and sister. They always had each other's back whether right or wrong. It was nothing for Eve to take off her earrings and throw down fighting like a man for her brother and vice versa for Rookie. Some people say blood thicker than water but they lived it.

"So Rah, what's going on man," Rookie sat down beside him.

"Man I'm chillin, for real. You know I'm on right."

"Yeah I heard. Deanna tell me how she barely see you wear the same outfit twice in shit."

"Oh you still mess wit her."

"Yeah. She writes me like everyday. Tell me what's going on and what not."

"So what about Shanice."

"Man I ain't heard from that bitch in like two months. Deanna told me she was about to beat her ass at the skating rink about three weeks ago."

"You need to leave them skank ass chicken heads alone. I told you them bitches ain't shit. When you out of sight you out of mind," Eve stood up. "I'm bout to get me a soda, what you want to eat."

"Get me the chicken tenders and some French fries."

"You want something Rasheid," Eve pulled some money out her pocket.

"Let me get the same thing," Rasheid realized he didn't eat breakfast.

"So who you cop from?"

"Older cat name Rodger."

Rookie just stared at him, "You talking bout Rodger, Rodger. Old head chubby nigga."

"Yeah man. The nigga cool as hell. Like a couple months ago my aunt stole like thirty-two hundred from me. So I just took a chance and went to his house and talk to him. Cause Dre had introduce me to him a while back."

"Hold up. You talking bout Dre? The one that be with Ric," he interrupted.

"Yeah man, Dre. Andre. The one with the Cadillac."

"Damn nigga you been doing some big things since I was gone."

"Yeah but check it," Rasheid said eagerly to get his story out. "Dre introduce me to Rodger and Rodger just start schooling me to the game. And the things he's telling me make sense. Some real shit. I go holla at him after my Aunt Tereesa stole my money and he front me like five O's. Telling me to bring him back thirty- five hundred. I went and took him his thirty-five hundred back like a couple days later and I've been copping from him since. And plus he selling me o's for like six-fifty. Every time I go to his crib he always dropping some jewels on me."

Rookie just sat there and looked at him for a second, "Man you know what the fuck this mean. You got the best connect in the city. Dog you can have this on lock. I bet you making a killing ain't you."

"Man some days I be getting rid of a O in a day."

"Damn! Out the projects," he said as Eve came back and put the food on the table.

"Out the projects," Rasheid grabbed his food and put it in front of him.

"So what's up wit the niggas out yo way. They ain't try to beef wit you or nothing."

"Nah not really," he bit into his sandwich. "Niggas grillin and shit but I don't got no major problem."

"Yo you got yo gat."

"Nah," he said with a mouth full of food.

"Man you can't be out there moving that kind of work wit no heat."

"Rookie eat your food before it gets cold," Eve pushed the food towards him and for the first tie he looked down at it.

"Sis this food hot as hell."

"Shit can't tell by the way Rasheid swallowing it," they both looked at Rasheid and burst out in laughter. Rasheid paid them no mind and kept eating. They continued to talk nonstop for the next time two hours topic after topic. Rasheid told him how it was at North Charleston High. Saying that the school was a joke, nothing but a fashion and car show. He told him about Tania which surprised Eve. Being that she knew her from school. They were like rivals. People would sometimes say they were the two finest girls in school. Rookie explain to them what was going on inside of prison. How there was always riots in the chow hall between Charleston boys and Columbia boys or Beaufort boys and Spartanburg boys. Basically whatever city felt they had to beef with the other. And how the c.o.'s treat them. But what really was on Rookie's mind was the fact that Rasheid had a connect to Roger. As he sat there and listened to Rasheid talk, he still didn't believe he pulled that off. He's been trying for a while to get a deal with Roger and just like that, his best friend got it without even trying. As Rasheid sat there talking nonstop, Rookie just studied him the whole time saying a few words here and there. In the back of his mind he was having a whole other conversation with himself. Rasheid got the connect he always wanted and Rasheid is his best friend. Which means when he gets out, if Rasheid still got that connect he is going to blow up. He might even be able to move some work out in the country too. As Rasheid continued to talk, Rookie just looked at him smiling on the inside. I knew I liked this nigga, he thought to himself as he envisioned his prosperous future.

"Santez, your visits over," the male correctional officer said.

Rookie looked at the c.o. and sucked his teeth as he stood up. Prison was one place that he knew he'll never be able to get use to.

"Aiight my nigga. I'ma be writing you," Rookie said mad that his visit was up so quick.

"Stay up Dog," Rasheid gave him a hug. "I'll be back up here to see you when I get a chance."

"That's what's up."

"Keep your head up Baby," Eve kissed him and gave him a hug. "You need some money?" she said as Rasheid looked up willing to offer some.

"I'm straight for right now. Y'all be easy. And Rasheid," he said as they made eye contact. "Be careful my nigga," the c.o. escorted him off.

"I got you!" Rasheid said loud enough for him to hear before the door was shut.

They rode home not speaking as much as they were on their way up. Rasheid knew what happened to Rookie could easily happen to him. He thought about what would happen if he was in that situation. He knew his aunt wouldn't be able to help him out. Being that he didn't have any other relatives, he wouldn't be able to depend on nobody else. So he didn't have no choice but to be careful. When he got back home he made his way to the block and in less than an hour he got rid of nine grams. Friday and Saturday nights were the best nights out the week. He was able to move five ounces per week and was making an average of fifteen hundred dollars per ounce. Him and Tania didn't see each other as much as they wanted to, but they made the best out of it whenever they got the chance. Which was about once a week.

Tania started to get inquisitive about him. Every time they were together, she'll notice the lump sum of money he pulled out. It wasn't a bunch of five's and ten's. He'll have a stack fifty's and twenty's. Now she wasn't a genius, but she knew he wasn't making that kind of money selling clothes unless he owned his own store. She drove East Montague coming from the post office after sending her brother and father some mail. She decided to surprise him by visiting him at his home. She found out where he lived from Sharika, one of Dee's girlfriend. He was too mysterious and she wanted to satisfy her own curiosity and see exactly who he was. She knew she was putting their friendship/relationship at risk for showing up at his house without his permission, but it was driving her crazy. She just had to know, did he sell drugs. She really hoped that he didn't, because if he did that meant that there really was no hope for the black men in America. Even the good ones with the most potential still turned to the negative lifestyle. As she got into the part of town which was called Macon, she saw how it earned the nick name Money Macon. She had never seen a neighborhood where every single street had nothing but crack heads, prostitutes and drug dealers. There were at least dozens of them all around. Tania locked her car door as she continued to drive around groups of people as they walked right in front of her as if they had the right away. When she got to the building where Rasheid lived, she stopped and looked around not seeing him anywhere. A couple of the guys noticed her, but paid her no mind once they saw she wasn't a threat or a crackhead. They thought she probably just came there to visit someone. Right as Tania was about to drive off, she saw a blue van drive up and Rasheid hopped out of the back putting some money in his pocket. She looked in the driver and passenger seat and saw that it was occupied by two middle aged black men who more than likely were drug addicts based on their appearances. She then looked back at Rasheid who was now looking at her with a shocked expression. He squenched his eyes to see if it was really her. Tania crossed her arm over her chest looking back at him.

"The motherfuckers a drugdealer," she said to herself as she watched him approached the car.

"What you doing here?" he asked.

She just looked at him while the image she depicted him to be steadily broke down in her mind.

"What are you doing here?"

"I live here," he sensed she wasn't happy.

"Don't play stupid Rasheid!" the tone in her voice caught the attention of people nearby. "What the fuck are you doing getting out of that van!"

"Hold up!" he said in a louder tone. "Who you talking to like that?"

Tania then realized she was acting outside of herself and tried to controlled her temper.

"I thought you said you sold clothes."

"Look," Rasheid scratched his forehead feeling as if he was being back into a corner.

"Can we go some place and talk about this. Some place other than here," Tania just sat there and looked at him. She wanted to give him a chance but then she thought what would be the use. She didn't want anything to do with drug dealers, but deep down inside she knew Rasheid wasn't that type of person. Or at least that's what she wanted to believe. As she was about to unlock the door, a white car pulled up on the

other side of the street right behind Rasheid. He turned around and saw
that it was another one of his clients.

"You holding Rah?" the missing teeth woman said.

Rasheid looked at the woman and turned back around to Tania. She
looked at the woman then back at him as she put the car in drive. Whatever
thoughts she had of listening to him, that women just confirmed the idea
that maybe she should just leave him alone and continued on with life as if
he never existed.

"Tania! Wait!" he said as she mashed down on the gas pedal. She
looked at him from the rearview mirror as he stood in the middle of the
road watching her drive off. She really wanted to give him a chance, but
then said fuck it. She would rather deal with hurt feelings in the beginning
then to deal with them months from now. Before she made a turn at the
stop sign to exit the neighborhood, she tried to get one more glimpse of
him in the mirror. No matter how much she tried to lie to herself, the truth
was that he already had a piece of her heart. She drove out of the
neighborhood with no intentions of ever coming back.

ChApter 10

R asheid sat in class and day dreamed about Tania as he waited for the bell to ring. He noticed two girls that sat in the second row from the front of the class kept whispering to each other then turning around and looking at him. They made it obvious they were flirting. He tried not to pay them any mind, though they started to get on his nerves. The bell rung as he rushed through the door with his book bag on his shoulder. Even though school was over the day was just getting started for him. He greeted every other person on the way out of the double doors. He didn't know half of the people who spoke to him, he just spoke back so it didn't seem as if he was being rude.

"Rasheid!" a girl's voice yelled out as he turned around and saw it was Deanna.

"Yo whassup Deanna," she looked even better than she did the last time he saw her.

"Hey," she went through her purse and pulled out a folded piece of paper. "This is from Rookie. I got it in the mail yesterday," she gave him the letter. He opened the letter, glanced at it then put it in his back pocket.

"Thanks," he was happy Rookie had a girl who was actually down to ride with him. As he was about to leave, he looked up and noticed for the first time the girl who was standing with her. She looked so beautiful his mind couldn't think of nothing else for a few seconds to come. The girl who obviously felt uncomfortable by Rasheid staring at her gave Deanna the eye as if she was ready to leave. Rasheid noticed what transpired between the two as he snapped back to himself.

"Rasheid you alright?" Deanna said in her high pitch voice with a slight smirk on her face.

"Yeah I'm cool."

"Do you know my girl Kiana?" she said as the girl looked at her as if she could cut her in half with her eyes.

"Nah, I've never met her before," Rasheid extended his hand to her.

"Hi," she said disinterested.

"Nice to meet you."

The girl stood about five feet two with a light complexion. She had her hair done in a wrap with brown streaks that complimented her eyes. Though it was evident that she was not eighteen yet, she had the body of a twenty-five year old woman. She had a mole on her right cheek and teeth was pearl white. Rasheid looked down at her open toe shoes and saw that she had the prettiest manicured feet he think he ever saw before.

"My mother's waiting for us outside," she made it clear she was ready to leave.

"Aiight Rasheid," Deanna said. They turned around and headed out the entrance of the school.

"Girl what's the matter with you. That's Rasheid!" Deanna said once they exited out the doors.

"Okay, and who is he supposed to be?" Kiana said more concerned about looking for her ride.

"Rookie's best friend. He got money and can dress his ass off."

"So does five hundred other nigga at school, you don't see me doing back flips over them."

"Whatever," Deanna held her hand up to her friend as they looked for their ride.

Rasheid just looked on. Realizing he was beside himself, he shook his head as he turned around and exited out the building. As he walked to his bus he heard someone yelled his name. He turned around and saw Dre standing on the schools walkway waving his hand in the air. Happy he didn't have to ride the bus Rasheid jogged towards him.

"Damn nigga, what you deaf or something," Dre shook his hand as he approached him.

"I could of barely heard you," he noticed some of the students staring at him and Dre. They figured he must be somebody important of Dre was picking him up from school.

"Yeah well let's roll out. I gotta holla at you bout something."

"What's up?"

"We'll talk," Dre walked a few steps ahead of him. "Y'all got some phat young girls running round this motherfucker here," he looked around the parking lot at the girls who were all walking in different directions. They all were looking back at him too. Most of them had the facial expression that read, you can fuck me for a ride home. Looking at his car and jewelry as if he was a celebrity. Dre opened the door to his burgundy ninety-three Cadillac Seville and hopped in the driver side as Rasheid got in the passenger scat. As he closed the door, he saw a white Mercedes Benz a few cars ahead of them with a pretty light skin older woman siiting in the driver's seat. He then saw Kiana getting in the front seat and Deanna sat in the back. Kiana and the woman looked almost like twins as Rasheid watched them drove off. Dre started the ignition, put the car in drive and stepped on the pedal, as the sound of Jay-z's Reasonable Doubt cd paid homage to his stereo system.

"So what's up wit chu," he turned the volume down a little bit.

"Nuttin. You know yo girl flipped out on me the other night."

"Who Tania?"

"Yeah. She just popped round my way, and I ain't never told her where I live," Dre eyes was back and forth on him and the road. "She seen me hopping out the back of this fien whip and started flippin on me."

Dre paused before he let his words come out," Tania's a good girl. She's going to make a good wife. But she's not caught into the fast lane era... I watched shorty grow up. Back in the day, she use to have a little crush on me. Ric use to always say he'll shoot me if he ever catch me fuckin wit his sister," he smiled as his mind reminisced. "But fo real you gotta look at it from her point of view. She watched the feds take her father away and now her only brother locked up for the same shit. So how she look fucking wit a nigga who's indulge into this lifestyle. Shit for the simple fact she even thought about fucking with a nigga like you says a lot on your behalf," Rasheid almost took what he said the wrong way. "Look at chu. You younger then her and you still in school. But I can see why she took a chance with you. Its not everyday you meet a boy from the projects who can do all kind of math problems in his head, spell almost every word in the dictionary and be down to earth. It ain't hard to see with the right push behind you, you'll have a bright future. And I know that's what she seen. Shit any bitch with some sense and want a future would snatch a nigga like you up," Rasheid thought they were giving him too much credit. "But yo, that's life. No need in crying over spilled milk. You feel me," he looked over at him as he pulled into the parking lot of a black owned tire shop. The tire shop was located right across the street from the projects. So of course the parking lot was the daytime hang out spot. Mostly everyone who was standing around talking, arguing, or joking with one another. There were females around as usual. Some walked around half naked and some just passed through pushing baby strolls with one or two or even three kids along with them. Dre drove up to a parking spot, put the car in park as a few people yelled out his name and walked up to him. Everywhere he went in the city he was like a local celebrity. "Yo, I'll be right back," he reached over to the glove compartment and pulled out a manila envelope which more than likely contained money. As he was about to open the driver door, he felt his pager go off. He grabbed it and looked at the number that paged him, "What the fuck is one one one," he opened the door and stepped out the car still looking at the number as two guys walked up to him and started talking. The three of them walked into the building. Rasheid laid his head back on the head rest and closed his eyes as he thought about everything that was going on. He tried to think about Tania but Kiana's face kept intercepting. It was just something about her that made everything else in his life obsolete for the moment. As his mind went back to Tania, he thought about everything Dre said about her. She was a good girl and if push came to shove, he would stop selling drugs to be with her. At least he thought so. As Rasheid let his mind traveled off, he was interrupted by Dre opening the driver's door getting back in the car.

"Hustlers don't sleep."

"I wasn't," Rasheid sat up in the seat. "I was just resting my eyes," he was a little disappointed he couldn't have no more time to himself.

"Well check this out. When was the last time you saw Rog?"

"Last week."

Dre started the ignition and backed out the parking lot. "Do it seem like he was acting strange lately?" he wondered if Rasheid was able to pick up on mix signals.

Rasheid thought about the last time he talked to him, "Nah… or if he was I couldn't tell."

As Dre was about to drive off, his attention went to his rearview mirror as he saw a white car drive up behind him then on his driver side. He looked at the two guys in the car and before his mind could think enemy, the guy in the passenger seat already had a shot gun aimed directly at him.

"You've been bless nigga!" the man shouted as he pulled the trigger. The loud sound of the shot gun sent everybody in the parking lot running and ducking for their lives. The bullet went straight to Dre's face and ricochet breaking the windows in the Cadillac. The impact knocked Rasheid into the passenger's door as he felt the glass smacked his face. For a second Rasheid thought he was dead until he felt the ringing from the gun shot in his left ear. He looked up and saw the busted wind shield of the car covered in blood, as he heard a bunch of commotion and cars screeching. He touched his face and looked at his hands seeing blood, but he felt as if the left side of his face was numb. He then looked over at Dre. He was laid back halfway off the driver's seat with half of his face blown away. Rasheid eyes almost popped out of his head as he watched him. He wanted to touch him. He wanted to yell out. But he couldn't move. He started seeing green and blue gush leaking out from where Dre's face used to be. He then opened the door and tried to run, but his legs gave out on him. He fell a few feet away from the car. He tried to get up but didn't have the energy. He laid there hearing police sirens far away but couldn't move. All he could think of for some reason was his grandmother. He closed his eyes and saw her cooking as she sang and hum to herself. He tried to yell her name, but when he opened his mouth no words would come out. Then he just waited for her to turn around but she never did. She just kept singing and humming while she cooked up a storm. Rasheid then felt tears coming down his face which he didn't have no control over. *Why won't she turn around* he thought to himself. He wanted to ask her why she left him. He wanted to say he didn't won't to be here if she's not with him. He wanted to go with her so bad as he saw how peaceful and at ease she looked. *Please Grandma take me with you,* he tried to say out loud but the words still wouldn't come out.

Hours later he woke up in the hospital wearing a gown with just his underwear under it. He got up and looked around the empty room then at himself. He felt his whole body then his face. After seeing that nothing was wrong with him, he got up and saw the bathroom door. That's when he heard the toilet flush and saw the bathroom door opened up. Tereesa came out the bathroom, and for some reason to him she was the most beautiful person in the world at that moment.

"Aunt Tereesa, what's going on?"

"You alright baby?" she walked up to him and felt his forehead.

"I was watching Grandma cook!" he said excitedly as if he was nine years old. "She was singing and I was trying to get her attention but she wouldn't turn around and look at me!"

Tereesa just hugged him tightly in her arms. She understood he was in a state of shock.

"I know baby. I know," she held him tighter as a tear came down her face.

"I was just trying to get her to turn around," he said softly as she gently rubbed his back. Just then there was a knock at the door. Two middle age detectives invited themselves in followed by a young black nurse.

"Oh you look just fine," she said as the detectives stood back and let her do her job. Rasheid looked at the women like she was crazy while the Tereesa continued to rub his back. "Just come back over here and rest yourself on the bed," she adjusted his pillow and fixed the sheets. "Now you got two detectives here and they want to ask you some questions," Rasheid sat on the bed as Tereesa sat next to him.

"Hello Rasheid," the detective extended his hand to him. "My name is Detective Matthews and this is my partner Detective Richardson," his partner shook Rasheid's hand also. That's when his memory kicked in and the whole scene played in his head. Dre got murdered. Up until now he thought it was all a dream.

The detective pulled out a small notepad and an ink pen, "Andre

Jenkins was killed today at approximately 3:52 p.m. and you were with him correct."

"Yes," Rasheid shook his head as the reality set in on him about his mentor being killed.

Detective Matthews continued to write in his pad, "How long have you known the deceased, Andre Jenkins?"

"About two years."

"Were you aware of any enemies or rivals that Andre had?"

"No," Rasheid shook his head.

"Did you see the shooter who was responsible for this?" the scene played back in his head when he saw the car roll up. Then he envisioned the person who shot Dre. A dark skin man with dreadlocks down to his shoulders, a face he would never forget. But he knew if he was to pick this person out in a line up or give the police a description of him, he'd be labeled as a snitch. That was something he didn't need on his jacket, but he also didn't want the man to get away with killing Dre. "I'm going to ask you this one more time, slower and clearer. **"Did-you-see-the-person-who-murdered-Andre-Jenkins**?" the detective said slowly but a bit louder.

Rasheid hated being pressured and that's exactly what was happening, "No," the guilt settled in on him as soon as the word left his mouth. The detectives looked at each other and then back at him. They sensed he was concealing information. They asked him other questions pertaining to the lifestyle Dre lived and people he dealt with. But none of the answers Rasheid gave them was helpful. After rewording questions they already asked. Tereesa got annoyed and started to let it show.

"How many times are you going to ask the same questions?" He don't know!" the detectives looked at each other and Matthews took out a card and handed it to Rasheid. "Thank you for your cooperation Rasheid. If you have any questions or would like to provide us with any information you think we should know, you can use that number to get in contact with us."

"At any time," the other detective added.

"You take care. And hope you get better," Detective Richardson said as they left Rasheid and Tereesa alone in the room.

"What you think?" Richardson asked his partner as they walked to the elevator.

"It's not what I think," his partner said. "The kid knows what's going on and I know he saw who shot this guy. There's no way possible that he didn't even get a glance at him. You can see in his eyes that he was lying," he pushed the elevator button while they waited for the door to open.

"So what. Another open and shut?"

"Unless another witness step up, or that kid opens his mouth I'm afraid so," the elevator door opened and they both stepped in.

⎯⎯⎯⎯⎯⎯⎯

Rasheid and Tereesa sat quietly on the bed as he reflected back on the day.

"Rasheid," she leaned her head on his shoulder, "I don't speak on a lot of things that you do because I know you're not a dummy. And you're getting older so you'll have to deal with what this world has to offer. But I would tell you this. These streets don't love you. These streets don't love nobody. What happened to Dre today could easily happen to anyone including you. I'm not going to tell you what to do because you're going to do what you want anyway. But I need you to be careful out there. I don't want nobody calling me three o'clock in the morning asking if I can come and identify your body. I know that I'm not the best example for you to follow but I do love you. And regardless of what you think of me I always will. You're the only sunshine I have in my life and even though I made some mistakes, I'll always have your best interest at heart," she rubbed her finger across the side of his face. At that moment she wasn't the drug addict, the thief and prostitute he became to despise. She was the Aunt Tereesa he knew before his grandmother died and right there they shared their first mother/son, aunt/nephew relationship. It felt good to the both of them.

⎯⎯⎯⎯⎯⎯⎯

The day of Dre's funeral, Rasheid had the same feeling he had when he went to his grandmother's funeral. He just didn't want to believe he was dead. He knew once he saw his body lying in the casket it didn't matter what he wanted to believe. The truth would be that he is dead and is never coming back. Rasheid saw Roger a few days earlier and thought about the reason Dre came to pick him up from school. He wondered why Dre asked questions about him anyway. Roger hadn't acted strange to him and if he did, he didn't notice it. When he went to Roger's house, he bought the usual five ounces from him and they talked for a while about Dre and everything else that was going on. Word got back to Roger that it was some Downtown boys. Dre had their part of town on lock, which meant they weren't getting the kind of money they were supposed to. What made it worse was that Dre was from North Charleston. It was just against the rules of the game for somebody out of another neighborhood to come to any other neighborhood or projects and sell drugs. Unless you got a life long bond or certain ties to that section of town or projects, you just can't do that.

After a couple days it seemed like nothing had changed. Of course people was still shocked about Dre's death, but business went on. There were still people getting high, which meant there were still people out selling drugs. In fact it seemed like since Dre got killed business picked up a little.

"You ready to go?" Tereesa asked. She was dressed in an oversize black dress barely coming down to her ankles. She had on a plain pair of black shoes with no heels.

Rasheid looked in the mirror as he adjusted his tie, "Yeah I'm ready," his mind was still distant off.

"Well come on cause you know the church gonna be crowded and I ain't trying to be standing up."

Rasheid took one last look at himself and left out the door following behind his aunt. When they got to the church it looked like they pulled up to the club with so much people standing in line waiting to get in. Rasheid saw a lot of familiar faces, some were people he saw at the party months ago. He and Tereesa stood in the back of the line as they listened to all of the yelling, crying, shouting and music coming from the inside of the church. They had the body viewing first, so the people who were standing outside the church were actually waiting to see the body. Even though there were a lot of people in line, they were moving pretty fast. Before they knew it, Rasheid and Tereesa were already inside the church. Most of the crying and yelling were coming from Dre's family. Everybody else who was not close relatives looked real calm. They were a lot of hustlers who came out to pay their respect and a lot of women too. Some dressed in the smallest and skimpiest outfits they could find as if they came to a party instead of a funeral. Rasheid saw two ushers taking a girl who he saw at Ric's party outside. She was yelling and screaming so much the ushers literally had to pick her up. He looked at her and shook his head. As they got to the casket, he saw that Dre was dressed in a purple suit. Then he saw a black scarf over Dre's face and pictures all around the casket, from when he was a child to an adult. The picture that made the biggest impact, was the picture they had in the front with Dre smiling holding his two year old son. Rasheid looked at the body and even though he couldn't see his face, he knew it was Dre. He looked down as Tereesa held his hand, then they both turned around to go find a seat. His mind was so distant, he didn't notice when he walked pass Tania. She was eyeing him down the whole time. Rasheid and Tereesa sat in the back row and listened to the reverend. They felt as if he was speaking to them.

"You see roses are supposed to smell good," the pastor said as people nodded in agreement and yelled out amen. "But if one rose stink, then I don't believe in telling you that, that rose smell good. I'm gonna tell you it stinks and I don't care how you feel about it! Because in order for you to fix your problem, you must first acknowledge it!" some people clap their hands and yelled out amen. "And once you acknowledge it you're either going to be alright with it or not alright with it. We're here to celebrate the life of Andre Leonard Jenkins. And ooh it was a young life. Twenty-two years old. You see I personally knew Andre. He use to sing on that very choir right there when he was ten years old," the preacher pointed. "And you what else I know? I know that he was a good person with a good heart. He was just lead in the wrong direction. The direction that the devil pointed to him and said it was alright for him to go down there. And us, we the parents are just watching them go down that lane. One by one. Others just like Andre are being taking over by the devil and we're just sitting there watching them do it," he yelled out. "And then have the nerve to want to complain when you see violence going on in your neighborhood or hear gunshots at night and turn around and call the cops on them. But I guess that's what we wanna see, a whole generation being locked in cages like animals or lying right here in front of you in a casket. Because that's exactly what's going to happen if you don't do something about it. If you want a change you can't hope for it, you can't wish for it, you have to change it. Because God only help those who help themselves!" he said as people clap their hands and some stood up while the relatives of Andre cried on as the pastor continued. After the service was over with, people exited out of the church row by row starting from the front to the back in order to minimize the crowding. As Rasheid was about to stand up, he saw Tania walking out. Their eyes locked on one another before she left out the door. When he and Tereesa got outside the church he saw her standing by her car and walked in her direction.

"Give me a minute Aunt Tereesa. I need to speak to a friend," he said never taking his eyes off of her.

"Alright," she pulled out her car keys and walked toward the car. Tania unlocked her door and turned around to see Rasheid walking in her direction. With mixed feelings build up on the inside, she opened the door and stood there waiting for him.

"How you doing Tania?"

"Hey," she couldn't help but notice how handsome he looked in his suit. "You alright. I heard you was with Dre when he got killed."

"Yeah, I'm alright. How about you?"

She shrugged her shoulders as her eyes wandered off. "I try not to question God's plan," her eyes got watery as her voice started to crack.

"But um… it's a little difficult sometimes. Especially when it seems everyone who I'm close to l end up losing them to the streets," she wiped the tears from her eyes. "Dre was like my brother. He was the one person I knew I could go to being that my father and brother is locked up. But I just…it's just that…" she broke down crying not able to finish her sentence. Rasheid went up to her and hugged her as she embraced him back letting the tears fall free from her eyes. After a couple minutes of releasing her tension, she wiped her eyes in Rasheid's jacket and looked up at him.
"Sorry about that."

"It's alright," he said not wanting to let her go. "Look, can we go somewhere else so we can talk."

She hesitated as they let each other go, "Yeah….we can do that."

"Let me go tell my aunt I'ma be home later."

"Alright," she got in the car. Tania questioned herself on what she was doing. She saw Rasheid in the rearview mirror walking towards her car, then closed her eyes and asked God to give her a sign on what to do. Rasheid opened the door, sat in the passenger seat and closed it behind him.

"Where you wanna go," she looked at him.

"It don't matter."

She stared at him for a moment, "I'm sorry about the other night."

"Nah it's alright," he waved his hand. "I ain't trippin off that," Tania eyes wandered down at the cd player then back at him.

"You wanna go to my house?"

"Yeah, we can do that," he said as she drove. They rode down the streets in silence, both being consumed by their own thoughts.

"You can sit wherever," she directed him to the chair or sofa. Rasheid sat on the love seat as he gave Tania's apartment a thorough inspection. The place was small but the furniture was nice and everything was clean and neat. She turned on the television to a movie that was on Lifetime then sat by him. He looked at her from the corner of his eye.

"What you thinking about?" she asked.

"Right now you."

"What you thinking?"

"Just thinking about how pretty you are."

She looked over at him. "How long you've been selling drugs?"

Rasheid looked at the t.v. then back at her. "About six months."

"I've known you about six months. What you start selling drugs when I met you?" she asked confused.

"Basically," he felt the need to air out his dirty laundry.

"But I thought you said you sold clothes."

"Would you feel better if I was doing that. Cause the clothes I was selling I was stealing it out the mall," she turned her head and looked at the wall disappointed. "Tania look," he grabbed her hand. "I don't know what you want from me. To be honest with you, I don't even know what I want for myself. But I do know I want you. How I know that? Because you're the first person on my mind when I wake up in the morning. The last person on my mind when I go to sleep. I think of you when I'm at school. When I'm in the streets. Every single day since the first time I seen you, you've been on my mind constantly. I know we got a age difference between us. I know how you feel about people who sell drugs. But I don't know what you won't me to do. I gave my grandmother my word that I'm going to graduate from high school. But I live with my aunt who's in a situation where she can't take care of herself so I got to be there to pick up the slack. She's the only family I got and the only family I know. I feel like I'm in a win/lose situation. It's an uncomfortable feeling being teased in school for having raggedy clothes, or about coming to school smelling stink because the water in my aunt's place been cut off for the past week. The preacher said something today that made a whole lot of sense. If you're being encountered with a situation that you're not alright with you're going to do something to change it. Now the way I changed it may not be right in the eyes of a lot of people, but that's only because they take the derogatory part of it and take off. And if you wanna be a part of that category and classified me like that, then I'll just have to deal with it. But first I got to survive. And until you or anybody else that can show me a better way to do this, for today not putting me in a position where I'm going to be hungry tomorrow. I'm going to keep doing this my way. And if I'm in the right or wrong I'm going to accept the penalty that comes with it."

Tania just looked at him before she spoke a word. He made her understood where he was coming from, but she also saw that he was trying to justify what he was doing, "So is it right for you to take the easy route because it seems like it's the best."

"This is not the easy way out. It do has it's advantages but it also have some disadvantages. I'm not doing this to get a name. I'm doing this so that I can eat, have a roof over my head and clothes on my back," he said as they were silent for a few seconds.

"So when are you going to stop," she saw that he had his mind made up. Plus he won her over by having motivation that every other black man should have in life, even if it do means going against the odds. Which is the same thing that attracted her to Dre. Having the qualities of being a provider.

"I don't know but it's definitely not going to be for the rest of my life….I just don't know if I can say the same about my feelings for you."

Tania didn't know if her mixed emotions came from the funeral or from the fact that she was really attracted to Rasheid. Her body was longing to be touched and caress. And more than anything she wanted to be held. They gave each other eye contact then drew themselves close enough to share a long intimate kiss. He felt her warm lips caress his mouth as she slipped her tongue inside his making it go into a circular motion around his tongue. Rasheid started to caress her thighs, sliding his hand under her shirt feeling how smooth her skin was. Tania then took off his jacket and tie then unbutton his shirt as he took it off and let it drop to the floor. They started kissing again as she pulled her lips away long enough to take off his shirt. Rasheid then started kissing her neck, then moved to her shoulder, fumbling with her bra as she turned around and unbutton it herself letting it drop, she gave him an eyeful of her thirty-four c cups. He then went down and gave one equal amount of tongue pleasure while she rubbed the back of his head gently.

Tania felt like she couldn't hold out any longer, "You have a condom?."

"Yeah," Rasheid remembered what Dre told him about always keeping one.

He went to his wallet and grabbed the condom as Tania took off her pants and underwear revealing every inch of her body to him. He just stared at her for a second.

"You need some help?" she broke his thought chamber.

"Huh. Nah I got it," he started to get nervous hoping that he won't disappoint her by not meeting her sexual needs. He then took off his pants and underwear and put the condom on. He eased his way on the top of her, softly kissing her chest as he gently slid his dick inside of her. As he slid it in all the way, Tania felt the other side of her coming back to life as she wrapped her legs around him kissing the side of his neck. Rasheid now feeling a little more confident, started to pick up the pace while he kissed her. Tania rubbed his back as she bit the side of his face. She then closed her eyes allowing her sexual face to take over moaning his name softly as her warm breath tickled his ear. Rasheid wrapped his mouth around her neck trying to contain himself from moaning out loud. As he closed his eyes and felt the rhythm of her warm breath brushing against his ear, he felt a familiar feeling taking over his body. It felt so good he couldn't fight it off as he released himself inside her, allowing his whole body to rest on top of hers while she still rubbed his back kissing him softly.

"I don't know if I can say the same about you too," Rasheid lifted his head up and looked at her.

"Huh."

She looked at him for a second, "I don't want you to leave," she said softly still looking in his eyes.

"I don't want to leave either," he kissed her. She pulled away from him and held his face directly in front of hers.

"I couldn't stop thinking about you too since we talked at my brother's party. You've been on my mind constantly....I think I love you Rasheid," she said softly.

"I know I love you," he said as they shared another intimate kiss. She then pushed his head gently on top of her chest while she rubbed the side of his face. They laid there naked for hours to come holding each other and having the best conversations of their lives.

Ch Apter 11

One Year Later

R asheid raced down the stairs looked around his living room then went into the kitchen.

"Baby I don't see it," he looked all around the kitchen.

"Did you look on top of the entertainment system!" she yelled out from the shower. Rasheid then raced to the living room and spotted his car keys on top of his fifty-two inch television.

"Alright, I found it Baby, I'm out. I'll be back to pick you up about two!"

"Okay, you be safe. I love you!"

"I love you too," he said as the phone rung before he got to the door. He then turned around to go answer it. "Hello!"

"When are you leaving?" the girl said in an upset tone.

"I'm leaving out the door right now Deanna."

"Well can I ride wit chu?" she said anxiously.

"No Deanna. Do you have a ride to his house?"

"Why can't I ride wit chu?"

"Deanna look, I gotta go. I'ma call you when I pick him up, bye," Rasheid hung up the phone then exited the apartment. As he walked outside, he was greeted by his outstanding paint job that always seem to catch him off guard since he got his nineteen ninety Cadillac Deville painted red. As he got into the driver's seat and backed out of the driveway, he let the sound of Notorious BIG song 'Mo Money Mo Problems' blast through his system. Since he and Tania moved in together and bought a bigger apartment, things were looking good. He was able to increase the amount of drugs he was moving as well as keeping a stable relationship with Roger. His name was getting a little bigger and it seemed he was getting more attention outside of school in places he wasn't familiar with. This made him realize that he had to stay conscious of his environment and the people he was dealing with at all times. He had seen first hand the results that would happen if he weren't, when Rookie got arrested and Dre got killed. He had loved the both of them but that would have never happened if they weren't caught slipping. He knew that just one slip on his behalf could result with him being dead or in jail. Above anything else in life his main goal was to stay focus. Since Dre's funeral, Tereesa tried to change over to another leaf. She had to go to rehab twice being that she relapsed after the first time, but when she graduated the second time she's been doing good since then. Rasheid was so proud of her, he put her into a newer apartment out the projects. Right after that, she got a job as a telemarketer.Realizing in four years she'll be forty and wouldn't have anything to show for herself, that's when she wished she would have took her mother's advice and went to college when she had the chance.

Rasheid drove down the interstate wondering what it would be like to have Rookie back home. He knew Rookie would want to get back in the game which he didn't think would be a good idea, with him just getting out, so he knew he had to deal with everything accordingly. He thought about all the possible pressure he could be put under in the next few days to come as he drove in silence to go pick up Rookie.

<center>~~~~~~~~~~~~~~~~~~~~~~~</center>

As he arrived at the correctional center he looked at his watch which read 12:52p.m. He parked the car and turned up the volume to the radio station promoting Jay-z's new cd Hard Knock Life. He couldn't help but to think of him and Rookie hearing the chorus sung between Jay-z and Memphis Bleek. "I done came up/ put my life on the line/ soaked the game up/now it's my turn to shine/time to change up/ no more second in line nine eight these streets is mine." He smiled as he nodded his head to the song. He thought it was funny how songs could relate to real life situations. He then saw the gates open up and saw Rookie walk out in an all white khaki outfit. He got out the car and walked up to him with a big smile on face.

"What's up my nigga," Rookie dropped his bag, walked up to Rasheid and gave him a hug.

"What's up," Rasheid said as they both firmly hugged each other. "Damn dog I see you got a little muscles now," he stepped back and looked at how built he was through his clothes.

"Yeah I've been doing a little working out. Yo that's your whip," Rookie looked around the parking lot and spotted the red Cadillac.

"Yeah man. You ready to roll out."

"You damn right. You was doing big things since I been gone," Rookie said as they walked towards the car and got in.

"Yeah you know. It ain't nothing to brag about," Rasheid started the car.

"Yeah whatever nigga. All I need is two o's and I'm back on. Oh yeah man! So when you gonna introduce me to Roger. Shit I heard that nigga had shit on lock since the eighties. Damn Dog! You got that Mase album. You gotta let me listen to this. I've been hearing this nigga killing them mixtapes," Rookie seemed so happy to be free he was not realizing how much he's talking. "Yo I'm trying to tell these niggas in here that Mase didn't get Puff rich. Big got that nigga rich. And how the fuck my nigga BIG died. Yo that shit fucked me up. That nigga ain't even get a chance to drop his album. I gotta get that Life After Death. I know that shit hard. Yo so what you got up in this bitch to smoke. I need a cigarette bad as a motherfucker."

"You smoke now," Rasheid looked at him then back at the highway.

"Yeah man," he read the credits on the Mase's cd. "I pick up that wack ass habit stressing and shit."

"Damn, well I don't got no cigarettes. But here, you can go by your own," Rasheid pulled a knot of money out of his pocket and gave it to him. Rookie's attention went straight to the money as he took it out of Rasheid's hand.

"This is what's up right here man," Rookie said as he counted back twenty-five hundred dollar bills. "You know what Ra. You the realist nigga I got right now. And that's my word I'ma ride wit you till the end. I'm for real nigga," he extended his hand to Rasheid. "That was some real shit you did paying for my lawyer. Even though I don't show it a lot I really appreciate that shit. On the real."

"That's what's up," Rasheid said still looking at the highway. "But you need to get ready for this party."

"Fo real man. I just want my peoples who been riding wit me on this bit to be there. I ain't even in the mood to see the rest of them niggas and broads yet," he put the money in his pocket.

"That's understandable. I'm only bringing Tania. I think Deanna got a few people from the school coming. Oh yeah, speaking of her please call her," Rasheid pulled out his cellphone. "That girl was nagging me all week long about you."

"That's my baby," he looked at Rasheid's cellphone. "This nigga got a cell phone."

"Actually that's Tania phone."

"Yo, you know I don't remember how your girl look."

"Well you'll see her tonight."

"She still work at that restaurant?"

"Nah, she's just in school."

"You pay for her to go to school?"

"Yeah," Rasheid said a little embarrassed. "She only got a little while until she get her degree. Then we talking about moving," Rookie looked over at him.

"Moving! Where y'all moving at!" he said still looking at him. "I don't know. She talking about Newport News, Virginia but I've been thinking about New York."

"New York! Virginia! Man y'all trippin!" Rasheid could tell that he wasn't too happy about the news. "Man if you know what's good. You'll stay yo black ass right here in the Chuck. Charleston, South Carolina. The best place to be on the planet earth," Rasheid laughed at him. "I'm serious man. Where you gone find the kind of hoes we got. These thick ass pork chop and gravy eating motherfuckers," he said as Rasheid burst out laughing and he joined in with him. "I'm serious, you can't find the shit we got in Charleston any other place."

"Man call your girl up," Rasheid said still laughing.

"Oh yeah that's what I meant to tell you to. You a scared ass nigga."

"Who!" Rasheid looked puzzled.

"Who. Nigga you ain't no owl. The day I got arrested when the cops was talking on the loud speaker. You almost shit on yourself. Think I ain't see your scared ass."

"You crazy man, you the one who was scared."

"Yeah whatever nigga. I'ma keep that between me and you," Rookie smile as he called Deanna.

Looking at the two in the physical aspect they both matured. They look more like they were in their late teens or early twenties rather than just sixteen years old. As Rasheid and Rookie drove up to Rookie's grandmother's house, there were already a house full of people waiting for his arrival. Deanna was the first to run out of the house straight into his arms as Rookie held her tightly in the air. Eve came out the house with her six week old son as Rookie went straight to his nephew to hug and kissed him. Mrs. Santez came out of her room with joy all over her face at the sight of Rookie. Rookie gave her a hug as they passed a few words back and forth to each other in Spanish. Rookie also met Eve's baby father Tremaine, whom he automatically didn't have a liking for. He knew he would have to deal with him in some type of way in the future. He also greeted everyone else at his house who were mostly from the neighborhood. As Rasheid watched his best friend speak to everybody at the house, he told him he had to go home and get ready. Rookie was feeling so much love he came and gave Rasheid another hug then went back to catching up with his girlfriend and family.

Rasheid came back home to see Kanesha stepping out of his apartment as Tania followed behind.

"What you over here starting trouble again," Rasheid said to Kanesha as he stepped out of his car.

"Huh. What you talking about Rasheid?" Kanesha said sarcastically as her and Tania shared an inside laugh.

"Y'all females is something else," Rasheid shook his head.

"Ooh, no he didn't. Straighten that Tania," Kanesha got in her car.

"I will," she said now with all all her attention on Rasheid. "So you had a safe trip," she wrapped her arms around his neck as he put his arms around her waist.

"Nah don't get off the subject now. I wanna no what you supposed to straighten."

"I'ma straighten you nigga," she said as they shared an intimate kiss not paying no attention to Kanesha driving off.

"My question is why you ain't ready yet," he pulled away from her.

"Oh. I'm still trying to figure out what to wear."

"All those clothes you got in that closet you can't figure out what to wear."

"That's what makes it so hard," she grabbed his head and lead him in the apartment. "Come on let's go inside. It's hot out here."

"Guess what baby," Tania grabbed some papers off the counter as Rasheid took a seat and flipped through the channels.

"What," she handed him the job application. He looked at the paper then back at her. "What you want me to do with this?"

"Baby that's a job application at a company called Behr right here in North Charleston. You can work their at sixteen and they start off paying nine dollars an hour," Rasheid let the papers drop on the glass table.

"Tania, what I told you about trying to find me a job. I don't need your help. When I find something that I like then I'ma take it," he said now looking at her.

"Are you even looking?"

"Don't start alright. So far it's been a good day, so please don't start," he put his attention back on the t.v.

"I'm not trying to argue with you baby, but I'm not trying to see you go to jail either," she sat down next to him.

"That's what you trippin off. Tania I told you chill, ain't nobody going to jail," she turned away from him and looked down at the carpet.

"Rasheid. You said you was only going to sell drugs until we get in a better position. So now we got a bigger place, two cars outside and money in the safe. So when are you going to stop?"

"If I knew I was going to have all this pressure on me I probably would have never started," he got up and walked into the kitchen.

"Don't walk away from me," she followed him. "And what is that suppose to mean?"

"Tania, you don't work. Who the hell is going to pay for you to finish school. Come on Baby think," he put his index finger to his head.

"You told me you don't want me working there anymore. I told you that I don't have a problem with getting a job."

"Yeah but when you work all you do is complain about how much money you don't have and how much bills you got. When you don't work you complain about you want me to stop doing what I do. I'm always out in the streets at night, I don't never be home. But I don't never hear you complain about that brand new 626 you got outside. Or all these clothes and shoes you got in every goddamn room of the house. You don't never complain when I throw money up in yo face," Tania tried to intercept but Rasheid cut her off. "Listen Tee, I know what I'm doing. Just sit back and let me take care of this," he put his hands on her arms as she tried not to give him eye contact. "Baby, I love you but right now I'm in the middle of something and I need you to be with me not against me. You think I wanna be out here every night. You don't think that I wanna be with you. I told you that I'm not going to be doing this forever and I mean that. It's just that right now is not a good time for me. So please believe me when I say this. Alright," she just looked at him then let her eyes wander off again. The two was quiet for a moment.

"You still coming to this party with me?" Rasheid broke the silence. Tania looked at him then walked off. "So is that a yes or no?"

"Can I finish finding something to wear," she said with an attitude. Rasheid knew times like this it was best to leave her alone. So he left to go take care of some business. About fourty-five minutes later he came back eight hundred dollars richer than he left. Tania still had an attitude so the communication between the two was to a minimum. Rasheid took a shower, got dress and they left out in her car with him driving. As they got to Rookie's house, it looked as if it was a block party going on. Eve hired a d.j., somebody put up a big banner that read 'Welcome Home Rookie.' The lawn was filled with people from school and the neighborhood who came to party. Tania and Rasheid stepped out of the walking towards the crowd as it seems they were the center of attention for the moment. Tania was dressed in a beige Polo dress and some matching sandals. Rasheid wore a white Polo t-shirt and black Polo jeans with white Air Forces. As he and Tania walked through the crowd, Rookie walked up wearing a wife beater showing off his muscles and prison tattoos.

What up Rah?" I thought you wasn't coming back," he said as he shook his hand.

"I just had to take care of a couple things," Rasheid grabbed Tania's hand. "This is Tania," he introduced them. She extended her hand to Rookie as he gave her a hug which caught her off guard.

"Tania, I heard so much about you. All this man been doing was talking bout you for the past two years," Tania tried not to blush as she looked over at Rasheid to read his expression. "I'm serious. I'm not lying. I can tell you everything about you. You're twenty years old, pisces. You go to Charleston University. Your name is Tania Melissa Johnson. You want me to go on," he embarrassed her. All she could do is hold a big smile on her face with hopes hc'll stop.

Rasheid pulled her to him with his arm around her waist," Alright man, you're embarrassing my baby," he said happy that Rookie indirectly gapped the bridge between them.

"I'm just keeping it real Tania. The man is in love with you," he said as Tania let her body relaxed on Rasheid's

"So what's up Baby Boy," Rookie playfully punched Rasheid in his chest. "Everybody over here. Come say what's up," he directed them to the section of the party where he was at. Sitting at the table was Eve, Tremaine, Deanna, Kiana and Chuck, Rookie's childhood friend who lived up the street. Rasheid unconsciously made eye contact with Kiana which Tania or nobody else noticed.

"Ayo Tremaine," Rookie said without looking at him. "Yo this my nigga Rasheid," he said as Rasheid walked up to him and shook his hand. "And this is his girl Tania," Tania waved at him not wanting to be in the spot light, sensing bad vibes from Deanna and Kiana.

"What's up Tania," Eve said to her forgotten rival.

"Hey Eve," Tania knew them speaking was just a front.

Rasheid and Tania sat down beside each other as Rookie entertained the crowd with talks about his experience behind bars. Kiana checked out Rasheid harder than she ever did before. She agreed that he was cute and could dress, but for some reason this particular night she was really attracted to him. She tried not to be obvious but she couldn't help it. She was turned on at how the lights gleamed off his jewelry and for some reason it complimented his dark complexion and low wavy temple fade. Every time he looked at her, she tried to hurry and looked away before he saw her, but she kept getting caught. Rasheid sensed she was staring at him and was starting to make him feel uncomfortable.

"Rah, why you so quiet nigga," Rookie said as all eyes went to Rasheid.

"I'm just chillin man."

"Y'all don't want nuttin to eat," Rookie said. Rasheid looked over at Tania as she shook her head no.

"Look man, you know my house is yo house so don't get all shy on me. If you need something just say the word."

"I'm aiight man."

"Tania you don't want nothing to drink?" Rookie asked her as she shook her head again. "And Tania, I know you ain't shy. All that talking you was doing that day at the restaurant," he said as she smiled. Rasheid's pager went off as he looked at the number and put the pager back on his belt. He whispered in Tania's ear as she cursed him with her eyes. Rasheid stood up and grabbed her hand and took her away from the crowd. Everyone could of detected what was going on.

"Look, I'm not going to be long."

"I said no!" Tania eyes could have cut him.

"Tania I'm not about to debate with you, it's only going to be about twenty minutes."

"What part of no don't you understand. You ask me to come to the party with you then you're going to leave me out here to go handle your little drug affairs. What the hell do I look like to you Rasheid!"

"Tania, I'm doing this for us!"

"No nigga, you doing this for you!"

"Look I'm not about to sit up here and argue with you."

"Fine then, I'm leaving. Give me the keys," she held her hand out to him.

"Oh so now you're going to leave me out here."

"You damn right I am!"

"You know what, here. If you wanna go. Go," he said as Tania snatched her car keys, stormed off to her car and slammed the door. When she got in she gave Rasheid one last evil look, started the ignition and drove off. She left him there looking at her as she disappeared down the street. Rookie walked up behind Rasheid.

"Girl problems huh."

"Nah that girl just got problems," Rasheid looked back at Rookie then at everyone else. "Yo I'ma need a ride. I need to take care of some business real quick. You think Eve would let you borrow her car for a minute," Rookie held his head down smiling. "What's so funny man," Rasheid said seriously.

"Nothing," Rookie said. "Let me go get the keys," he walked away smiling to himself.

"I'm saying man, what's so funny," Rookie continued to walk off as he shook his head. Rasheid kept looking at him until he accidentally made eye contact with Kiana. They both looked away quickly. Rookie came back within minutes with the keys to Eve's Nissan Sentra. They both got in the car and drove off.

"Yo, whassup wit yo girl?"

"You know she trippin about me hustling and shit."

"How the hell she trippin when you payin for her to go to school."

"That's what I be trying to explain to her. But she be on some other stuff, talking bout I'ma end up in jail or something crazy," Rookie was quiet for a moment.

"on the real Rah. Shorty really love you. If she willing to sacrifice y'all being broke over you taking a risk with your life out here in these streets, that should tell you something," Rasheid looked over at him then out the window. He made a vow to himself to stay focus and that's exactly what he was going to do. Stressing over Tania was only going to get him sidetracked.

"You understand what I'm sayin?" Rookie said.

"Yeah, but right now I'm own a mission. And I ain't trying to play both sides of the fence."

"I feel you Dog, you know, the choice is yours and regardless of what I'ma still be on your side. I'm just saying as a friend I'ma tell you what you need to hear instead of what you want to hear."

Rasheid listened to Rookie talk until they got to his apartment. They shook hands as he stepped out of the car to get in his. He took a trip to

West Ashley. As he drove into the neighborhood which was predominantly white, he stopped in front of this three story house. A middle aged white man stepped out and made a transaction with him. He gave him six hundred dollars as Rasheid handed him the product. He then walked back to the house with a satisfied look on his face as Rasheid went back to his car and drove off. He had a few middle class clients just like the man who he just did business with. One of them made up ten of his customers in the projects. He was still maintaining decent grades in school. His relationships with Tania was kind of rocky. But the one area he did excel in his life was getting money. Sometimes he was just amaze to count anywhere from nine hundred dollars to twenty-four hundred dollars per night. He'll tell Tania he was going to stop soon, but deep down inside he felt that he was lying to her as well as himself. He got back to the apartment and saw that Tania car was there. When he got up stairs to his bedroom, she was under the sheets and could tell by the way she was laying down that she wasn't asleep. He put his money on the dresser, took his clothes off and on top of the sheets trying not to disturb her. As he let his mind traveled his body fell asleep without him realizing it.

Rasheid woke up the next morning to see Tania getting ready to go to church. There's some grits and eggs on the stove for you," she looked at him through the mirror while she put her earrings in her ear.

"Thanks," he said half awake. I probably wanted to go to church with you," he walked over to the toilet to pee. Tania didn't respond. She sprayed on some if her perfume scenting up the whole room. Rasheid flushed the toilet and stepped out of the bathroom looking at her.

"You still mad at me?"

"No," she said with no facial expressions.

"So why you ain't woke me up to see if I wanted to go to church with you?"

"She turned around and looked at him," Rasheid you only went to church with me one time. Why out of the blue you would want to go this morning."

"Still, you should at least check to see if I wanted to go," he said as he washed his face and brushed his teeth. Tania grabbed her purse and car keys.

"After church I'm going to check on my mother and probably take her out to eat. I should be back sometime this evening," she then walked off.

"Tania," Rasheid said as she turned around and looked at him. "I love you."

"I love you too," she said sincerely as she walked out the room.

Rasheid got dress, went downstairs ate his breakfast and left out the house. He went straight to Roger's house with hopes that he'll catch him in a good mood. Afterwards he was going to do his usual routine out the projects which he wasn't in no big rush, knowing that Sunday mornings were usually slow. When he pulled up to Roger's yard he seen a gray Lexus parked out front. He then saw Roger and some guy talking. The more he studied the two, it looked like they were arguing. He was skeptical at first about getting out the car, but that's when the two of them looked in his direction. The guy gave Rasheid a he sharp look as he got out and walked towards them. The guy who was dressed in some jeans, a silk shirt and some alligator shoes, turned back to Roger and finished what he was saying, Rasheid over heard them.

"I never expected that out you," he said with his hands across his pelvic area.

"Rino, we've been doing this for years man. You know I-."

"That's why I never expected it out you. Peace," Rino walked off calmly. As he walked off he stared Rasheid down without blanking his eye. Rasheid looked back at him as the guy got in his car and drove off, giving him one last look. *So that's Rino.* He thought to himself as he watched the Lexus drove off. He's smaller than I thought. Roger walked in the house as Rasheid followed him.

"What's up Roger?" he stepped into the living room. Roger didn't say anything. Instead he walked into the backroom. "Yo Rog, I'ma need the usual," he yelled out welcoming himself to a seat.

Roger walked out the back room counting some money, "I'm charging ten-fifty a O."

"Ten-fifty a O," Rasheid said as if he was speaking a different language. "That's almost double price."

"That's my price take it or leave it," he walked into the kitchen still counting money. Rasheid looked puzzled for a moment. He shook his head then looked at Roger who was now in the kitchen looking through the cabinets. He started to walk out the house but decided against it. It was no secret Roger had the best cocaine in the city, and he knew if he walked out he could possibly be taking a chance on cutting ties with that.

"Rog, I didn't even bring that much money out the house." "Well how much you got!" he said impatiently as if this whole conversation was starting to annoy him.

Rasheid took the roll of money out of his pocket, "I got about fifty-six hundred dollars on me."

"Give me the money Rasheid," Roger took the money from him then went to the backroom. Minutes later he came back, handed Rasheid his eight ounces then went back into the kitchen.

"See, I knew you love," Rasheid joked but the expression on Roger's face was still serious. "Well I'm out. I'ma holla at you later on this week," he said as he left out the house. Roger gave him no replied.

Rasheid drove to the projects thinking about what he seen transpired between Rino and Roger. He figured Roger more than likely messed up some money that he owed Rino. That's probably why he raised his prices. Then he pictured Rino whole persona. He wasn't happy at all. What if Rino cut Roger off. That would mess up a whole lot of things. He started to ponder on the thoughts of that being his reality. Then shook it off as he turned up the volume on the radio. When he got to the projects, he parked his car and went and joined Dee who was seated on a crate.

"What's up Dee?"

"Ain't shit. What's up with you?"

"Chillin. Money slow so far?"

"Its aiight. Bout to pick up in a minute."

Just as Rasheid commented he saw one of his clients drove up. He hopped in the back seat as the car drove off. Minutes later he came back with him still seated in the back placing money in his pocket. As soon as he got out the car, he saw another one of his clients drove up and before he knew it, customers were coming were coming through left and right. In just a couple of hours he went through almost two ounces. He knew for the next few hours business was going to be jumping. Then around four or five o'clock things would start to simmer down, being that people would have to work in the morning. Rasheid had one of his clients drop him off at the corner store so that he could get a soda. When he came out, he took his time walking back to the block, letting a million things stroll through his mind. He thought about Tania and what Rookie was saying to him the previous day. He really wanted things to go smooth, between them, but he knew in order for that to happen he would have to stop doing what he do. And no matter what Tania said, he knew if he was to stop selling drugs right now, within the matter of months they were going to be broke. He heard a car driving up behind him and he moved to the side of the road looking back at the same time. He saw the gray Lexus slow down until it came to a stop right behind him. He bent down and saw Rino in the driver's seat.

"Get in," Rino said with authority. Rasheid hesitated at first then opened the door and sat in the passenger seat as Rino drove off. Seated inside the car was like being in their own world. The ride was so smooth it felt like an airplane on the road. Rino turned the music up to the point where it wasn't loud, but you didn't have to strain to hear it. He then took an already rolled blunt out the ashtray, lit it, took a couple of pulls then passed it Rasheid.

"I don't smoke," he turned down the offer. Rino looked at him.

"That's good," he put the lit blunt back in the ashtray. "So let's get straight to the point. A lot of people don't understand the importance on discipline and persistence in this game. Being discipline set the foundation for you to be in control," he said keeping his attention on the road. Rasheid was all ears. "When you can control your thoughts you can control yourself. And when you can control yourself, then you can control others. There ain't too many people who can do that. But I've been hearing how you conduct yourself out here in these streets. And I honestly think that you have what it takes," Rasheid just looked at him wondering what he was talking about.

"Okay...so what you want from me?" he asked desperately wanting to know why him and Rino was having a conversation.

"Grab the bag off the floor behind your seat," he turned around looked at the bag then picked it up and put it in his lap.

"Open it," Rasheid unzipped the bag and he thought his heart stopped when he saw the two kilos of cocaine and a brand new nine millimeter lying on the top of it. He looked over at Rino then back at the bag. "You know what to do with that?" he was speechless. He literally didn't know what to say. He wanted to tell him that he didn't think he was the right man for the job. He felt it was too much responsibilities. But he also knew that this is an opportunity that don't come around everyday. This could be his chance to stabilize himself financially. Besides his pride wouldn't allow him to tell this man he didn't think he could do it. He then zipped the bag back up.

"Do you know what to do with that?"

"Yeah," he prayed he wasn't making a mistake. "I'm

not making you feel uncomfortable am I."

"Well I need sixteen thousand off each key. Whenever you need me, call this number," he handed him a card and a paper. "And whenever I need me, call this number," he handed him a card and a pager. "And whenever I need you I'm going to page you. Code three four, four, three," Rasheid put the pager and the card in his pocket.

"You got anything you need to ask me."

"Um…yeah, when you gonna be looking for the money?" "I'll be

to see you Friday," he looked at him. "Alright," he hoped he

didn't disappoint him.

"Where's your car?"

"Down the street," there was no more conversation between the two. Rino dropped Rasheid off as his car, as he stepped out with the bag.

"Friday."

"Friday," Rasheid said as Rino drove off. He then hopped in his car and drove off as he seen Dee looked at him, wondering why he was getting out of the car with Rino. Rasheid got home and saw that Tania was not there yet and calculated that he had about a hour or two before she showed. He put the bag on his side of the closet and sat on the bed strategizing. As he was thinking and idea hit him. It was something he had to be real cautious about, so he knew he would have to take careful steps in order to make it happen. He picked up the phone, dialed some numbers then put the phone to his car.

"Hello," Rookie said on the other end.

"Yo Rook what's up. This Rasheid."

"I know your voice nigga. What's up," Rasheid paused for a few seconds.

"You trying to make some money."

ChApter 12

72 Hours Later

"**R**asheid," Rookie looked at him. "We got fifty thousand dollars in front of us right now," Rasheid suddenly felt paranoid.

"You sure your grandmother ain't coming down here."

"I done told you, this is my section of the house. Ain't nobody comin down here. Plus the doors lock anyway," he said as his attention went back to the money.

"Aiight, I'ma go ahead and put this thirty-two thousand up. So that leaves what," Rasheid said as he did the math in his head. "Eighteen thousand four hundred. So that'll be nine thousand two hundred a piece," he looked at Rookie who was still looking at the money.

"Cool wit me."

Rasheid paired up with Rookie so that he could help him sell the two kilos by Friday. The word got out that they were selling ounces for nine hundred dollars and halves for four hundred and fifty. Rasheid's biggest worry was getting Rino his money back. Wednesday night they had the money they owed Rino plus three-fourths of a kilo to themselves.

"Look at all this money," Rasheid said amazed after they spread the cash out on the table in the basement of Rookie's grandmother's house. "So what you gonna do? You're gonna hold on to the rest of the work until tomorrow?"

"Yeah, I guess. If that's what you want."

"Aiight then. Help me put this money up so that I can go home and get ready to go to school in the morning," Rookie just looked at him.

"Rasheid, why the fuck is you still stressing this school shit. Motherfuckers go to school so that could get a good job that makes money. What's your excuse?"

"Rookie I told you, that's a promise I made to my grandmother."

"I mean I feel you right," he put the money in the bag. "But to me it seems like you defeating the purpose. I mean we got more money on this table than most teachers make in a year."

"Rook," Rasheid said with an attitude. "I told you it's personal. So drop it. "He already had to fight with himself to continue to go to school. He didn't need nobody else adding fuel to the fire.

"You right. Your life. So you gone come through tomorrow when you get out of school," Rookie quickly changed the subject.

"Yeah, I'ma do that," Rasheid put the rest of the money in the bag. He then adjusted the gun in his waist under his belt buckle, shook Rookie's hand, grabbed the bag and walked to the door. Walking around with that big gun stuck to his waist was something he had to get used to.

"I should be through about four o'clock tomorrow."

"Do that man," Rookie said recounting his money. "Lock the door on your way out," he said without looking up.

"I'ma talk to you tomorrow," Rasheid said as he lock the door and closed it behind him.

"Peace."

As Rasheid got home, he opened the door, looked around his apartment that Tania kept so neat then quietly went upstairs. When he got in the room he saw Tania lying down with her eyes closed and assumed she was asleep. He opened the closet door, put the bag all the way in the corner, then took his gun out and placed it on the top shelf. He laid some clothes over it, then opened the bag, took out nine thousand two hundred dollars and put seven thousand of that in his safe. He took the rest out an placed it in the dresser. He then sat on the bed and took off his boots.

"So you carrying guns now," Tania said.

Rasheid looked over at her then took off his shirt, "Don't you supposed to be asleep."

She then sat up in the bed and turned on the lamp, "I got a question for you Rasheid. How can you stay up all night until two maybe even three in the morning and then be productive in school all day," he looked at her and could tell she wasn't asleep at all.

"Look Baby, I'm tired. I've been up all day. Can I please take a shower so that I can get some sleep."

"Sleep. Oh now you wanna get some sleep. If you really wanted to get some sleep, you would of came home at a decent hour so that you can get some sleep."

Rasheid walked towards the shower without commenting.

"I notice you got more money than usual. So what's up with that?"

"Tania, we can talk about anything you wanna talk about tomorrow but right now I just wanna get some sleep," she looked at the roll of money on the dresser, looked back at Rasheid as he entered the bathroom then turned off the lamp and laid back down. When she heard the shower come on, she turned the lamp back on and picked up Rasheid's pants and searched through his pockets. She then looked through the numbers of his old pager and saw so many different numbers that she just turned it off and took out the card he had in his other pocket. The card had an Atlanta area code with no name. Just a number. She made a mental note of that and put the card back in his pocket. She walked over to the closet and got a closer look at the gun. It was a new a brand new Smith and Wesson 9mm. She quickly flipped through the bills and estimated it was about two thousand dollars, put the money back on the dresser, turned the lamp off and laid back down in the bed. She wondered exactly what was going on in her life. She fell in love with a hustler. A vow she made to herself that she would never do. Involved with a person who sell drugs, and she's in love with Rasheid, who's becoming a known drug dealer in Charleston. As the tear rolled down her cheek she quietly said a prayer, asking God to rescue him from the lifestyle that's ahead of him which right now he's to blind to see. Rasheid got out of the shower came to the bed, and laid down. He put his arms around her waist as she laid her hand on top of his as the tears continued to fall from her face.

After about forty-five minutes of Tania trying to wake Rasheid, he finally got up washed up and ate a toast egg and cheese sandwich she made for him. Then he got ready for school. He put on a pair of Ralph Lauren jeans with a white and blue collar shirt to match and his white Air Forces with the royal blue check. As he brushed his hair and put on his necklaces, watch and rings, he looked in the mirror as Tania walked up behind him.

"You going to school or a fashion show," she knew the fast ass girls at North Charleston High would be trying to get at him and for the first time she thought would there be any competition for her.

"You have a nice day too," he sprayed on some cologne.

"Rasheid don't do that to me."

"Do what?" he turned around and looked at her.

"Make me out to be the enemy."

"I'm not making you out to be nothing Tania."

"Yes you are. Everybody wants the finer things in life but that's not what life is all about. Rasheid, you're not going to be able to do this forever."

"I understand that Tee, and I'm not trying to do this forever," he put down the cologne and checked his appearance one last time in the mirror.

"So when are you going to stop."

"Soon," he walked up to her and kissed her on the mouth without her forming her lips to be kissed in return. "I gotta go," he left her some money on the dresser from the previous night. "The money is on the dresser. I'm out," he raced out the room.

"Are you going to be home this evening."

"I don't know baby, I'ma try to. I love you," he said as the door slammed behind him.

"I love you too," she said to herself as she grabbed the money off the counter and looked at it as she sat on the bed.

Rasheid drove up to the student parking lot and got out with his books in hand as he made eye contact with some students who tried to act like they weren't watching him. It wasn't a secret to his peers that he sold drugs but too them he was to anti-social. It was only a select few that he actually conversed with. Deanna was one of them and he had a few other females that he felt comfortable with. He had a couple of guys that he associated with but none of their conversations were personal. This made him even more mysterious to his peers and also his teachers. Some of his teachers recognized that he rarely wore the same outfit twice, but that was nothing new with the students at North Charleston High. Alot of them who weren't nickel and dime hustlers had jobs at restaurants or grocery stores and would spend their whole check on clothes just to keep up with the style. North Charleston carried the reputation to be known as a car and fashion show. The teachers also noticed for him to have the least activation as far as with the involvement of the class, he scores the highest on all his test but isn't consistent with doing homework. So in their eyes that made him stand out. As Rasheid headed to class he heard someone yelled out his name.

"Hold up Rasheid!" Deanna got out the passenger seat of Kiana's brand new Toyota Avalon. She walked up to Rasheid with Kiana walking behind her. "You not going to be holding my man hostage every night."

"What you talking about Deanna," Rasheid joined them as the three walked to class.

"I'm talking bout the last few nights he keep telling me that you and him got business to take care of. I know you better not be taking my man to no bitch house," Rasheid looked at her as if she just stated a dumb comment.

"Deanna, you know that's not even my style. You don't even see me out there like that."

"Oh I'm not worrying about that, cause I heard that girl got you on lock," she joked him. He now realized that she just wanted to talk to him.

"Yeah whatever," he brushed off her statement.

"Um-huh. So what you gonna bring her to the prom too," she said now having Kiana's full attention.

"I don't know," Rasheid said as he looked up and saw a group of guys standing on the side of the hallway eyeing him down as if they were looking for trouble. He recognized all their faces and didn't have a liking for any of them. Especially the one they called N.O., a nickname he went by which stood for his initials, Nehemiah Owens. He was a little taller than Rasheid about six-one with gold on the top and bottom row of his teeth. He went out of his way to let Rasheid know that he didn't like him by saying little comments to initiate a conflict between them. But Rasheid never took the bait, he just looked at him as if he was a little boy trying to start a fight with a grown man and walked away without his pride getting involved. That made N.O. even more furious. As the three walked up, Deanna and Kiana felt the tension coming from the group of guys which made them feel a bit uncomfortable.

"Whassup Kiana," N.O. said. "I done told you bout hanging round dem busted ass niggas," he looked directly at Rasheid as Deanna put her arms around his with hopes he wouldn't stoop to their level of ignorance. Rasheid looked back at him as Deanna nudged him and they continued to walk to class. Kiana looked back at the four guys and rolled her eyes at them. "Well fuck you then bitch! I'll buy you from your man then sell you back to that nigga!" he said as he and his partners burst into laughter. That made Deanna turned around and roll her eyes at them.

"Wack ass project niggas get on my nerves," she said irritated.

"They can't get no girls so they always trying to dis em'," Kiana said feeling a bit embarrassed. Rasheid knew the statement he made was indirectly towards him. He looked at Kiana then at Deanna and decided he wasn't going to tolerate it anymore. He turned around and let his books drop to the floor as he walked towards N.O. and the group of boys he stood with. Deanna tried to grab his shirt but he continued to walk in their direction. They all stood at guard.

"You got something you wanna say to me," Rasheid stood face to face with N.O.

"Nigga fuck you!" N.O. brandish a pocket knife holding it by his side. "Bitch ass nigga. So what you gone do."

"Rasheid," Deanna yelled nervously as she pulled his arm. "Come on. Let's go to class."

"Yeah nigga. Listen to your broad or leave this bitch on a stretcher," N.O. glared at him. Rasheid knew he didn't have no wins so he stepped back as Deanna wrapped her arm around his.

"But since you want a shot at the title, I'm gonna give you what you looking for!" N.O. yelled out as Kiana, Rasheid and Deanna continued to walk in the opposite direction. They had everyone in the hallway disappointed. They were hoping that there was going to be a fight.

"Rasheid, you know can't be following up with them clown ass niggas," Deanna said seeing how pissed off he was.

"It's cool. I ain't trippin. Look I'ma holla at y'all," he walked into his class not being able to hide his anger.

"See you later," Deanna said as her and Kiana continued to their class. "I can't stand N.O. black ugly ass, "Kiana said with an attitude. "He always trying to start something, knowing damn well he can't fight. I wish Rasheid would of beat his ass."

"It look like he was standing up for you."

"Whatever," she was to mad to blush.

"Keep on playing. You gone let Rasheid pass right by you."

"Deanna, the boy already have a girlfriend."

"So, what the hell is that. I'm trying to tell you that Rasheid is that nigga."

"I'm not about to mess up the relationship he got going on with that girl."

"Why not. That bitch don't know what kind of nigga she got. You see how they was acting at the party the other day."

"Deanna, that boy don't even pay me no attention."

"Damn Kiana, do I have to teach you everything," she said seeing that her friend was naïve as they came. "He almost got his ass stabbed over you. If he didn't think nothing of you, he wouldn't of reacted when that nigga called you a bitch," Kiana just walked along with a smile on her face. She wasn't raised in the hood like Deanna. She's the only child of her mother and father who raised her in the suburbs. They're originally from Detroit. They moved down t South Carolina three years ago when her father got a better contract as on architect. Her mother was a real estate agent and the two grossed over two hundred thousand dollars a year. So Kiana didn't have a financial problem unlike sixty-five percent of the students that went to school with her.

"Well if he didn't have a girlfriend and I wasn't talking to Seafus maybe something could happen. But that's not the case," Kiana stopped at her locker to take out her books.

"Don't get me wrong. Seafus is sexy but I know at least twenty girls he done fuck in the school. So what you think he gone do wit chu," Kiana looked at Deanna and rolled her eyes. "Don't get mad at me girl. I'm just stating the facts. Plus that nigga don't got nowhere near the kind of money Rasheid got. And trust me I know. I did my homework," Kiana closed the locker and they walked towards their class.

"All you think about is money."

"That's not all about," Deanna said in a tone loud enough for her to hear as they shared a laugh and entered the class.

When Rasheid got out of school, he caught up with Rookie to check on the status of the product that he left him with the right prior.

"Yo Rah, dis shit crazy. I got rid of nine ounces since ten o'clock this morning," he took somme money out of the glove compartment of this ninety-three Nissan Maxima. Rasheid wasn't paying no attention to what he said, he was too busy looking at his car.

"Rook. You ain't been home a week yet and you already bought a car. And Maxima at that."

"Man Rah, I had it get it. That was a offer I couldn't refuse. A nigga told me all he wanted was fourty-seven hundred. So how the hell I was suppose to turn that down."

Rasheid looked around then scratched the top of his head, "I'm just sayin man. Don't bring too much attention to yourself. You just got out. Remember."

"Nah I'ma lay this bitch back in the cut. I ain't even gonna be driving like that," he handed Rasheid some money. "Shit I might let my girl drive round fo real," he pondered on the thought. "Her ass wouldn't like nuttin better."

"Ahh man, guess what happen today," Rasheid looked at the number that paged him and went back to the conversation.

"What."

"That punkass N.O. pulled out a knife on me."

"I know you ain't talkin bout punkass Nehemiah Owens."

"Yeah," Rasheid put the money in his pocket. "Him, Q, Lil Marv and D-Roc," Rookie started to get aggravated. "Them skittle ass niggas don't want no beef! They don't got no money! Don't got no broads! I betcha all they do is walk around and try to look hard all day. School bus riding ass niggas." Rasheid looked at another number that paged him. "If it wasn't for Deanna, some shit probably would of pop off," Rookie looked at Rasheid long and hard. He knew the four guys Rasheid spoke on and he knew if they had the chance to get at Rasheid they would do it in a heart beat. Especially if they could get away with it. He wanted to put an end to that problem before it even started.

"So what you trying to do. You wanna ride on these niggas." Rasheid looked at him and saw he was serious.

"Hell no! For what. They ain't even on my level."

"Rah, if you let them niggas get away with that, they gone feel like they can get away with more than that. Man you too big to let a small timer play you like that."

"He got one more strike, and he's out," he didn't want to go the violent route but he would if he had to.

"That was his one more strike. Rasheid listen, you don't sale nickels and dimes no more. You got access to keys. If you let people see bitch ass niggas lie that disrespecting you and they know you got money, then you ain't gonc bc nuttin but a target for niggas to try to make a come up on."

"I mean you know, that maybe the case. I can't say that I disagree but I got a lot of shit going on right now. I got a lot of weight on my shoulders. I don't need no unnecessary attention. All that's going to do is start a domino effect of some bullshit," he looked at his pager again and saw Tania was paging him. "And I'm trying to avoid as much bullshit as possible."

"Welcome to the game," Rookie looked Rasheid directly in his eyes. "It comes with the territory. And if you ain't trying to ride on these niggas then I will," he got in his car and started the ignition. "I got some business I got to take care of. Make sure you get at me," Rookie drove off feeling a little upset of how easy going Rasheid could be sometimes. Rasheid shook his head at him then got in his car and drove off.

ChApter 13

~~~~~~

D owntown Charleston Doc and Easy sat in Doc's Q45 Infiniti and talked with each other as they watched the children play in the park.

"So what the fuck is up with Rodger?" Why did Rino cut him off?"

"You know that nigga was smoking that shit on the low for years. Him and them white broads. Somebody said he fucked up a lot of money or coke. One of the two," Easy said as he rolled up the blunt.

"So who you think got the connect?"

"Ain't no telling. I heard about a nigga in Hollywood name Jay. But he mainly be out the country. Plus I think he got a outside connect," he brushed off the crumbs of marijuana that fell on his Gibaud jeans. "I can't wait to catch that nigga slipping. Oh check this out. My little cousin from North Charleston was telling me bout some young nigga he go to school with that's suppose to be getting money. Some nigga name Rasheid."

Doc looked over at his friend, "So you think that nigga stupid enough to fuck wit a nigga in school."

"They say he got that butta and he lettin it go for nine hundred a O."

"Nine hundred a O," Easy had his friend's full attention. "You ever seen him before."

"Not a day in my life," Easy said lighting the blunt. "Oh yeah but my cousin said that Dre use to fuck with the nigga like that," Doc looked back at his friend sharply when he heard that name.

"He selling O's for nine hundred and he knew Dre," doc contemplated in the idea. "Might have to check this young nigga out. What's your cousin's name anyway."

"N.O. matter of fact I'm bout to call him up in a minute," Easy passed the blunt to Doc.

─────────────────

Rasheid got off the interstate following the directions that Rino gave him. After about twenty minutes of driving he found himself in the country side of Mt. Pleasant while he looked at the number on the house and then back at the paper and saw that it was correct. This was not a place he expected to see Rino living at. As he got out the car and walked up the driveway he got a closer look at the money green ninety-six Cadillac Seville that was parked in the driveway he knew he seen it before. He just couldn't remember where. He rang the doorbell and a young light skinned woman who looked as if she was in her mid-twenties opened the door.

"Hi," Rasheid said to her. She just stared at him. "I'm looking fo-."

"Come on in," the woman cut him off. He stepped inside the house and looked around as she closed the door and guided him to the section of the house Rino was in. As he stepped into the room that reeked of weed smoke, he observed RIno sitting down in a casually dressed shirt and pants with some bedroom slippers watching Jeopardy. He looked over at Rasheid then cut the t.v. off as his lady friend left them alone. Rasheid didn't know what it was but as Rino sat there in his casual clothes and slippers his whole aura seemed powerful.

"Mr. Rasheid. What's going on man," Rino directed him to a seat.

"I'm alright," he put the bag with the money in it on the floor beside him. He was nervous but didn't have a clue why.

"So you had any problems?" Rino pointed at the bag.

"I probably had a problem counting it," he tried to make a joke as Rino just stared at him. After a few seconds pass he let off an easy laugh as Rasheid joined in with him.

"So that's all my money right there," Rino stop laughing.

"Yeah," Rasheid shook his head.

"Well can I have it."

"Oh yeah!" Rasheid jumped up and gave him the bag. Rino unzipped the bag, glanced in it then looked back Rasheid as he zipped the bag back up and put it on the floor. He then sat back in the sofa and studied him.

"So what's up man?" How you doing?"

Rasheid looked around then back at him, "I'm fine."

"You sure."

"Positive. How about you?"

"I'm doing fine. Thank you," he readjusted himself in the sofa. "You know Rasheid. I've been hearing good things about you for a while now. You know Rodger speak real highly of you," he took a piece of chocolate out the candy dish then offered one to him.

"No thank you," Rasheid wish he'll stop beating around the bush. The anticipation was killing him.

"So being that I took an interest in you, I had to do some research. You know, have my people check you out. To see if you was actually worth investing in," he bit a piece of the chocolate.

Rasheid looked confused for a moment.

"Who's your people?"

"It's too late to worry about that now, because if I wanted you dead, you would have been dead by now," he laughed which Rasheid didn't thought was funny but he had a slight grin on his face anyway. "But what's important is that now your apart of a team. And not just a teammate. A major player. So you're going to have the status that a major player have," he said as they both looked at each other. "Rodger got rid of nineteen bricks a month for me. So do the math, at sixteen g's a key, that's over three hundred thousand dollars a month. My question is do you think you can come close to that," Rasheid felt a big lump in his throat as Rino read the expression on his face. "You got any type of experience with children?"

"No," he wondered where that question came from.

"Well I have six children. And I don't want them to have no false image of what the world has to offer. So I hide nothing from them and I also push them as far as they can go. When they were babies I seen in their eyes that they were afraid to walk on their own. So I stood them up on their feet and stepped back with my arms reach out for them so they can step into it. Every step they took closer to me, I took a step back. After a while they started to get frustrated but they continued to try to reach me without realizing that they're walking. They have the essential and the potential that they need, all they needed to do was do it," Rino stood up and walked towards the door. "Sit tight for one second. I'll be right back. Rasheid looked around the room then he checked his pager and saw that he had three pages he missed with Tania being one of them. By the time he put the pager back on his waist Rino had reentered the room with the black bag in his hand. He gave the bag to Rasheid then sat back on the sofa. "That's seven bricks in that bag. So that's one hundred twelve thousand dollars I need back," Rasheid just looked at him and wondered how he seemed to keep putting himself in these crazy predicaments, "Rasheid, I'm not forcing you to do this and if you don't want to, feel free to walk out right now," Rino pointed to the doorway. Rasheid just sat back in the sofa.

"It's not that," he tried to figure out the right words to say. "It's just that I never dealt with this much money and before and to be honest with you," he let his eyes wander around the room. "I just get a little nervous," Rino shook his head as if he comprehended.

"That's understandable. And I appreciate your honesty. That's a part of human nature. Especially when your around something that you're not familiar with. But being that you're on a higher level now it's going to be a whole lot of other shit your not familiar with coming at you. So you need to continue to stay focus and be as humble as possible. I feel like I shouldn't have to tell you this but I'm just making sure. When some niggas get a little money, they start to feel their untouchable. They don't last. Some niggas fall victim to pussy. And if a man's weakness is between a woman's legs he don't last. You have others who I don't know why but wanna try the same shit the selling, seeing first hand how it destroys other people's lives and of course you know they don't last. Soon some people are going to be expecting you not to last. You probably got some out there right now that's praying on your downfall. And the only one who can prove them right or wrong is you," Rasheid was all ears. "All I can do is guide you. But you get to choose rather you succeed or fail...and if I thought you was a failure, I would of never wasted my time with you."

Rasheid looked over at Rino then suddenly felt the pressure of the world on his shoulders. He stood up and grabbed the bag as Rino walked with him to the door.

"Be careful. Stay focus and conscious. And if you need to talk to me about anything, remember to call that number."

"Alright," Rasheid said to him as he walked to the car and got in. As he drove through the countryside of Mt. Pleasant and got back on the interstate, he thought about the seven kilos of cocaine in the trunk of his car. Then he thought about Tania. He knew that meant he was going to be spending less time with her which is also a future problem. He got on his cellular phone and called Rookie to tell him he was on his way.

"We got to hurry up man. I got motherfuckers lined up right now. Shit we might get rid of this shit in about three, four days," Rookie said as him and Rasheid cut and bag the drugs.

"I'm hoping at least two weeks."

"Two weeks! Rookie looked back at him. "Shhh, nigga mark my word, less than seven days. Seven bricks in seven days.

"Rook," Rasheid stopped what he was doing and looked at him. "Remember to keep a low profile."

"Man I ain't just start doing this. I'm serious about this shit, this ain't no game. And I'm going to prove it. We gotta win/win. The goal is to get rich without going to jail.

"Yeah that's the plan."

"All we gotta do is stay on track…and we gone have to hurry the fuck up because time is money," he said as Rasheid laughed at him.

Rasheid and Rookie toured all through the city of Charleston selling their product. Throughout the whole weekend besides the sleeping they weren't able to have two whole hours to themselves. They were picky with some of the people who the sold to. They could sense when some people was just bad business and they tried not to have any type of dealings with them. But even with being choosy to some of their clients by Sunday night or early Monday morning the two counted over one hundred thousand dollars. As they split up the money, they went their separate ways with hopes of meeting up the next day.

When Rasheid got home, he looked at his watch that read almost three o'clock. So he decided that he wasn't going to go to school. He figured one day out from school wouldn't hurt him. When he got in his apartment he quietly went upstairs to see Tania either asleep or pretending. He put the money in the safe and took off his clothes then went in the shower. When he got out the shower he saw Tania changed position she was now lying on her back with the sheets halfway down exposing the top half of her body. Rasheid then realized that a few days passed since him and Tania had sex and he was starting to feel an urge for it as he continued to watch her. He bent over and kissed her lips. Still no movement came from her as he went down and kiss her again.

"I have to go to school in the morning," she said with her eyes still closed.

Rasheid laid down next to her, "That means I can't kiss you."

"That's exactly what that means."

"You my girl," he kissed the side of her face as he wrapped his arm around her. "And if I wanna kiss you I'ma kiss you."

"Not taking into consideration that by you kissing me can wake me up out of my sleep which could also be a hindrance for my day to come."

"Damn Baby, you don't gotta get all technical on me," he said as he slid away from her and laid on his back.

Tania laid on her side now facing him.

"Rasheid. We don't never spend no time together. We supposed to have a relationship and it seems like that's the last thing on your list to worry about."

"It's not that," Rasheid looked at the ceiling. "It's just that I'm trying to build a future for us. Being put in the different situations I done been through, it makes me look at life from a different perspective. I don't want to go through no more hard times and I don't want to see you go through none either. But I got a plan, by the time you graduate it's going to be a wrap for me. I'm trying to move away from here then maybe I can go to college and work on my career," he said as he visualized his thoughts. "We gonna have more than enough money. And I probably might go to law school."

"But what if something bad happens by then…Rasheid I can't go through none of that no more. Why don't you just stop now. I know we got more than enough money. And if we don't I'll just get a job. I'm not a stranger to working."

He looked at her then back at the ceiling.

"And where you gone work at to pay for the shit we got. The rent, the car notes, both of our car insurances. On top of that you still gotta pay for tuition and we gotta eat. Let's be real, that don't make sense," he looked over at her. As those words left Rasheid's mouth Tania suddenly felt trapped. As she let the reality settled in, she knew he was speaking the truth. If he was to stop hustling and they both got jobs, it wouldn't be enough to take care if their living conditions. She put her hand on the top of his chest realizing that he was the only way she could live out her dream. "Rasheid," she whispered as he looked over. "Just promise me you'll be careful."

"I will," he said as he turned over to kiss her as she closed her eyes and wrapped her arm around his neck.

Rasheid slept in the next morning for the first time since he could remember. When he got up it was after eleven o'clock and by the look of the room he could tell Tania was long gone. He got out of bed, got dress and went to the kitchen and fixed a bowl of Cinnamon Toast Crunch and turned the t.v. on BET. When he was finished he took the roll of money that was on his dresser and left out the house to go catch up with Rookie. As he stepped outside, the sunny eighty-five degree weather was a beautiful greeting as he press the alarm button on his car.

"Excuse me," a female voice yelled out. Rasheid turned around and saw the light complexion girl who lived next door to him standing in her doorway with just a t-shirt on barely covering her big ass and exposing her juicy yellow thighs all the way down to her pretty manicured feet, "Can you do me a favor?"

"What's up," he tried not to look at how beautifully curved the girl was. "You think you can help me lift something real quick?"

Rasheid just looked at her knowing if he go inside with her, it'll probably be trouble, "It'll only take one minute. It's just me and my baby in here and I can't lift this dresser up," he hesitated for a second, press the alarm button on his key chain and walked in the girl direction. She eyed him down until he was face to face with her. He looked down at the girl who not only had a nice body but her face was just as pretty.

"How you doing," he put his keys in his pocket.

She welcomed him in the apartment him in the apartment and closed the door.

"I just need a little help with this dresser."

Rasheid looked around her house and saw it was neat and clean.

"My name is Shonda." "Alright.

I'm Rasheid."

"I know who you are," she guided him to the room. He suddenly felt a set up as he followed behind her. "I just need a little help carrying this dresser to my daughter's room."

"Rasheid picked the dresser up and felt that it weighed no more than twenty pounds. He looked at her then took it to the next room as she requested. She walked in the room behind him.

"I was thinking it'll look good right here," she bent over and picked up one of her daughter's stuff animal. While she was bent over he got a peek of her hairy pink flesh between her legs. She had no underwear on and bent over again giving him another peek of her hairy bush, this time giving him an eyeful.

"That girl is always leaving her stuff animals all over the place," she said as she picked up the other one then put it on the bed. Rasheid erection grew noticeable through his jeans catching her attention.

"Well I gotta go take care of somethings," he tried to leave out the door.

"You sure you can't stay awhile," she stepped in closer to him and rubbed her breast against his chest.

Rasheid felt his lust taking over and he knew if he stayed another second he'll fall victim.

"Look, I gotta go," he stepped outside as he took another look at her before he walked away. The temptation was almost too much to resist. But he knew he couldn't have sex with his next door neighbor. He don't need no unnecessary drama. He got in his car took a deep breath and drove off.

Rookie hung up the phone just as Rasheid pulled into his driveway.

"What's up man," Rasheid got out the car.

"What's up school boy," Rookie put the phone in his pocket. "What you playing hookie today."

"I figure one day wouldn't hurt."

"Yeah. Well check this out. I'm bout to make a run out Ashley Phosphate real quick. I got a nigga who trying to cop."

"Well I'm going to get about twelve. I've been getting pages all morning," Rasheid followed Rookie into the basement. When they got out they were greeted by Tremaine who pulled up in his candy apple red Lexus. Tremaine was brown skin with cornrows coming down to the middle of his back. He had a reputation for getting money and having the ladies but mostly for being a lunatic.

"Rookie and Rasheid. What's going on little homies," he stepped out the car.

"What's up," Rasheid said after he noticed Rookie completely ignored him.

"I'ma go take care of that. I'ma try to be back around seven o'clock. You got the keys to the basement right," Rookie shook Rasheid's hand.

"Yeah I got it."

"Aiight then I'm out," he pulled out his .45 glock checked the clip then put it back in his waist. His intentions was to imitate Tremaine. Tremaine thought it was cute. Rookie got in his sister's car and drove off. Rasheid went to put the bag in the trunk closed it back then opened up the driver's door.

"Rasheid, let me holla at you for a minute," Tremaine walked in his direction.

"What's up," Rasheid sat down in the driver's seat.

"What up big timer. I hear you got shit on lock out here."

"Well you know how that go. Believe half of what you see and none of what you hear."

Tremaine smiled at him then walked in closer lowering the tone of his voice, "Look man. I know what time it is with you. Word is that you got North Charleston on lock," Rasheid looked up at him to see where the conversation was going. "But where your troops at man. What the fuck is you gonna do when bullets coming at you from every angle. I know you ain't depending on that little shit you got on your waist. And yo homeboy Rookie, he a good nigga and all be he ain't but one man and he damn sure ain't immune to bullets."

"So what's your point man," Rasheid got irritated that Tremaine exposed his weakness.

"My point is that you need me just like I need you. Every nigga in this city know who my young niggas are. And they know their as ruthless as it gets. Now let me get down wit yo network as I put you down with mines. We can all get money. How can you lose."

Rasheid thought about what he said. He knew the people Tremaine was talking about and what he spoke of them was the truth. They went by the Blood Brothers and had a reputation a mile long for robbery and murder. He really didn't want no dealings with them but he knew it would be an advantage to have them on his side.

"Let me get back with you on that," he closed the door and started the ignition.

"I'ma talk it over with Rookie."

"You do that," Tremaine walked off. "Cause we can have a bright future together."

Rasheid drove off as he thought about Tremaine's proposition.

"You straight," Rookie said.

"Yeah," Rasheid opened the trunk to retrieve the black bag. While Rasheid walk to the side of the house to enter the basement Rookie just stood there looking around making sure everything was alright and the coast was clear. When they got in the basement Rasheid put the bag on the floor as Rookie locked the door.

"What you got," Rookie took a seat by Rasheid.

"Ten."

"Ten!" Rookie said shocked.

"Ten," Rasheid opened the bag to display the ten kilos of cocaine.

"Bet," Rookie pulled up the carpet then opened the safe. Rasheid started putting the product in the safe.

"You know what Rookie. You could have been a hell of a carpenter," he admired how Rookie installed the safe in the floor.

"You know I was thinking that same shit. My pops was a carpenter. I just took the trade up in prison just so they could take some points off my level but then I took a liking to the shit.

"So why didn't you get a job as a carpenter than," Rasheid stood up and grabbed the empty bag.

"The same reason you didn't get a job at whatever it is that nerds do," Rookie laughed at his own joke then took a seat on the sofa as Rasheid joined him.

"Yo," Rasheid looked at him. "I'ma put Tremaine down. Plus I'm need some help moving these keys."

Rookie frown his face disapprovingly.

"We don't need him. Me and you and can do this shit."

"What I'm sayin is that it'll be better if I had him on my side. I'm not trying to get my hands too dirty and I don't want you to get yours too dirty either," Rookie just looked at him not understand where he's going. "Listen Rook. Do you understand how much money we gone be playin with. Rino just gave me ten keys. That's over three hundred thousand dollars. You trying to tell me with figures like that I shouldn't have an army. All I'm doing is fronting Tremaine a brick. And I think it's going to be worth it in the long run…Then that'll probably take some of the pressure off me. I done made a lot of money out here and I don't even have time to spend it."

Rookie looked over at Rasheid, pulled out a Newport and lit it. He knew Rasheid was speaking logic it's just that he already hated the fact that Tremaine got his sister pregnant. He didn't want to do business with him to.

"It's your call man. But I'm letting you know if any of these niggas ever get in my way I got to have em. Tremaine or the Blood Brothers and I don't give a damn how many niggas they done robbed and killed."

"Okay good," Rasheid said happy he convinced him. "We got a meeting tomorrow."

"Who is we?" Rookie looked at him.

"Me, you, Tremaine and the Blood Brothers."

Rookie looked at Rasheid then took a long drag from his cigarette and blew the smoke in the air as he shook his head.

Rasheid and Rookie pulled up to the house where Tremaine and his crew awaited their arrival. They got out the car and looked around the suburban neighborhood then went up the stairs to ring the doorbell. Tremaine opened the door and greeted both of them as they came in and took a seat. The Blood Brothers were all seated on the sofa.

"Aiight yo," Tremaine closed the door and stood in the center of the living room. First let me make the introduction. Rasheid this is C.J., Black, L-Note and Tee. Y'all this is Rasheid. "Tremaine said as Rasheid got up and shook all of their hands with Rookie following suit. "And I know y'all know Rookie."

C.J. stood about six feet two with a medium built and a bald head. He was the biggest robber out the group. With him it was all about taking money. There was rumors that he once murdered a guy for whatever reason but there was no proof of it and much wasn't said about it either. Black who was originally from Miami, Florida moved to Charleston when he was about twelve. Three years later his mother died of aids and he didn't have no other family members to go to. The state then took him in and he became a foster child and ever since then he's been a loose cannon, not carrying about anything. A twenty year old trigger happy kid who gets a kick out of watching other people suffer. He met up with C.J. and Tee in the foster home and besides his step brother that still resides in Miami, they were the only family whom he ever acknowledge.

L-Note probably was the most dangerous one out of the crew. At twenty-two years old, it's a known fact that he already killed seven people. When he was eighteen years old he was at a red light waiting for it to turn green, when he saw the car pulled up next to him the with the guy who stabbed him in his leg when they were fighting a few weeks prior. Without even thinking about it, he got out of the car, walked up to the car he was in and shot him right in his head. His brains was blown all over the steering wheel. Days later he got indicted on first degree murder and went to trial facing a life sentence. Nobody wanted to testify against him so he ended up having the case dropped due to lack of evidence and was free on all charges. After that people started calling him L-Note due to the fact he was supposed to get life in prison. He was already a bit on the crazy side but after he beat the murder case he felt like he was that much more untouchable.

Tee who was the younger brother of L-Note did follow right in his footsteps. He probably was the biggest threat to society out of all of them because unlike the rest, he didn't have a conscience. And being the youngest out the group he carried the worse reputation. At seventeen years old he robbed, stole and killed. He was known throughout North Charleston and Summerville and even though he was the craziest what a lot of people didn't know was that he was also the smartest out the group.

After everyone greeted each other, Rasheid and Rookie took a seat while Tremaine stood in the center.

"Aiight. Check it out. Everybody got a position. We're going to be moving the majority of cocaine through this city. Rasheid supplying the work and we moving it. I'm trying to have North Charleston, Downtown and West Ashley on lock. I done figured out a method to where we can move at least twelve keys per month," he said looking at Rasheid. "The only thing that's holding us back is us. With a year every man in this room should at least be holding six figures," he looked around the room.

"Less than a year," Black said.

"So if anybody got any objections or issues, put it on the table right now."

Everyone looked at each other then at Rasheid.

"Who gonna be responsible for taking care of the money," Rookie asked.

"Me," Tremaine said. "You cool wit that?"

Rookie looked over at Rasheid then back at Tremaine. "It ain't my call so fuck it," Rookie said.

"Rookie if you got something you wanna say then now is the time to get it off your chest."

"You don't have to worry about that. If I had something to say believe, I'll say it," Rookie said with a little animosity.

Black and C.J. looked at each other than at Rookie.

"You straight man," Rasheid asked knowing something was bothering him.

"I'm good," Rookie pulled out a Newport then lit it.

Rasheid sensed the vibes that the Blood Brothers was sending Rookie and right then he saw a future problem.

"Aiight then let's get this money," Tremaine broke down the plan on how they was going to take over the city.

A couple days later Rasheid took a hundred and sixty thousand dollars cash to Rino who in returned gave him another gave him another ten kilos. Rino was a little shock how quick Rasheid sold the product. He knew he was going to come around but he didn't think it'll be that soon.

Rasheid pulled up to the car lot and got out looking around. He was fascinated by looking at all the Mercedes, BMW's, Jaguars and Lexus on the lot. Then a middle aged white man approached him while he was still eye shopping.

"Hey," the guy looked at him with a big smile on his face.

"Hi," Rasheid pulled the card out his pocket. "I'm looking for Carl Sedar."

"And that'll be me," he extended his hand to Rasheid. "You must be Rasheen."

"Rasheid," he corrected him as he shook his hand.

"Oh sorry bout that Rasheid. Tremaine told me about you. I've been doing business with him for years," he put his hands in his pockets and stepped closer to Rasheid as he lowered his voice. "Whenever you doing business with me, you don't have nothing to worry about. I can make it look like your just a college students who parents bought you a car. Catch my drift, he nudged Rasheid with his elbow.

"Yeah," Rashied said shocked by seeing even middle class white folks could be crooked.

"So tell me what you like," he spoke back at his normal tone.

"That's not an easy choice," he looked around the car lot again.

"Yeah, tell me about it," the salesman smiled.

"But I do like that gray Benz over there," he pointed.

"Good choice," he spoke now in his sales pitch voice, "Nineteen ninety-seven CLK four thirty Mercedes Benz. You want find too many people in the city with that. And you can bet your bottom dollar on it," he said as they walked over to the car. The more Rasheid studied the car the more he fell in love with it and he knew he had to leave off the lot with it. "Stay right here. I'll go get the keys," he pat Rasheid on the back then walked off. Rasheid just stood there looking at the car knowing he had a winner. After all the paperwork was done, Rasheid had the salesman to drive his Cadillac behind him while he drove off in his brand new Mercedes Benz. When he got to his house, the salesman parked the Cadillac, shook Rasheid's hand and congratulated him on his new car then got in the new car with the other salesman who followed them and they drove off. Rasheid took another look at his broad new car then went inside.

———————————

"Ma, where do you want the potatoes to go at?" Tania asked as she helped her mother put the groceries away.

"I don't know Tania. Find a spot where it could fit. I don't know why you bought me all these groceries in the first place."

"Because you need some food," she turned around and looked at her mother.

"But I don't need two hundred dollars worth," the fragile woman sat down and lit a cigarette.

"That's not two hundred dollars," she put the food in the refrigerator. Her mother studied her while taking long drags of the cigarette.

"That boy must be treating you real good. You spending his money like water."

"No I'm not," she said defensively.

"Girl, you forgot who you talking to. I know money when I see it," her mother had a slight grin on her face," he got you an apartment and a car. I was born at night but it damn sure wasn't last night," she flicked the ashes in the ashtray. "You still ain't bought him up here to see me yet. What you ashamed to bring him over or something."

"Ma, I live with him and I barely see him."

"Well I guess you don't need to see him. As long as he giving up that up that money you know he doing alright," she laughed at her own joke.

"No Ma. I can't be in a relationship like that. I need more than just money," she took a seat by her mother. "I wanna go places, have fun. You know, live like normal people. The only time I get a chance to talk to him is after midnight and most of the time he's too tired to talk," she leaned back in the chair expressing herself hoping her mother would understand. Her mother put out cigarette, crossed both of her hands on top of the table then looked at her.

"Do you love him?"

Tania nodded her head.

"Well you need to work it out. Y'all are still young and got a whole lot more of living and learning to do. Experience is the best teacher in life. Trust me, I know. He's gonna make some mistakes, your gonna make some mistakes, he's gonna make some more. But you can't let those mistakes discourage you because your gonna miss out on how beautiful life could be. You find out where you went wrong and try to fix it so you can keep moving on. Cause what don't break you down is only going to build you up. So if you really love him then try to thick it out," she said as Tania listened closely to every word. Just then she felt the vibration from her pager go off on her waist. She checked it and saw that it was Rasheid.

"Speaking of the devil," she pressed a on her pager then put it back on her waist. "Rasheid paging me. I gotta go," she grabbed her purse then headed to the door.

"Ha-ha. Only two things that make you move like that, true love or some good dick," her mother laughed displaying her mouth with no teeth.

"Bye Ma," Tania tried not to blush. She walked back to kiss her on her cheek.

"Bye Sugar," her mother watched as she left out the door as she reminisced when she was that age. "And don't forget to write your daddy and brother!" she yelled out.

"I won't!"

⁓⁓⁓⁓⁓⁓⁓⁓⁓⁓

Tania drove down the street and cursed herself for not bringing her umbrella as she watched the rain fall down. When she got to her home, she seen the Mercedes parked outside and wondered who Rasheid's company was. She hoped it wasn't one of his drug dealing friends. She reached under her seat grabbed some old school papers and held it over her head to prevent the rain from messing up her hair due. She then walked briskly to the door.

"You could have least brought an umbrella to me outside," she took off her jacket but then got caught off guard by the lobster smell. "Are you cooking?"

"Technically no. I bought it. I'm just preparing it for you," Rasheid poured her drink in a champagne glass.

"Is that wine?"

"Nah," he smiled. "Grape kool-aid." Tania

laughed at him.

"Rasheid, you are ghetto," she walked up and admired how he prepared the lobster meal.

"Thanks," he said sarcastically.

"Who's car is that out there?"

Rasheid continued to poor the drinks making sure both glasses was even. He didn't say word.

"Rasheid," she said in a serious tone. "Whose car is that outside." He then looked up at her.

"It's mine."

Tania held her hand up to Rasheid as she closed her eyes.

"Rasheid. I know you didn't went and bought a Benz."

"Look Tania we straight. Everythings straight. So you don't got nothing to worry about."

"Nothing to worry about! Rasheid you went and bought a Mercedes Benz. You're barely seventeen years old. Don't you know the police is going to be all over you when they see you in that car!"

"You not listening Tania, you don't have nothing to worry about. I got everything under control. Now can we just eat and try to have a nice time. You always talking about how I don't spend no time with you and here I am trying to be romantic and you messing up the groove," he said walking towards her. "Now trust me. You don't have nothing to worry about," he grabbed her by her waist and tried to kiss her but she turned her face. "Gimme a kiss," he nibbled on her cheek.

"No," she tried not to let him butter her up.

"Girl gimme a kiss," he said now nibbling on her neck and rubbing her butt.

"You know you done stumble across a gold mine," Tania couldn't help but smile as he took advantage of it and stole the opportunity to kiss her. She gave in and kissed him back.

"Now can we please eat?" It took me almost all afternoon to get this ready and you wanna come with all this telling, talking about a car," he said in almost a whining tone.

"Boy shut up," she smiled at him as they enjoyed their meal and had a genuine conversation for the first time in months.

The next day Rasheid pulled up to school in his brand new Mercedes Benz as he had everyone in the student and teacher parking lot attention. All the girls was in ooh's and ahh's while he seen jealousy in some of the guys eyes but they still couldn't take their eyes off the car. Deanna jumped out of Kiana's car and ran up to Rasheid.

"Boy I know you ain't went and bout a fucking Benz!" she looked inside the car with her hands on the window as if she never seen a Mercedes Benz before. "Uh-unh. Let me see the inside! she said as Rasheid slammed the trunk putting the bookbag on his back. "Open the door Rasheid!" she said anxiously.

"Hold up," he unlocked the door.

"Girl want you stop acting like you never had nothing," Kiana walked up acting unimpressed.

"Bitch this is a four-thirty Benz. You better act like you know!" Deanna said looking all around his car.

Rasheid looked over at Kiana which she could of sense but tried not to look back. He had to admit she was one of the finest girls in the school. He figured a little harmless flirting wouldn't hurt.

"So what's up Kiana?" he said walking up to her.

She waited months for him to reapproached her, and now that he's doing it her brain won't react quick enough to send the right words through her mouth.

"Hi," she said trying not to blush.

"So how you been doing?"

"Fine."

"Rasheid! What you suppose to put on top of this a laptop! Rasheid looked over at Deanna who was playing with the special features in his car.

"Deanna," he said calmly. "Please don't break nothing in my car."

"Nigga I'm not gonna break nothing," she said still fiddling with the gadgets.

"That girl's crazy," he said getting back to Kiana. "Tell me about it," Kiana looked at her friend.

"So what's been going on with you though?"

"Nothing much, besides school and chilling with my girl."

"You don't talk like you from round here."

"You mean I don't talk geechie," she smiled as he did too. "I'm not. I'm from Detroit."

"Oh so you a Detroit playa."

"Nah. I ain't no playa," she continued to smile.

"So what happen to your boyfriend?"

"What boyfriend?" she acted as if she didn't know who he was talking about.

"Ol boy I use to always see you with, I can't remember his name," Rasheid said trying to recall what they call him.

"You talking about Seafus."

"Yeah, Seafus that's it. I thought that was your boyfriend."

Kiana shook her head, "He's not my boyfriend," she said now looking directly in his eyes as he looked back in hers.

"Oh for real."

"Boy Rasheid you done fuck the game up with that one," Deanna said walking up to the two. Rasheid pressed the alarm button on the car as they heard the bell rung.

"I already got two tardies. Let me hurry up and get to Mrs. Cunningham class before she write me up," Deanna said.

"You mine if I walk you to class Kiana," Rasheid asked seeing that she had a lost for words. She looked over at Rasheid asked seeing that Kiana had a lost for words. She looked over at Deanna who eyes were telling her yes.

"No, I don't mine," she said as she felt a little bit of nervousness.

"Well I'ma catch y'all two later. I gotta go," Deanna walked off as she gave Kiana that look.

"So how you like living down here."

"Okay," she said as they took their time walking to class.

"How long you been living down here?"

"Almost three years now," Kiana looked up and saw N.O. walking in their direction staring at Rasheid. She looked at Rasheid who observed N.O. as well. The two stared each other down until they were a few feet from one another.

"You got a problem with your motherfucking eyes nigga!" N.O. said aggressively.

Rasheid didn't say anything. He just met his gaze back.

"You ready for your chance of a lifetime nigga. Just like I though! Bitch ass nigga!" N.O. said as the two stood face to face.

"I don't got time for no chumps," just as the words left Rasheid's mouth N.O. punched him in his face causing him to take a few steps back. Without thinking Rasheid dropped his bookbag and the two threw hate makers at each other as a crowd came from out nowhere gathered around. N.O. was caught off guard at Rasheid having more fight in him than he thought. Every punch he threw him, Rasheid met him back with an equal if not more powerful blow. He then tried to grab him and that's when Rasheid struck him on the side of his face as he fell to the ground. He tried to get up but it was no use. Rasheid met him with another punch followed by another one as he fell back on the floor. The hall monitors busted through the crowd grabbed Rasheid and pinned him against the locker as the other two picked up N.O. off the floor and held his hands behind his back as if they were the police. The crowd was ecstatic, laughing and cheering as other hall monitors muscled their way through the crowd and tried to control the group of rowdy teenagers.

"Alright, the shows over! Get to class before I start taking names!" one of the hall monitors said. Kiana stood in shock from all the commotion watched as the hall monitors escorted Rasheid to the principal's office.

ChApter 14

~~~~~~

Rookie was at the corner store slash drug spot talking to his childhood friend Chuck.

"Man who the fuck taught you how to roll a blunt," Rookie took the blunt from him.

"I'm not into that fancy shit. As long as the bitch smokable," Chuck said exhaling the smoke. "I heard Rasheid went and bought a Benz."

"Yeah, me too," Rookie said not wanting to get into the conversation.

"I thought that's your boy."

"He is," he said looking around.

"So is y'all wit the Blood Brothers," Chuck said taking the blunt from Rookie.

"Damn nigga, what you wearing a wire or something. Or these fucking questions like you the police," Rookie took a seat on the hood of his Maxima watching the crowd of people around him.

"Nigga don't try to play me. I wanna know why you ain't put me down yet," Chuck said with an attitude.

"Timings not right yet," Rookie looked at his watch as if he had somewhere to be. "Plus, I ain't got no say so right now. It's a whole lot of shit in the air and ain't no telling which direction it takes when it touch," he pulled out a wad of cash out his pocket. "Hey Lil Marvin," he yelled out the kid who came running as he peeled off a ten dollar bill. "Go get me a ham and cheese sandwich, some barbecue chips and a bottle of Sprite. Keep the change."

"Thanks Rookie," the boy said running into the store.

Rookie then observed a forest green and gold Q45 Infiniti pulled up. Two guys who got out and walked in their direction.

"You know these niggas," Chuck said in a low tone steadily eyeing down the two guys.

"Hell no," Rookie reached for his glock then checked to see of it was on safety.

"Yo, what's up man," one of the guys said to Rookie. "You know me," Rookie shot back.

"No need for the hostility," the guy shown him no sign of intimidation. "My name is Doc and this my homeboy Easy," he said as Rookie looked at the guy who was just standing there with his hands across his pelvic area not saying a word.

"We trying to meet Rasheid. And people saying you the closest thing to him."

"Who's people?" Rookie said.

"People. The streets." "Where y'all from?"

"The E," Doc refered to the Eastside of Downtown.

"Well check this out," Rookie scratched his head. "Rasheid ain't here right now and I don't know when I'ma see him again."

"Well you gotta a pager number?"

"Let me get yours," he sensed some bad vibes from the two. Doc wrote down his pager number and gave it to him.

"I'ma holla at chu man," he shook Rookie's hand then they walked off.

Rookie just looked at them as they got in their car and drove off.

"Them niggas don't seem right, do they," he looked at Chuck then back at the car.

"I don't know but that quiet nigga look familiar as a motherfucker." Rookie looked at the car as they drove off.

"I don't think I seen him before."

Rasheid walked out of the school building balling up the suspension paper and throwing it in the waste basket. He got in his car and drove off. Being that it was before noon he decided to go see his Aunt Tereesa since he hasn't seen her in almost a month. When he got to her apartment he saw that the Volvo was clean on the inside as well as the outside for a change. He looked at the door and Tereesa opened it on his second knock. Her eyes lit up when she saw him.

***

"Hey Baby!" she stepped outside to give him a hug. After his aunt left the drugs alone her natural beauty started back glowing.

"Hey Aunt Tereesa," he hugged her back.

"Come on in," she walked inside behind him. "You hungry?" she closed the door.

"Nah, I'm alright," Rasheid took a seat then looked around his aunt's apartment.

"Don't you suppose to be in school?" she walked into the kitchen.

Rasheid looked up at her.

"I got suspended."

Tereesa stopped in her tracks and looked at him.

"What you get suspended for Rasheid?"

"For fighting. But it wasn't my fault. This boy hit me first."

Tereesa took a seat by her nephew.

"Negative things happen when you deal out of negativity," before she said another word she held her head down in embarrassment. "I blame myself for everything that's going wrong in your life."

"This ain't your fault-."

"Rasheid," Tereesa said with a tear in her eye. "Baby I'm so sorry for the life I've forced you to live. I pray the Lord put in your heart to forgive me. If not sooner than later."

"Aunt Tereesa, it's not your fault," he put his arm on her shoulder. "I guess this is the way-."

"Rasheid," she cut him off again. "I had a dream the other night that you was twelve years old and you just moved in," she wiped the tears from her eyes. "And you was calling me while I was laying down. And at first I was too tired to get up. But when I did get up it felt like it took forever to get to you. And when I finally got to your room some guys had you tied up in a rope choking you. And as I tried to move towards you I was suddenly frozen and they continued to choke you and all I could do was stand there and watch. That was one of the worse dreams I can ever remember having," she scared Rasheid as much as she was. Rasheid just looked away for a minute not knowing what to say.

"That do sound scary," he broke the silence.

"Rasheid listen. I want you to stop selling drugs, cause ain't nothing good is gonna come out of that," she said as she read Rasheid's facial expression which wasn't in accordance with what she was saying. "You could even move back with me. We can start all over. And live like Mama intended for us to."

"Aunt Teressa," he said searching for words. "I-I can't do that right now. I got a whole lot on my plate," he said avoiding looking at his aunt. "I got my own life, you know me and Tania still trying to straighten out what we got going on," he said now realizing he's hurting her feelings. "I just can't do it Aunt Tereesa," she looked at him then put her hand on his chin pointing his face in her direction.

"Well you gotta do something Rasheid. Because the lifestyle you living is gonna catch up to you."

Deanna jogged towards Kiana trying not fall in her high heels.

"Hold up Kiana! Damn," Kiana stopped turned around and waited for her.

"Girl, I heard Rasheid beat the hell out of N.O. Everybody's talking bout it."

Kiana didn't say a word. She walked on once Deanna caught up.

"So what happened?" Deanna asked intrigued. "Did Rasheid swell him up. Bust his lip."

"Is that all you care about!" she snapped.

"What you mean if that's all I care about. Rasheid my boy," Deanna said in defense. Kiana just walked on.

"Unh-unh. I know Ms. Thing ain't strung out on that nigga already."

"Ain't nobody strung out on nothing," she said showing her Detroit city girl side. "I just don't see why Rasheid got in trouble when N.O. started the whole thing. He just walked up to him and started saying slick shit out of his mouth then punched Rasheid for no reason," she said as they walked out the double doors into the student parking lot.

"And what happened after that?"

"Rasheid whipped his ass. They was punching each other real hard in the face then N.O. fell to the floor. Rasheid never stop hitting him then the hall monitors came and broke it up. N.O. never got a chance to get off the ground," she said unlocking the door then pressing the automatic lock so Deanna could get in on the passenger side.

"Damn."

Kiana sat in the driver seat and unlock the door so Deanna could get in on the passenger side.

"Now you really can't lose with him. He look good, got money, drive a Benz. Can't leave that out and he can fight. Shit you can't beat that wit a bat."

Kiana put the car in drive and drove off thinking about Rasheid as Deanna talked her ears off.

"Yo what's up Jay," Rookie got in the passenger side of the guys Cutlass Supreme.

"What's going on with you Rookie," the dark skin heavy set guy said as he handed him a knot of money. "Here we go," Rookie took the money out his hand.

"Four and a half," he gave the man the product in return.

The guy opened the bag licked the tip of his thumb, tapped the cocaine, and licked his thumb.

"Boy this some good shit you got here," he closed the bag then wiped his tongue in his shirt.

"You know I deal wit nuttin but the best," Rookie said with confidence counting the money then putting it in his pocket. "Aiight Jay. I'ma holla at you Baby," he stepped out of his car.

"Aiight Rook. You take it easy," he said as he drove off.

Rookie took out a Newport and lit it up. He turned around and saw Rashied pulling up in his brand new Mercedes Benz as everyone just stared. If anybody was getting and attention right then Rasheid stole it for the moment. Rookie leaned against his car as Rasheid hopped out walking in his direction. Everyone looked on as if he was on the red carpet.

"What's up?" Rashied said approaching him.

Rookie just looked at him still smoking the cigarette.

"What's up nigga. What the hell is your problem."

"When you copped the Benz?"

"Day before yesterday. You like it," Rasheid said looking back admiring his car. "I'm straight. We straight. But we got bigger things to talk about then my car." Rookie looked away as he continued. "Now Tremaine just about finished selling those keys and if you finish I might can make that trip to Rino early this week." He said checking his pager. "How you looking anyway?"

"I don't got that much left. "Rookie watched the cars pass by. "Oh yeah. That's what I meant to tell you," he said recalling what happened earlier.

"Oh yeah me too," Rasheid said recalling his altercation with N.O. "I got the rumbling with N.O. today."

Rookie looked at him shocked.

"What happened!"

"The nigga was running off his mouth and he had the nerve to steal off on me."

"And what you do."

"Gave him what he was looking for," Rasheid said calmly. "The people suspended me for ten days though.

"You know what man," Rookie shook his head with a slight grin. "I don't know what to say about you."

"What you mean you don't know what to say about me."

"Cause that should have been the first thing that came out of your mouth when you saw me."

"It was nothing but a fight," Rasheid said.

"It's bigger than just the fight!" Rookie got louder. "How come I'm always the last to know about shit that happens to you or decisions you make!"

Rasheid looked around at the attention Rookie brought to them.

"Rook," he said in a lower tone. "Lower your voice man. You high. You trippin."

"Nigga I ain't trippin!" he got even louder. "You trippin. Tremaine and the Blood Brothers knew about you bringing them in with us before I did. I didn't even know you had a car. A bitch told me that this morning. Now what if something would of happen to you in that car and all they could say that it was a nigga with a gray Benz. How the fuck was I suppose to know it was you!"

"Rook, I understand what you saying but you getting just a little-."

"Man fuck that!" he said as Rasheid looked around and saw that everyone was looking at them. "Don't let this shit change you. I've been doing this shit my whole life. You haven't, so please don't let this shit change you Rasheid."

Rasheid was upset with Rookie's comment but he tried to control his temper.

"First of all," his voice was still calm. "Before I made a decision to do anything with Tremaine I came to talk to you. Matter of fact, you the reason we didn't agree right then and there. And secondly ain't shit changing me. You know where I came from. You know how I use to live. Motherfuck the Benz. I don't give a fuck about that material bullshit. I just bought it cause it look nice. If you think I changed then maybe you need to take a second look cause it might be you who changing. So don't come to me with that bullshit. I gotta put up with it enough at home with my girl. I be damn if I'ma be doing it with you too," the two held eye contact with each other for a moment. Rookie looked at the sun setting as he inhaled the smoke from the cigarette. He then looked back at Rasheid.

"My bad man," he said in a much calmer voice. He held his hand out to Rasheid as she shook it and hugged him at the same time.

"You aiight," Rasheid said letting him go. "We brothers man. We suppose to argue every once in a while. "Rookie smiled at him then tossed the cigarette.

"I got about four o's on me right now and like nineteen back at the safe. I'll probably sell out that shit tomorrow."

"That's what's up. Just holla at me when you get done," he took the money from Rookie.

"Come by the house and get the rest."

"Yeah, I'll probably be by first thing in the morning," Rasheid said not having enough space to put the money in his pocket.

"You do that man, I'll see you in the morning," Rookie shook his hand one last time.

"Aiight man, in the morning."

Rasheid drove down Rivers Avenue and turned into a gas station to fill up his tank. As he got into the parking lot he noticed all eyes were on him. He knew he wouldn't be driving his Benz as much. The attention he got from driving it was crazy. He filled the tank up, went and paid for the gas and came out the store in time to see C.J., one of the Blood Brothers pulling up in a Ford Explorer with the music blasting. When C.J. saw him, he parked the car and got out to acknowledge him.

"Boss man Rasheid. What's going on?" he approached as the two shook hands. He kind of resembled the rapper Fredro Starr out of the rap group Onyx.

"Ain't nothing man, what's up with you?"

"Bringing life out of death," he used an acronym for blood. "Yo," he said in an up north accent. "We making a killing with this shit out here. Man I don't know where the hell you got this work from but now we got more customers than a Chinese restaurant," him and Rasheid shared a laugh. "I ain't never seen no hard move this fast before."

"Gotta be the best at what you do. No need for half stepping."

"Yeah that's what's up, but yo, that's your whip," C.J. checked out his car.

"Yeah that's me."

"I see you. I see you. Hopefully another six months of this and I'll be pushing something like that," he rubbed his hands together. "But yo I got my peoples waiting on me and I know you got things to do so I'm bout to be out," he shook his hand and walked off.

"Alright C.J. I'ma holla at you man," Rasheid walked back to his car. He looked around wondering how time move so fast. It was already pitch dark.

"What's up Rasheid," a guy said whom he wasn't familiar with at all.

Rasheid looked at him suspiciously, "What's up."

The guy continued to walk in his direction, "I thought you said you was gone holla at me."

Rasheid just looked at him, "I don't think you know me."

"I don't but you know my bitch," he brandish a nine millimeter and aimed directly at Rasheid's abdomen. "If you try to run or scream I'ma kill you," Rasheid looked around from the corner of his eyes, he couldn't believe that he was getting robbed in front of a gas station and no one noticed. "Be easy and you'll live to see another day. Now hand over the keys and give up the loot," the guy said in a voice a little above a whisper with the gun still pointed at his stomach. Rasheid now gaining back his confidence felt like everything was going to be alright.

"Ay look man," Rasheid rubbed his face then looked the guy directly in his eyes. "It's obvious you got me fucked up with somebody else," the guy looked at Rasheid like he was crazy. "But being that you don't know no better, let this be a fair warning. Don't ever try this again," the guy then felt something poke him in his back and without looking around he knew it was the barrel of a gun.

"Now drop the gun or I'ma kill you," the voice said as the guy tried to look over his shoulder to try to get a peek of the person. "I said drop the motherfucking gun." The guy knew that he was in a no win situation dropped the gun then held his hands by his side.

ChApter 15

R ino got up from his seat and closed the blinds, "So how long you got
suspended out of school?"

"Ten days," Rasheid sat down looking at him.

"Perfect timing. I'ma need you to take a trip to Virginia for me.
Richmond," he paced the floor as Rasheid listened on. "You're going to meet
a guy there that's coming from New York. He's buying keys for twenty a brick
and he's buying twenty-five. This is a big move that you about to make so
I'm gonna need you to be extremely careful. Richmond is a tough city and if
you ain't on point them niggas will kill you out there. So take every move
with caution," he handed Rasheid a pad and an ink pen. "Write this down.
You'll get on 95 north and you won't get off until you're in Virginia. You'll
take 95 north all the way up and get off at Jefferson-Davis. That'll take you
through Chesterfield County. Then your gonna get off on Walmsley Blvd.
Then Your gonna get off on Orcutt Lane which connects BroadRock to
Hull street. Keep straight until you get to Southside Plaza which is where
Hull street and Belt Boulevard meet. Right there in the parking lot of
Long John Silver there's going to be somebody to meet you. Am I moving
too fast for you?" he said as Rasheid's was still writing.

"On paper no. Now when I actually get there I don't know."

Rino smiled at him and continued to pace the room. Rasheid listened
closely, "It's only complicated if you let it be. So don't let it be. Your driver's
license straight right," he nodded his head. "You're going to be driving one
of my cars. An Oldsmobile. Not flashy at all. Perfect engine, it'll ride
forever. And Kisha is going with you too," Rashied then looked up at him.

"Who's Kisha?"

"Kisha!" Rino yelled out.

The girl came through the door and looked at Rasheid without saying a word. It was the only girl who he ever saw around Rino.

"This is Kisha. Kisha as you know this is Rasheid," she nodded at him. "Now Kisha is your cousin, and y'all going to visit y'all aunt who lives in Southside if y'all are stopped and questioned by the police. This is the address," he gave Rasheid a card with a Southside address on it. "Now Rasheid I'ma need you to dress down. Don't wear nothing flashy. Matter of fact I don't even won't you to wear nothing name brand. Go buy you an outfit from Wal-Mart, shoes too. No jewelry or none of that shit. I want y'all to look like some common country ass niggas. Now it's going to be about a seven or eight hour drive. Get there, make the exchange and get back. We don't got no room for mistakes. And I'ma give you fifteen hundred off each brick. So go get you a good night of rest in and be back first thing in the morning ready to roll. Okay," he said as Rasheid stood up.

"Alright."

"You alright?" Rino asked.

"Yeah," Rasheid tried not to sound nervous.

"You sure."

"Yeah, I'm sure."

"Well I'll see you in the morning," Rino said as he shook Rasheid's hand and watch him walk out the door.

Tania got out of her car and opened the trunk to grab the groceries. She heard a bunch of laughter which caused her to look in the direction at her next door neighbor. She saw two girls around her age sitting on the lawn in patio chairs looking at her whispering to each other and burst out in laughter again. She looked behind her then back at the girls. She ignored them as she realized they were talking about her. She got her groceries together, closed her trunk then headed to the door as she heard them burst out in another laughter.

"Stupid ass broads," she said to herself as she struggled to open the door. She got inside, took the groceries to the kitchen, press the intercom button on the phone and heard that Kanesha left two messages. She then got started on dinner. As she took out the pots, she heard the phone ring. She went and answered it while holding the phone to her ear with her shoulder.

"Hello."

"What you don't know how to call nobody," Kanesha said. "Hey girl, what up," Tania started running water in the pot.

"What's up with you. And how you ain't told me your man Rasheid was big time."

"What you talking bout?"

"Rasheid. Shit from what I heard he run the whole Charleston."

Tania frowned her face as if Kanesha was exaggerating. "I don't know but all that. Just because he bought that Benz don't mean nothing," she tasted a little bit of the sauce then poured it in the pot. "I mean we got money but ain't like we millionaires. And what made you say that anyway. Where you getting your information from."

"You heard of them crazy ass niggas called the Blood Brothers."

"Yeah!" Tania stopped when she heard that name. "Wasn't one of them on the news a few years ago for killing that man at the red light and they ended up dropping the charges cause everybody was scared to testify against him."

"Yeah, that's the one the call L-Note and that nigga is crazy too. But anyway I was at Tashima house in Trailwood getting my hair done and her crazy ass brother Jamel came in and told us how they beat the hell out of some boy who tried to rob Rasheid. So you know that nigga knows everything that goes on in North Charleston."

"Uh-unh," Tania now listened closely to every word.

"So he was telling us how the Blood Brothers and some nigga name Tremaine now sell drugs for Rashied. And you know how broke niggas love to talk about another nigga getting money. He starts to talk about how Rashied got North Charleston and West Ashley on lock. Every bitch in the house that night was trying to see Rasheid," she excluded herself. "And everybody like how the hell is this young ass nigga getting all this money and this bitch ain't even told me he was on like that."

Tania was now mad. She was mad that her girlfriend had more info on the man she was living with than she did. And mad because he was getting too deep into something he supposed to be getting out of soon. Just then she heard Rasheid's keys in the door.

"Kanesha that's Rasheid now, so let me call you back later. And thanks to girl."

"You know I got your back," she said as they hung up the phone.

Rasheid then walked through the door.

"What's up Baby," he wiped his feet off then walked up and greeted her with a kiss.

"Hey," she tried to act as nonchalant as possible. "What you doing home so early," she put her attention back to the food.

"What, I can't come home early," he stood behind her and kissed her neck while he rubbed her side. "What you cooking?"

"Some spaghetti."

"My favorite."

"I thought collard greens, fried chicken and macaroni with cheese was your favorite."

"Girl whatever you cook is my favorite," he kissed her one last time and walked off.

"Hold up Rasheid."

"What's up," he turned around.

Tania just looked at him. It was hard for her to believe he was the type of person her friend was saying he was. He still looked innocent in the face. Just like the day when she first seen him in the restaurant. He was a little bigger. A little maturer. He now had a mustache with a little peach fuzz under his chin. But he still had the same innocent look. She looked him directly in his eyes.

"Do you have the Blood Brothers selling drugs for you."

He looked at her suspiciously, "Who told you that?"

Right then she knew what she heard was true.

"Rasheid why are you messing with them crazy ass boys. Don't you know they kill people!"

Rasheid just looked at her, "Tania who the hell told you that."

"It don't matter who told. I'm asking you a question Rasheid!" she yelled. "Just what the hell are you doing! You bought a Mercedes Benz, running around with killers! What are you trying to do end up dead or in jail. Go ahead and tell me now so that I want be surprised. Because one of them is going to happen."

"What I'm trying to do is get us some money!" he evened his voice tone with hers.

"And what's the price your willing to pay for that! Your life!" Tania covered her face with her hands trying to calm down. "Rasheid," she spoke now in a softer voice putting her hand by her side. "Baby, you know it'll kill me to see your face behind bars. I don't have the strength to come visit you in prison."

"Tania what the hell is you talking about, ain't nobody going to prison!" She shook her head at him, "You just don't get it. When are you going to stop this," she looked at him with sympathy in her eyes.

Rasheid rubbed his forehead then scratched the top of his head.

"Soon Baby. Real soon. I promise," she just looked at him.

Rasheid thought that he might as well tell her the news about him leaving town.

"Um-," he tried to break it to her easy. "I'ma take a trip to Virginia for bout a day."

"For what," she said in a soft tone.

"Business. Straight business. That's it."

Tania just looked at him and walked off wiping her eyes.

"Dinner will be ready soon."

Rasheid was about to say something then thought against it and walked to his room. Tania then rested her hands on the counter with her face down crying to herself.

———————————

Rasheid and Kisha drove down I-95 in silence for hours. Each being consumed by their own thoughts. Rasheid battled with his thoughts between Tania and business but he also was enjoying the ride. It was like for the time being he was free which made him thought about traveling more often. Kisha then reached to the side of her purse and pulled out a nail filer and filed her finger nails. He looked at her from the corner of her eyes. She was nowhere near bad looking. But you could definitely tell that she had some skeletons in her closet. Her eyes told the story.

"So where you from?" he said something to her for the first time since they got in the car.

"Evanston," she continued to file her nails without looking up.

"Oh yeah. I got peoples out there. You know Jon-Jon?"

"Nope."

"You nervous?"

"Nope."

"So you done this a few times already?"

She stopped filing her nails then looked up at him.

"I'm here to do business with you. Not to socialize," she said as she went back to filing her nails.

Rasheid respected her wishes then searched the radio for a better station.

As they entered the city of Richmond he paid close attention to the signs following the directions Rino mapped out for him. As he drove through the streets looking at all the buildings, the alleys and the people, he was surprised he never heard of Richmond, Virginia. He lost count of all the guys he passed that couldn't have been that much older than him driving Lexus and Benzs. So he knew a lot of money was definitely flowing through this city. As he drove down Hull street he saw the sign that read Belt Boulevard ahead of him then he saw the shopping center and turned into the parking lot. Kisha then put on some chap stick checked her portable mirror of her face real quick then put the mirror down.

"You ready," she said as she fixed her hair.

Rasheid took the glock .45 from the secret compartment Rino showed him, put it in his pants then looked around.

"Yeah"

Kisha just looked at Rasheid for a second.

"Look," she said. "Rino asked you to do this because he trusts you. Not just trust that you're a reliable person. But he trust that you know how to handle a situation. So in case you don't know, the shit were doing could get us life in prison. So what you need to do is calm down, stop looking so nervous and just be easy and please don't make Rino look bad."

Rasheid just looked at her like he didn't know she could talk.

"So are you ready to do this?" she tried to motivate him.

Rasheid smiled at her, "Yeah I'm ready to do this."

"Aiight then, let's do it. Open the trunk for me," they both got out the car. He opened the trunk as she retrieved the bag purse that contained the twenty-five kilos of cocaine. He closed the trunk and followed her lead into the restaurant. As they got into the restaurant, he followed her to a table in the far corner where another female was sitting at waiting patiently for them with a bag just like Kisha had.

"Hey girl," Kisha said to the girl as she sat directly across from her with Rasheid taking the seat next to her.

"What's up, what the hell took y'all so long," the girl said with a smile. "I ain't order cause I was waiting on y'all to get here. Here watch my bag let me go use the bathroom," she got up and walked to the bathroom.

"Let me go grab some toothpicks," Kisha said to Rasheid as he stood up and let her out. Seconds later Kisha returned and took the seat the other female sat in while the other female came and sat next to Rasheid. The waitress came and they all ordered and ate holding a fake conversation with each other and then they paid for their meal and left. Kisha left with the bag full of money and the other girl left with the cocaine. By Kisha playing her position so well made Rasheid step up to play his. The restaurant wasn't packed but it wasn't empty and the way the three acted it off there was no type of suspicion held to them. Rasheid and Kisha drove back safely to South Carolina with five hundred thousand dollars cash in the trunk of the car. Kisha looked over at Rashied then back out the window.

"You did good," Rasheid looked over at her then put his attention back on the highway.

"You did good too," she smiled to herself with her face pointed out of the window not letting him see.

Ch Apter 16

~~~~~~

R ookie and Deanna laid naked on the bed passing the blunt back and
forth to each other.

"So how is school going?" Rookie inhaled the weed smoke. Deanna
took the blunt from him and put it to her mouth.

"It's alright. Ain't been no big fights this year except for Rasheid and
N.O…... I'm glad Rasheid beat that nigga ass cause he swear he hard."

Rookie laughed at her.

"Baby, I wish you would come back to school. When you was there
that shit use to be fun as hell. Now it's wack for real. You know I don't
even be chillin with that much people no more. Shit the only people that
I really talk to in school is Kiana, Trish and Rasheid."

"That's good," Rookie took the blunt from her. "You don't need to be fuckin
wit them clowns anyway," he coughed up the weed smoke.

"Well I don't. But I be trippin off Kiana ass. You know she like Rasheid
right."

"For real," he said unaware.

"Um huh. And I think he like her too. They would make a cute
couple."

"Rasheid got a girlfriend," he took the blunt from her.

"Fuck that bitch. You remember how stuck up she was acting at the
party. That bitch act like her pussy is made of gold."

Rookie laughed at her letting effects of the marijuana take over him.

"So how long you think it's going to be until we move in with each."

"Ain't no telling. Bout a couple months."

"Cause I can't wait until I have my own house. And I'm gonna need something no less than a Acura Legend."

Rookie looked down at her.

"Well I'll settle for a Camry," Deanna said jokingly looking back up at him. He just stared at the ceiling. "What. You saying I can't have a Camry."

Rookie didn't respond.

"If you and Rasheid is partners and Rasheid riding around in a Benz, you mean to tell me you can't at least get me a Camry."

"Look Deanna. Shit is crazy right now. The money ain't a problem. The problem is I don't know what tomorrow holds. Especially since Rashied done bought these other niggas in. So before I start spending money like that I'ma just wait awhile and see how shit plays out. I said I'ma get the whip and crib and I'm gone get it. I just need a little more time."

Deanna rested her head back on his chest.

"You promise?"

"Yeah," he continued to stare at the ceiling.

<hr>

Rasheid got home to see that Tania already left for school. He took the bag upstairs and emptied all of the hundred dollars bills on his bed and just looked at the money for a moment. He then went to his safe, pulled it out the corner, laid it on the bed and went to lock the bedroom door. He unlock the safe and poured all the money on his bed. Then he done what he's been itching to do for awhile. Count his money. He took the rubber band off all the rolled up cash he had, separated the hundreds, fifties and twenties then started counting. Twenty-eight minutes later he thought his mind was playing tricks on him realizing he counted over three hundred and forty thousands dollars. He couldn't believe that all of the money belonged to him and he could do whatever he wanted. He neatly put the money back in the safe and laid back on the bed looking at himself in the ceiling mirror. He decided to treat himself. So he picked up the phone, dialed some numbers and put the phone to his ear.

"Yo," the voice said on the other end.

"What's up Boy, this Rasheid."

"Oh what's up nigga."

"Ain't nothing. What you doing?"

"Bout to hit the block as usual. Why what's up?"

"Go ahead and hold off on that for awhile. I want you to ride some place with me."

"Aiight," he said a little puzzled. "You need me to bring the ski mask."

"Nah," Rasheid laughed. "Ain't nothing like that. Just a little gift from me showing my appreciation from that situation from the other night."

"Okay," he said shocked. "What, you gonna come pick me up or you want me to meet you somewhere."

"Nah, I'll be there to pick you up in about a hour. So be ready." "I got chu," he said as they hung up the phone.

"Ayo man, how the fuck you let this nigga beat yo ass."

N.O. frowned his face as he looked away from his friend, "Man I done told you the nigga sneak me," he said to Q, Junior and D-Roc as they sat in the living room listening to their friend.

"That's not what Tasha said," Junior said. "She said y'all shot a fair one and that nigga whip yo ass."

"Shut the fuck up Junior! You always trying to co-sign some shit. Listening to what that stupid ass bitch said!"

"Nigga don't get mad at me cause you let that soft ass nigga beat yo ass," Junior said standing.

"But you can't do it," N.O. said standing up face to face with his friend. "So what's up," Junior said pushing him. N.O. pushed him back almost making him fall. Junior then tried to grab him but Q held him back.

"Y'all niggas chill the fuck out!" Q stood between the two. "Chill out Junior!" the two looked at each other still wanting to fight. "Sit y'all ass down," N.O. and Junior both took a seat. "This bitch ass nigga got y'all niggas fighting like y'all strangers. Now check this out," he said taking a seat. "Easy and Doc want this nigga dead. But we don't got to take it that far. All we got to do is shake that nigga up, put him in the trauma unit or something, take all his shit and he gone want to roll out."

"But what if he don't. What if he try to retaliate," D-Roc said speaking for the first time.

"Man we talking about Rasheid. Ain't but so much he can do. And if he want to go to war then fuck it, we kill his ass," Q said looking at all the faces around the room.

"Don't he got the Blood Brothers working for him?" Junior asked.

"Man fuck the Blood Brothers," N.O. said. "What you scared of them nigga or something. Shit them niggas blood pump just like mine."

"I ain't scared of nann nigga in Charleston," Junior said to him.

"Aiight, aiight," Q tried to break the two up before they begun again.

"So this is what it is. We gone fuck this nigga up take his shit and everything should fall in line after that. So stop making this shit harder than what it is. And if that nigga Rookie step up to the plate then he get the same treatment. And with Rasheid out the game, the money gone speed up. So does anybody got a problem with it," he looked around the room at the four faces. Aiight then good, lets do it," he said putting the beer bottle to his lips.

"Excuse me, do you mind if I speak to your manager," Rasheid said to the sales clerk.

"Uhh- sure, let me go in the back to get her," the young lady said walking to the back.

"What you up to," C.J. asked.

"I'm tryin to get a job," Rasheid said to him with a slight grin on his face.

"Anyway," he turned his head knowing that wasn't the truth. I wanna know what you're really here for."

"You'll see," he said as a middle age black woman came from the back looking closely at him and Rasheid.

"How may I help you?" she asked.

"Yes ma'am," Rasheid stepped in closer talking in a professional tone. "My name is Rasheid and this is a friend of mine C.J. and we were wondering could you close the store down for no more than two hours so that we could do a little private shopping?"

The manager and C.J. looked at Rasheid like he was crazy.

"I plan on spending no less than twenty-five thousand dollars."

The woman facial expression quickly changed.

"Your spending twenty-five thousand dollars," she looked Rasheid directly in his eyes.

"Yes ma'am."

"In here," she pointed down.

"Yes."

On a Thursday afternoon she figured the most the store will make was about two thousand dollars in two hours. She was a little skeptical about doing it but as she looked at Rasheid something was telling her that he wasn't playing.

"Claire," she said to her employee who came running while she still had her eyes on Rasheid.

"Yes," Claire said.

"Go put up the close sign. Don't let no more customers in and when these few customers leave out pull down the gate," the girl looked at her then at Rasheid and done what she was told. C.J. burst out into a silent laughter, play punching Rasheid on his arm. He would of never guessed that Rasheid could close down a store in the mall. As of right then was the most joy he ever experienced in his life, feelings like he was somebody, like he established something in life. At that moment he wished his mother could see him.

After all the customers left out of the store, the sales clerk pulled the gate down and assist Rasheid and C.J. as they tried on all type of clothes and purchased dozens of sneakers and boots. After awhile some of the noisy customers in the mall gathered around the gate wondering if Rasheid and C.J. were rappers. About two and a half hours later when they were finished shopping and done tried on just about everything in the store, they went to the counter and Rasheid paid for all the attire which came up to almost twenty-nine thousand dollars. The manager checked the money to make sure it wasn't counterfeit, then took the money to the safe in the back and helped them bagged up all their items. She continued to look at Rasheid, since they closed the store. She never took her eyes off of him for no more than a minute.

"Are y'all some rappers," she said folding up some shirts and putting it in the bag.

"Yeah," C.J. said before Rasheid had a chance to say a word. "I'm the president and CEO of T.T.S. Records and Rasheid is the first artist on the label. He'll be dropping his debut album real soon so y'all be on the look out for that," it took everything in Rasheid's will not to burst out in laughter as C.J. said it with a serious face.

"Oooh," the manager brighten her face. "So that explains why y'all got all this money. Cause at first," she said in almost a whisper. "I thought y'all was some big time drug dealers," Rasheid and C.J. both laughed at her.

"T.T.S.," the sales clerk said. "What that stands for."

"Threat To Society," C.J. said.

"How come I never heard of that before," she said still putting clothes in the bag.

"Oh you will soon," C.J. said seriously as Rasheid bottled up his laughter.

"What's up Greg?" Easy said as he came and stood behind the guy in line at the convenient store.

"Oh what's up Easy," the guy turned around and acknowledge him.

"What, you don't fuck with a nigga no more. Shit I ain't seen you in a few months, "the guy paid for his food and stepped to the side.

"Nah ain't like that E. I just been busy making a few moves."

"Yeah, I know," he put two beer bottles on the counter. "I be seeing you. I heard you do business with them niggas out North Charleston now," he referred to Blood Brothers.

The guy held an embarrassed look as Easy paid for his items and they walked out the store.

"E look," the guy tried not to offend him. "Ain't nothing personal." Easy nodded his head assuring him he understood.

"But you know them niggas got the best product in the city. And I don't even fuck with them niggas in North Charleston like that but I got a daughter to feed."

"I feel you man. You don't owe me no explaination. I just wanted to make sure we still cool," he reached out to shake the guy's hand.

"Oh yeah man," he said relieved shaking Easy's hand. "Ain't never no love lost. But yo I got some business I got to take care of. I'ma holla at you," he said walking to his car.

"You do that," Easy popped the top to his beer bottle as he watched the guy get in his car. "Dime piece hustling ass nigga," he said to himself before he put the bottle to his lips. He walked over to the driver side of his Infiniti and got in.

"Man, this Rasheid nigga is starting to get under my skin," he said to Doc who was just getting off the phone with one of his mistresses.

"Man I been told you this nigga in our way. We need to go ahead and pluck him off the map," Doc said putting his cellular phone in his pocket.

"Doc," Easy looked over at him. "We can't keep killing people just because they got a better connect than us. Look at what happen with Dre. And that was just last year. Now this nigga Rasheid just came up out of nowhere. So what, you wanna kill him too."

"I'm looking at longevity. Check it out. Dre was connected to Roger. But now Rodger out the game. Dre is dead. But this nigga Rasheid blew up and that faggot ass Tremaine jumped on the band wagon. And just about everybody in the city copping from these niggas. Now what if we bless this nigga Rasheid. Tremaine gone be ass out and where does that leaves us. Cause ain't like motherfuckers gone stop smoking crack. Then we'll be able to move this shit like we suppose to. Cause it don't make no sense for us to move a brick in two months. That shit is crazy.

Easy looked at his friend as he allowed himself to go into deep thought on what he said.

"First let's see how N.O. and them lil niggas handle the situation. They say they gone handle it," he looked away then back at his friend. "Let's just see what they do first."

Rasheid wasn't too excited about being back in school after his suspension but it did felt good to be greeted by Kiana this morning. She was the only girl he consider being with besides Tania. He thought the reason he liked her so much was because her and Tania shared the same characteristics. Kiana seemed loyal and trust worthy with a big heart just like Tania and they both was fine as hell. They both had beautiful complexion with a nice body. They both could stand next to Beyonce or Mya and share the spotlight if not out shine them. But lately him and Tania's relationship was getting real rocky. They only said a few words to each other within the past week. She wasn't even giving up no pussy. He had to sex up a couple of his groupies then hoped that they wouldn't go run their mouth after they were done. He had enough rumors going around about him, he didn't need no more. But throughout all he figured he lived a pretty good life compared to the other kids in school. He had a nice home, two nice cars, enough clothes to go months without wearing the same outfit twice and on top of that, he had money. He just wished him and Tania was on better terms.

"So Rasheid," Mr. Williams brought his attention back to class. "I see that you're still on vacation. Maybe you can tell us what the answer is?" he said with a big smile.

Rasheid looked around the class as everyone looked at him. He sat up in his chair and cleared his throat.

"Um could you repeat the question?"

"Sure," Mr. Williams looked down at the book. "Plates are large sections of the planet Earth's what?" he said looking at Rasheid smiling with his hands behind his back. Rasheid looked back at him as everyone looked on sensing he was about to humiliate himself. Rasheid thought hard before he answered the question.

"Um, plates are large sections of the planet Earth's upper mantle and crust."

Mr. Williams held a shocked look on his face. He couldn't believe Rasheid answered the question correctly. He then looked around the class seeing all eyes were on him. Feeling a little embarrassed he continued with his lesson. Most of his teachers at North Charleston High acted as if they had something against him. They heard rumors through the other students that he was supposed to be a big drug dealer and assumed it was true by the way he dressed and what he drove. Only five percent of the teachers at North Charleston could afford to drive a Benz. Some of them hated the fact that he's not even eighteen yet and he's flaunting one around town. The bell rung and everyone got their belongings and headed out of class. As Rasheid walked out of class he saw Kiana coming in his direction. Just like that all thoughts of everything else cleared his mind.

"Where you heading at," he stopped in front of her as everyone in the hallway looked on.

"I was coming to meet you," Kiana tried to hold in her smile but was unable to whenever she was around Rasheid, he made her felt as if she was a three year old child at a Barney show live.

"So what you about to get into?" they walked side by side towards the exit of the building.

"Nothing but drop Deanna off and go home and do some homework."

"Well I was thinking maybe we could go get something to eat and you know kick it for a little while before you go home."

Kiana heart skipped a beat. She tried to calm down and not sound too anxious when she answered him.

"That's only if I can ride in your Benz," she smiled at him as they walked out the double doors.

"What, you gonna leave your car here?"

"I'll just let Deanna drive it to her house. I mean if that's cool with you," she said in a joking way. "I know you're a busy person and what not," he held his head down smiling.

"Yeah, you straight."

"Well let me see if I can find Deanna," Kiana turned around and looked for her friend. Just then Rasheid thought his eyes were playing tricks on him. He took a second look and saw that his eyes did not deceive him. Someone was sitting on the hood of his car. He then walked briskly toward his car as Kiana turned and observed what was happening. Her instinct instantly kicked in as she wanted to yell Rasheid's name, but the words wouldn't come out her mouth. As Rasheid got closer he saw that it was N.O. sitting there as if he had a point to prove. He threw his bookbag to the ground ready to show N.O. he wasn't the one to be fucked with. The closer he got, he noticed N.O. smiling at him. Then he saw four doors opened on the car next to him and automatically felt a setup. Before he could even get his thoughts straight he saw guys running in his direction with crowbars and some other weapons he didn't have time to recognize. He tried to runaway but that's when N.O. greeted him with a hard object directly to his forehead knocking him immediately unconscious.

ChApter 1 7

Kiana tossed and turned in her bed all night. She tried to fight off the memory of seeing Rasheid covered in a pool of blood. The more she tried to fight the more the picture stayed in her mind. She never seen no one took a beating like that throughout her whole life. She remembered freezing up not knowing what to do as she seen all those guys beat down the lover of her dream. She took off the blanket, looked at the clock that read 1:41 a.m. and decided to call Deanna. She dialed the numbers and put the phone to her ear listening to it ring. Deanna picked up on the third ring.

"What's up Kiana," Deanna sounded like she couldn't sleep either.

"How you knew it was me. Oh I forgot, caller i.d. So what you doing?"

"Listening to Donnell Jones make love to me on my stereo. Why, what you doing? Thinking about Rasheid."

"I couldn't stop thinking about that since it happened. Did you see how bloody he was. I couldn't even recognize him. And you seen how long it took the ambulance to get there. Shit he could of died out there," Kiana said feeling as if she was about to cry again. "What he did to them anyway?"

"Girl them niggas just jealous. Jealous of who he is and what he got. When I talked to Rookie earlier he said that Rasheid was going to be alright. He said that the doctor said he took a bad beating but it looked worst than what it was. But don't worry. They think they got off on Rasheid but their time is coming. North Charleston is about to bring some bloody nights."

"What you mean?" Kiana hoped that it wouldn't get worse.

"What you think Rookie gone let that shit ride. Shhh, you'll see. A lotta shit bout to go down and I can promise you that. Plus Rasheid got the Blood Brothers with him too. I can guarantee you, you ain't heard the last of that."

Kiana listnened on. She thought that Deanna was exaggerating a bit. Rasheid didn't seem like the type to have status like that. He seemed too innocent. Too sincere. Though when you looked in to his eyes or better yet when he looked into yours, he made you feel like you were in the presence of someone special.

"Deanna," Kiana said softly.

"What."

"Can I ask you a question?"

"What's up?"

"Does Rasheid really sell drugs?"

"Oh Lord," Deanna covered her eyes.

Rookie leaned against his car and lit a cigarette. He knew this day was coming. Though he dreaded it came so fast.

"So what you gone do?" Chuck said to him.

He didn't respond. He just kept smoking his cigarette. He looked up to see one of his faithful clients pulling up. A white boy name Russell. He was the typical white boy in Charleston whose parents had money and tried to lead him into a successful direction but went astray and decided to go down the path drugs paved for him. Rookie had in his mind that he wasn't making any sells but since he liked Russell he figured he'll make an exception. Rookie walked up to the car and bent down poking his head in the driver's window.

"What's up Russell?"

"What's up Dude?" Russell said not looking like his usual self.

"What yo white ass doing over here this time of night," Rookie already knew what he wanted.

"I need a boost," he handed him a roll of cash. Rookie looked at the money and smiled putting it in his pocket.

"I'll be right back," he walked over to his car. Before he even got to the car Russell drove off. Rookie looked at him driving down the street confused. He walked in the middle of the street looking both ways.

"Where the fuck that motherfucker go to?" he said to Chuck still looking puzzled in the middle of the street.

"What chu say to him?" Chuck said.

"I ain't say shit to that nigga. He gave me the money and I told him to…" he stopped in midsentence sensing something wasn't right. "Hold up," he thought out what happened. He then took the money out his pocket that Russell just gave him and looked through it. Just as he held the money in his hands he saw the blue lights before his mind could even think the words set up and police. He tossed the money and tried to run only before realizing that they already had him circled. It was about six or seven North Charleston police cars with cops getting out the cars running up to him and Chuck with their guns out screaming spread your hands and get on the ground. Rookie mind quickly flashed to the time when they busted him and Rasheid coming out the restaurant. He held his hands up as he got down on both knees with Chuck following him. The police ran up to them putting on the hand cuffs. As he felt the locks on his hand for some reason he had a feeling it would be a long time before he seen his freedom again.

"I'm alright Tania," Rasheid said to her as she adjusted the pillow under his head. She ignored him and took a seat beside him. He laid on the sofa as she put tea tree oil on his bruises. He spent two days in the hospital and this was first day back home. He didn't look as bad as the rumors said he did though he did took a beating. He had stitches going across his forehead and under his right eye which was still swollen. He had two fractured ribs and minor cuts and bruises on his chest, stomach and back. But what really got to him was his headache that didn't went away since he woke up in the hospital.

"Rasheid, you need me to get you anything from the store?" Tereesa said with her arms across her chest.

"I'm alright Aunt Tereesa," he said with his eyes closed. When Tereesa learned that Rasheid was in the hospital she came as quick as she could being by his side all throughout his visitation hours. Through the time her and Tania became close.

"I go it from here Ms. Tereesa if you wanna go home and get some rest," Tania stated with her attention on aiding her man.

"Rasheid you sure you don't need nothing," Tereesa asked. She felt a bit jealous but in a good way. She was glad Rasheid had somebody who had his best interest at heart, but she hated the fact she failed to do so.

"Yeah, I'm fine Aunt Tereesa ," he answered. "Just go home and get you some rest. I'ma call you later on this week."

Tereesa walked up to him and kissed his forehead right on top of his stitches.

"You better," she slightly touched Tania's shoulder then walked to the door.

"Okay bye Ms. Tereesa. Thanks," she said still putting the oil on Rasheid.

"Y'all take care," Tereesa exited through the door.

Rasheid tried to sort out how he was going to take actions. He figured N.O. thought that they accomplished something big when really it was nothing but some inconvenience. His mind was really on Rookie and the half of brick the police knocked him off with. He wasn't really worried about him snitching or the money he just knew if things didn't go in the right direction Rookie could get a lot of time. But first and foremost he had to take care of N.O. and his crew. If he didn't he knew every hungry punk in North Charleston would see him as a target whenever they needed a come up. That was a reputation that he couldn't have.

"What you thinking about?" Tania asked as she put fresh band-aids on his stomach.

"Nothing," he lied.

"Well you know what I'm thinking about?"

"I probably could guess," he said with sarcasm.

"Rasheid, if that wasn't a wake up call for you to leave this lifestyle alone then I don't know what she was," she put down the tea tree oil and alcohol pad and leaned over him with her arms rested on the back of the chair holding her faces inches form his.

Rasheid braced himself for what was about to come.

"So what your gonna do? Let your ego get you into a world of trouble. Or even worse get you killed. Rasheid," she gently touched his lip. "I know who you are. I know you're a good person with a good heart. But what I love most about you is your drive and ambition. Now just imagine if you can put that motivation to something productive," she rubbed his head. "Now I came to realize that you don't feel comfortable working a regular job. So I've been thinking…why don't you open up your own business. I've been talking to this guy who's in class with me and he's into real estate. He's been explaining to me about some of the things he do and I don't have a complete understanding about it yet but so far it sounds interesting as well as lucrative. Something you should think about. And if you don't want to do real estate I'm pretty sure we could find some other type of business venture to get into." That did sound like a good idea and Rasheid did thought about going into business for himself but that was later down the road. He had some important issues to get out of the way first and opening up a business right now was going to take a lot of time that he didn't have.

"That's a good idea baby," he said with his eyes still closed.

"So your gonna try to open up your own business?" she silently blushed.

"Naw, I'ma try to open up our business. Just not this very minute," her happiness slowly dried up. She waited for him to roll in with the excuses. Rasheid opened his eye and looked at her.

"I don't know how to say this Tania. But there's a lot of things that I have to straighten out before we even move in that direction. I already know what you want me to do and that's leave all this behind. I got people under me as well as over me and if I just walk out right now I'ma put a lot of people lives in jeopardy and if I do that, that'll be real selfish on my behalf."

Tania looked away from him. "What if you get killed the next time."

Rasheid closed his eyes and tried to block her out. He hated thinking about death.

"I'm serious Rasheid," she looked at him. "What if you get killed next time. You talking about putting other people lives in jeopardy, well what about mine. Have you ever thought about that. What if someone wanted to get to you through me."

Rasheid struggled to get on his feet. He then slowly walked to the stairs. He knew what she was saying was true but couldn't take no more pressure.

"Where you going at?" she got louder. "The truth hurts doesn't it!" He didn't comment, he just limped his way up the stairs.

"I'm trying to help you Rasheid," she said as her voice started to crack. "But you act like you don't want my help," she walked to the stairs and watched him enter the bedroom and closed the door behind him.

"What am I suppose to do Rasheid!" she yelled at the bedroom door. She then sat on the steps with her hands in her face.

"Okay so they beat the nigga up. What the fuck is that suppose to do," Doc said to Easy sitting in the pool room of his house. Easy took a sip of the beer, put the bottle on the pool table, closed his left eye and aimed for the two ball in the corner pocket. The ball went in.

"This nigga Rasheid ain't no threat," he came up from the shot.

"Don't sleep nigga. Any man who got money is a threat." Easy held his hand up to him as he went on to explain.

"A nigga who moving keys like that is not suppose to have a little nigga like N.O. able to touch him just like that," Easy held the tip of the pool stick like it was a mic. "He's weak. The niggas he run with is weak. Even if they do retaliate on N.O. which they probably will, the point is this nigga is still weak. You gotta keep in mind, he's a teenager. I don't even think he's eighteen yet. All he doing is hiding behind that money. So why this nigga beefing with little ass N.O. we gone take North Charleston by surprise."

"And then," Doc said not seeing how that plan was going to get them through the door.

"It ain't no and then. The whole time we was trying to figure out a way to find this nigga Rasheid slipping but we was the ones slipping not realizing that the whole time he was slipping in our face. All we got to do is muscle this nigga out our way. And if he wanna act froggy and leap," Easy said taking a shot at the four ball in the side pocket. "Then we might have to set his appointment."

Doc leaned back in the chair thinking about what Easy just said.

Rasheid knocked to the door twice as Kisha opened it for him.

"What's up," he said. She nodded as he stepped in the house and closed the door behind him. She then took him to the room where Rino waited. As usual Rino sat in the sofa casually dressed still looking powerful. Rasheid took a seat and the two shared eye contact for a moment.

"So how you feel," Rino finally broke the silence. Rasheid tried to hold in the embarrassment he felt but Rino automatically saw straight through it.

"The best men are the men molded from faults," Rasheid just looked at him understanding exactly what he was trying to say. Rino knew what happened but Rasheid went on and explained anyway. After hearing the words from his mouth he went ahead and gave Rasheid the tools he felt he was missing.

"Like I said earlier, The best men are the ones molded from faults. Do you know anything about the civil war?"

Rasheid nodded. "A little."

"Well let me break down the science. The civil war was a war between the Unions and the Confederates. Abraham Lincoln was the president of the Union and Jefferson Davis was thee president of the confederate. It was a war basically over power and money. Ulysses Grant was a general for the union. Now Ulysses Grant lost many battles but won the war. And he didn't win it over by asking nicely. He took what he wanted. He used the opposing side weakness against them and it became power for him. But in order for him to do that he first had to learn what he was up against. Then take every move with extreme caution. All you need is a bunch of fools who's willing to bust their guns to win a battle. But only a thinking man can win a war. I didn't choose you to work for me because I like your charisma or think you're handsome. I chose you to work for me because you can think. When I first met you, I told you when some men get a little bit of money behind them, they start to feel as if they're untouchable. You remember that?"

Rasheid nodded.

"Well don't fall into that category. You got caught with your hand on your dick and the only good thing that came out of that situation is that your still breathing. So now that your still breathing you still have a chance. You're not a nickel and dime hustler. You distribute kilos of cocaine. Territory comes with that, that you must be willing to protect at all times. So you can't afford to be taking hits like this. Now I know you got what it takes. But it's not about me, it's about you. If you don't think you're cut out for this, then you need to go get you a job at a grocery store or something. Now if you know you got what it take to step up and master this, then you need to do it. This ain't a game. This your life."

Rasheid took in every word Rino gave him slowly. He knew he was being insulted and praised at the same time. He stood up and him and Rino embraced each other before he left out the room. As he stepped out the room he noticed Kisha standing by the door who probably listened to every word that was said between the two. He continued to walk to the door. Kisha followed him outside and closed the door behind her. Rasheid just looked at her.

"You just lost a lot of respect in the streets," she said to him. "So in order for you to relapse, your gonna have to come back twice as hard. I can see in your eyes that you have the power to take over this city. It just hasn't been brought out you yet. You need to expect that a lot of dudes gonna be gunnin for your crown. Because people don't fear people. They fear people's reputation. You still have the power to change that over. It all lies on you. Stand your ground. And don't let these bitch ass niggas make you out for a sucker," she turned around and opened the door. She then turned back around and looked at him. "I'm rooting for you," she said before she entered the house and closed the door. Rasheid stared at the door for a second got in to his Cadillac and drove off.

ChApter 18

"In every project, in every hood on Montague all out in Liberty Hill, Dorchester, Rivers Avenue, Ashley Phosphate throughout all North Charleston. I only want our people moving our work and I'm not trying to hear anything else. West Ashley and the country is pretty much at ease. And I don't give a fuck about Downtown.

"Yo Rasheid," Tremaine interrupted him. "There's a lot of money Downtown."

"I'm not trying to be greedy about this. I'm trying to be smart. We stepping on enough toes as it is, no need for no unnecessary bullshit just for some extra doe. We gone eat the food we got on our plate before we ask for seconds. Yo C.J.," he turned around facing C.J. and L-Note. "Don't kill these niggas. We don't need no bodies. Just give em something to think about while they're laying on that hospital bed. And don't close your eyes. In case they want a part two. I need this structure solid," he looked around at all the faces in the room." I'm talking bout so solid water won't be able to soak through. I got one man down, so we gonna have to pick up the slack. Ain't no half stepping and ain't no room for mistakes. It's out there all we have to do is go get it. Time is money and we can't afford to lose either. So I gotta go check on some things. Use the code to page me if you need to holla. And if nobody don't got nothing to say on that then I'm out," he looked around at all the satisfied faces. He then shook their hands left out the house and drove off in his Delta eighty-eight Oldsmobile. He bought it the day prior to keep a low profile. Eighty percent of the cocaine being used in North Charleston and West Ashley came from Rasheid. They had crack houses with look outs on the corner who were getting paid by the hour. It was like the drug world had their own government with their own language and signals. It started out in North Charleston and West Ashley then it spread through Hollywood and parts of Mt. Pleasant. Rasheid knew that if his plan continued to succeed he'll be seeing his money tripled in no time. But it was not all about money, it was about having the ability to take charge and take over.

Rookie sat at the table and lit his third cigarette as he listened to the detective threats go in one ear and come out the other.

"So Reginald," Detective Morris said. "Or Rookie which ever you prefer, cause frankly I don't give a damn. Because after this trial is over and the judge sentence you to twenty-five years in prison, your name is gonna be Ramona."

Detective Ryans bottled up his laughter, "Take it easy on the kid," he said.

"Kid!" Morris yelled getting up from his seat. "This ain't no kid! This is a fucking drugdealer!" he screamed in Rookie's face. "Eighteen ounces of crack cocaine! A unregistered .45! A unregistered .38! And on top of that he's a convicted felon with three years on probation!" Rookie blew the smoke in the detective face. The detective grabbed his wrist and twisted it almost causing him to scream out in pain. "Listen to me you punk motherfucker!" he lost his temper and talked so closed to Rookie he spat in his face. "Now you got two choices. Either you cooperate and give me some fucking names or I'll see to it that you don't get out of prison until my great-grandson is elected mayor!"

"Calm down Jake," Detective Ryans pulled him back. Detective Morris walked off as Rookie waved his wrist back and forth to get the blood circulating back through.

"Mr. Santez," Detective Ryans tried to take a much smoother approach than his partner. "We understand that there are code to the streets that can't be broken. But there's a difference in being loyal and being stupid," Rookie took another pull of the cigarette and blew the smoke in the air. "You are facing twenty-five years in prison. But we are willing to make a deal with you where you'll be back in the streets by the time your twenty-one rather than forty-three. Now do you know these two," he took two photos out of a folder and placed it in front of Rookie. It was a recent picture of L-Note and C.J. With no facial expression he looked up at the detective and shook his head. The detective then pulled out two more photos. It was the two guys that approached him at the corner store about meeting Rasheid. Doc and Easy.

"How about these two," again Rookie looked up at him and shook his head. He then pulled out more photos. Some of the pictures was guys he knew and some he just seen before but just about all was in some way connected to the drug game. He just shook his head photo after photo.

"He's lying. That motherfuckers lying through his teeth," Morris said.

Detective Ryans put the photos back in his folder and sat on the desk looking at Rookie.

"Well how about if I toss around a few names. See if they sound familiar huh."

Rookie shrugged his shoulder inhaled his cigarette one last time then put the butt in the ashtray.

"Tremaine Johnson."

"Don't ring a bell."

"Chad Brown."

"Don't ring a bell."

"Kemone Ford."

Rookie shook his head, "I don't know who that is."

The detective just stared at him knowing he was lying.

"Well how about Rasheid Willis," he said slowly.

Rookie looked up at him as the other detective placed a big smile on his face. Still with no facial expression he stood firm.

"I never heard of those people before in my life."

"You ask for it so you're gonna get it!" Morris stormed out of the room. Ryans got off the desk and followed his partner.

"When you decided to talk, we'll listen," he said before he left out the room.

Rookie then lit up his fourth cigarette.

That's that nigga Junior right there," one of C.J.'s young soldiers said to him with anticipation for revenge. C.J. slowed down at the intersection and eyed the guy down. He seemed to have his full attention on a conversation on the pay phone. C.J. parked the s.u.v. directly behind him and the four guys hopped out. Junior didn't even noticed a they walked up behind him and tapped his shoulder.

"Phone check nigga!"

He turned around just in time for the closed fist to meet him in his face. He tried to run but it was useless, C.J. picked him up as if he weighed no more than fifty pounds and dropped him on his head. People in the neighborhood and at the corner store was looking at what took place but nobody dear say anything. Their motto was if it didn't have nothing to do with them or their family it was none of their business. Each of C.J.'s soldier grabbed an arm and a leg and they took Junior around to the dumpster and beat him merciless. One of the soldiers picked up an old t.v. and smashed it in to his head knocking him unconscious but that didn't stop the beat down. After about thirty minutes of punching, kicking and hitting him with every type of object they could find, they rested for a while and looked at the unconscious Junior who was beaten beyond recognition. They then stripped him butt naked and tied both of his arms to a nearby tree with a sign around his neck stating, 'This is what I get for fucking with Rasheid.' C.J. and his soldiers thought it was hilarious as they got back into the vehicle and drove off.

"So what's up Shorty. You gone give me the number or what?"

"I already told you I got a man," Kiana looked around with hopes that Deanna would hurry up out the store.

"You ain't got to lie," the guy said leaning in her car window. "And even if you do got a man, that nigga a fool for letting you out his eye sight. See if you was my girl," he eased himself closer to Kiana. "You'll never have to worry about being alone. I'll be your shield, your comforter and your provider. I'll be the one you cuddle up with in the middle of the night."

"Ill" Kiana almost said out loud as she looked at the guy with total disgust in her face.

"Reggie what you doing?" Deanna walked out the store with her bags. The guy looked up at Deanna.

"Oh what's up Deanna, I ain't seen you in a minute."

"I know you ain't trying to holla at my girl with all them baby mamas you got."

He looked at Kiana and smiled then gave Deanna a look as if he wanted to say bitch shut the hell up.

"Naw yo. I only got two kids. You know how broads is these days. Always trying to jock a nigga for his bread."

Kiana who was now relieved Deanna was out of the store started the ignition and put the car in drive. The guy stood up and stepped back from the car.

"Maybe I'll catch you another time," he said.

"Maybe," she thought otherwise.

"Yo Deanna. Tell Rookie I said keep his head up." "I will," Deanna waved at him as Kiana drove off.

"What the hell, you was in there buying the store?"

"Please," Deanna looked at the receipt then put it in her bag. "Just like when you at Bloomingdales. It take you all day just to buy two shirts."

"What you brought anyway," she tried peak in her bag.

"Dolce and Gabana blouse and skirt to match," she showed her outfit. "I'ma where it Saturday when I to go see Rookie."

"Don't you think you need to save as much money as you can. If Rookie going to be in jail for a while you know you're going to have to take care of this baby by yourself."

"He's getting out," she wasn't trying to face that reality.

"I'm just saying Deanna," Kiana put her hand on top of hers. "Its better to be safe than sorry. I'm only telling you this because I'll hate to see you in a bind." It was a long pause between the two. "So what did Rookie say?"

She didn't respond.

"Deanna," Kiana looked at her then back at the highway. "What did he say?"

Deanna turned her head the other way.

"You didn't tell him did you," Kiana said disappointed already knowing the answer.

Deanna turned and faced her.

"I'm going to tell him this weekend."

"So Rookie doesn't even know that his girlfriend is three months pregnant with his child. Kiana said.

Deanna looked at her best friend then rolled her eyes looking back at the window. She sometimes wished that she didn't tell Kiana all her business.

It wasn't long before the Blood Brothers and their crew caught up to a couple of the other guys that was connected to the incident with Rasheid. They too got beat down in similar ways and it didn't take a rocket science for the people to know that it was behind Rasheid. The only ones that were missing was Q and N.O. That was until L-Note found out the address to where Q's mother lived. Him his brother and a couple of their workers crept up to house wearing all black with ski masks. L-Note knocked to the door and signaled for everyone to stay down until the door opened.

Janice Singleton a very religious woman and a single mother of two. Twenty-one year old LaQuan whom everyone called Q and thirteen year old Jessica. Janice was getting out of the shower when she heard someone knock at the door. She wrapped the robe around her still damp body and walked to the front door bare feet still drying her hair.

"Why do you have the t.v. up so loud for?" she said to her daughter who was looking through an Eastbay magazine. She reached for the remote control and turned the t.v. down.

"Who is it?" Janice said as she looked through the peep hole but couldn't make out who it was in the dark. She heard the voice say something she also couldn't make out. "What is Johnathan doing now," she assumed it was her next door neighbor. As she opened the door L-Note then pointed the nine millimeter to her face as the four guys burst into her house.

"Where the fuck is Q!" he said with the gun aimed directly in the center of her forehead.

"No! Mommy!" her daughter screamed out running for the safety of her mother. One of the guys picked her up and held the gun to her head.

"No!" Janice cried out. "My baby!" she tried to run to her daughter's rescue. L-Note then struck her in the back of her head with the gun. She fell down as the blood poured from her head. She knew she was wounded but all of her feelings was numb as she tried to get to her daughter. "No! Please God don't let them do this! Not to my baby!" Janice cried out.

"Bitch shut the fuck up!" L-Note smacked her in the face with the gun.

"Now where the fuck is your son!" He pinned her down on the floor with his hand wrapped around her neck and the gun pointed to her face.

"I don't know!" she screamed. "I swear to God I don't know!"

"Nah bitch! You know where he at! You ain't getting off that easy!" he signaled two of his workers. "Trash the crib. Since this bitch don't want to talk make her ass pay."

"Please!" Janice tried to catch her breath. "Take whatever you want, just don't hurt my baby. Please Lord don't let them hurt my baby!"

"Bitch shut the fuck up with that religion shit!" Jessica felt like she couldn't move as she helplessly cried watching the guy torment her mother. L-Note's soldiers trashed their whole house. Breaking the cabinets, throwing dishes and glasses all over the place. They turned over the refrigerator, ripping up their pictures and breaking the furniture. When they were through, L-Note signaled for them to leave. They didn't harm the little girl. Not physically anyway but they did harm both of them mentally "Hope you got your black dress ready. Your son got a funeral waiting for him," L-Note said before leaving out the door. The girl ran up to her mother crying and buried her face in her chest.

<hr>

Tania drove through the neighborhood of Trailwood and stopped in front of the single wide trailor and blew the horn for Kanesha. After the second blow Kanesha came down the steps and got in on the passenger side of Tania's 626.

"What's up," she said to Tania as she drove off.

"Hey."

Kanesha put her pocketbook down on the floor as she looked at her friend. She could have detected that she wasn't in a good mood.

"So how is Rasheid doing?"

Tania shrugged her shoulders.

"You do know it's about to be a lot of shit going on around here behind that. They beat the hell out of some boy last week and tied him to the tree butt naked with a sign around his neck saying something about this is what I get for fucking with Rasheid."

"Are you serious!" Tania almost slammed on brakes.

"Yeah girl I'm serious. Where you been at. Everybody been talking about that. Now that he got them Blood dudes with him he basically run Charleston."

"Whose he?"

Kanesha looked over at Tania, "Rasheid. Yo man. That's who."

Tania frowned her face as she listened to her friend.

"I heard that he had something to do with them dudes breaking into that lady house and beating her and her daughter up last night."

"What dudes broke into who house?"

"Damn Tania. You live under a rock or something. Some dudes broke into some lady house who live in the Wailing. Beat her and her daughter up. And they trash the house."

"Are you serious! And you think Rasheid was behind that?" she said hysterically.

"I don't think so," Kanesha held a puzzle look on her face. "But that's what everybody saying. They say Rasheid couldn't find some nigga name Q so he send some dudes to get at his mother. I don't know if its true or not but that's just what I heard," Kanesha looked out the window.

Tania drove in silence as Kanesha continued with her gossip.

"Y'all did what!" Rasheid couldn't believe what he was hearing. L-Note just told him and Tremaine what they done to Q's mother and sister. "Please tell me you're joking," he held his head down in disbelief. "Tell me you bullshitting with me L-Note. Because I know you got more sense than that."

L-Note flopped down on the sofa showing his rebellious side, "Man you told us to handle the situation so that's what I did," he thought he was going to get praised instead of scolded.

"I didn't tell you to fuck with the man mama and sister!" Rasheid yelled surprising everyone. "Think L-Note! Think!" he pointed his index finger to his temple. "The police is already suspicious about that shit that happened with me," he indicated how they questioned him when he was in the hospital. "And y'all gone run up in his mama house and torture her and her daughter. You don't think she's going to the police! Huh! And you don't think the police is going to point that shit to me!" Rasheid stood up and paced the floor. "L-Note, that was not a smart move," he said as he tried to go into deep thought.

"It wasn't," Tremaine commented for the first time. His attention was mainly on weighing and bagging the cocaine.

"So what the fuck was I supposed to do!" L-Note yelled out getting fed up.

"You was to supposed to think!" Rasheid even his voice tone with his. L-Note turned his head and frowned his face. Rasheid continued to pace the floor wrecking his brain. He then took a seat trying not to allow his emotions to take over. He looked at L-Note and Tee who was holding the expression of children who just disappointed their parents then at Tremaine whose attention was still on weighing and bagging the drugs.

"Where's C.J." he asked.

They all looked at each other then back at him not having an answer.

"Yo, make sure you don't lose this nigga," C.J. said to Black. He then put on his ski mask and took out his gun.

"Shit, it don't look like he's going no where no time soon," Black tossed his cigarette out the window as he watched N.O. conversed with a prostitute on Spruill Ave.

"Hell no. I'm not going for that shit again. You still owe me twenty dollars from last week. Now either you pay me in advance or I ain't fucking wit chu," the woman said leaning in the driver seat on N.O.'s hooptie.

"Bitch, I ain't giving you no money in advance. What the fuck I look like to you."

"Well fuck you then nigga," she walked off. Just as she stepped away from the car N.O. regretted he said those words. The skirt she wore revealed her butt cheeks as she walked away. He then laid back in the seat and took a long sip of his beer. As he laid back with his eyes closed then opened it back, his attention then went to his rear view mirror which was a second too late. Before he could take another breath he was at gun point through the passenger and driver's window.

"Get yo bitch ass out the car nigga," C.J. said through the passenger window.

N.O. looked at C.J. then at Black. Knowing he had no wins he tried his hand anyway taking a swing at Black with the bottle. Black blocked his arm as C.J. opened the door and smacked him in his face with the pistol. He then grabbed him by his neck and dragged him out of the car on the ground. Black quickly ran on the other side. N.O. tried to get up and run away but Black went across his face with the pistol. C.J. then kicked him in his stomach taking all of the wind out of his lungs.

"A-aiight, a-aight," he managed to say after catching his breath. "It wasn't me man. It was-," C.J. smacked him in the face again with the gun causing him to spit out gulps of blood.

As N.O. continued to plead for his life that intensified the anger of Black and C.J. as the continued pistol whip him C.J. stood up feeling tired of hitting him with his gun and watched on as Black tortured him.

"I'm sorry man!" N.O. cried out not able to take no more lashes with the gun. "I'm-I'm sorry man," he pleaded holding up both of his hands up looking back and forth from C.J. to Black hoping they'll have pity for him. "That's my word you don't have to worry about me fucking wit y'all niggas no mo. Just please man don't hit me no mo."

Black looked up at C.J. and started laughing as C.J. stared at N.O. with hate in his eyes.

"Please man, don't hit me no mo," he said to Black.

"Shut the fuck up!" C.J. kicked him in his face with all his strength causing his head to hit the wheel of the tire. N.O. instantly closed his eyes and laid back on the ground. C.J. and Black just stared at him for a moment. They looked at each other then back at N.O.

C.J. nudged him with his foot but got no type of movement from him.

"Damn," Black said. "I know we ain't kill the nigga."

C.J. grabbed his shirt and tried to pick him up then let him drop. N.O. still didn't move. He just layed there looking as if he was asleep. C.J. then put his gun in his waist and bent down to check his pulse. He felt around N.O.'s neck feeling nothing, he then stood up.

"Let's go," he said to Black still looking at N.O.'s lifeless body. "This nigga dead."

Black looked at N.O. put his gun in his waist and looked back at C.J.

"Well this ain't good," he said.

C.J. looked at Black, "Man let's go," they both made sure no one was around then took off their mask and walked back to the car as if nothing happened.

Ch Apter 19

Rasheid sat in class thinking about his drug operation while Mr. Williams mouth away about something that was irrelevant to physics 2. He thought about Tania and how their relationship went from bad to worse. They gotten to the point where they literally wasn't speaking to each other. He planned on making it up to her before something happened between the two that he regretted. Just then someone knocked at the door which made everyone looked to see who it was. Mr. Williams walked to the door and opened it as two hall monitors exchanged words with him in a low tone. He then stepped out the class and closed the door. Seconds later he came back in the class and stared at Rasheid.

"Rasheid, you're wanted down stairs in the main office," he said without blanking an eye.

Rasheid detected something wrong as his mind flashed to Tania then to his Aunt Tereesa. He then thought the worse, thinking one of them was in a car accident or the house caught on fire. He glanced at Mr. Williams who was still staring at him then walked out of the class taking over a nervous feeling. The two hall monitors escorted him to the main office. Mr. Williams closed the door and stood in front of the class.

"You see class. Living the fast life may look good on the outside. But sooner or later it will catch up to you," he walked over to his desk with his hands in his pocket as if he foreseen this whole thing was going to happen. "I got a feeling you all want be seeing Rasheid again for a long time," he said before he took a seat at his desk. The students all looked at each other confused.

Rasheid walked down the hall hoping that neither his girlfriend nor his aunt was seriously hurt. As he came around the corner he saw the two uniformed police officers standing in the office. They looked up just in time to see him walk through the door. Rasheid's heart started beating faster as he walked up to them.

"Are you Rasheid Willis?" one of the officers asked looking him up and down.

"Yes," he answered.

The officers then pulled out his handcuffs.

"You're under arrest for breaking and entering during nighttime with the intent to commit robbery, malicious wounding and second degree murder of Nehemiah Owens," he said putting he handcuffs on Rasheid.

Rasheid looked puzzled for a moment. He was caught off guard on the arrest but was really surprised to find out about the death of N.O. He wanted to speak up on his behalf but knew it was useless seeing that they were going to arrest him anyway. So without a word, he allowed them to put him in handcuffs and escorted him outside to the police car. Students and staff members watched on knowing that was going to be the big talk for the rest of the week.

"Damn," C.J. said to himself as L-Note watched the cars passby. "Fuck! Fuck, fuck, fuck!" he looked at L-Note. "You know shit about to roll down the hill right."

L-Note shook his head.

"Naw. He'll be alright. One thing I found out about fighting that murder case is that in the court, they have to prove you did it. Not just to say it. They don't got no evidence Rasheid did none of that shit. Finger prints or nothing. We just need to make sure that bitch and her daughter don't point him out," just then one of their regular clients drove up and C.J. signaled for one of his youngins to serve him.

"When was the last time you holla at Tremaine?" C.J. asked him.

"Day fo yesterday. We down to like three bricks."

"Damn. So something got to happen. Cause we damn sure can't have this nigga locked up," the youngin came back, put the money in his pocket and listened on to their conversations. L-Note then observed an unfamiliar s.u.v. driving slowly towards them. It then came to a stop. They looked at the four heads in the vehicle. The passenger window came down and Doc stuck his head out the window.

"Heads up!" Doc yelled out. "Y'all trespassing. Y'all niggas got till Friday to get off the block."

C.J. and L-Note looked at each other then back at him as if he was speaking another language.

"Well at least they got heart," C.J. said.

"Nigga get the fuck out here!" L-Note spat at them.

"Like I said nigga!" Doc said in a more aggressive tone. "Get the fuck up off the block before-," was the last words he said before L-Note took out his glock 9mm and started shouting through windows of their vehicle. Easy sped off as all of his passengers ducked for safety. L-Note ran in the streets still shooting the gun at them. After the clip was emptied, he stared down the streets with fire in his eyes until the car disappeared. He then walked back to his seat.

C.J. took a sip of his beer, "Who the fuck was those clowns?" he said unimpressed by their actions.

"I don't know and I don't give a fuck! Niggas thinking shit sweet huh!" he said getting madder by the second. "It's time for murder season out this motherfucker. Rasheid ain't here to save these motherfuckers now."

Before he had a chance to get adjusted in his seat he heard the bullets before he could have seen where they were coming from. Easy came right back this time three of his passengers shooting machine guns as bullets flew everywhere leaving L-Note, C.J. and their youngin no choice but to run for cover. C.J. ran behind an abandoned car pulling out his .45 as the bullets flew pass him. He ducked down not moving a muscle until it was over with. When he figured the coast was clear after hearing them drove off, they all got up checking each other.

"Fresh you straight?" L-Note asked out of breath.

"Yeah," the young boy said traumatized.

"Ha ha ha, I like that," C.J. laughed like a mad man. "These niggas want it now they got it," he cocked his gun and walked to his car. "Make sure the lookout is and point!" he yelled out. "If anybody comes through here whose not a fien or a resident I want every motherfucker in the car dead. And I don't give a fuck who it is. L-Note get them niggas up off the block for right now. It's time for war," he got in his car and drove off.

"You look good," Rookie said to Deanna.

"Thanks," she blushed as she sat on the other side of the Plexiglas. "So when are they gonna let you."

Rookie dropped his eyes. He was hoping the question wouldn't come up during their visitation.

"I don't know yet."

Deanna sensed that he knew something he wasn't telling her. She tried not to panic.

"Well it's going to be soon?"

"I don't know," Rookie still avoided looking at her.

"Well what do you know!" she snapped.

Rookie looked up at her. "I crapped out. That's what I know. These motherfuckers want me to snitch on Rasheid. I know that too," he paused for a few seconds. "But I know that I ain't going out like no bitch."

Deanna turned her head already knowing where the conversation was going.

"Deanna you think I want to be in here. You don't think that I rather be with you. But I ain't no fucking snitch. I can't have that shit over my head. If I gotta do time I'ma do it like a soldier and not like no little hoe," Rookie tried to convince her as himself.

"Stop talking like that." "I'm
only being honest."

"Stop talking like that Rookie!" she yelled out. "You are not going to do time! Do you hear me. You're not going to do no time!" she broke out in tears.

"She's taking this worse than me," Rookie thought.

"Look baby," he tried to butter her up. "I ain't said I'm giving up. Believe that I ain't going down without a fight. I got some money saved up this time so I'll be able to get a good lawyer. So just be easy. Everything gone be alright. And as long as I know that I still got you. I'm gone be alright," he smiled "Alright."

Deanna looked up at him wiping the tears from her eyes.

"Well I need to know that you're going to be there for us."

"I'ma always be here for you baby," he assured her.

"Not just me but for us," she wiped her tears with a napkin.

"I'm here for us Baby. I'm not about to crack for nothing," he patted his chest.

"I hope not. Because we need you."

"Who's we," he thought this case might have her going a little crazy.

Deanna looked down in her lap then back at him.

"Rookie I'm pregnant."

Rookie's whole facial expression changed. Deanna just looked at him.

"Pregnant?" he said confused. "What you mean pregnant."

"What I mean is that you're going to be a father."

The words ate straight through his heart like a knife.

"Are you sure? How far along are you?"

"I'll be there months next week."

"Pregnant," he said in a loud whisper still in shock.

"So you mean to tell me you're going to be a father behind these walls." He didn't hear her last comment. He saw still in shock.

"So Grandma why did you become a teacher?" Rasheid asked putting the dishes in the sink.

"Because I felt as if it was my calling," Mrs. Willis said washing the dishes. "It was a gift I was blessed with. To teach and help others understand."

"So what do you think my gift is?" he looked up at her.

"I don't know Baby. That's for you to find out. Whatever it is that you have a desire to do in your heart."

"I think I want to be a lawyer," he said anxiously.

"Well that's where it starts. In your mind. You can do whatever it is that you put your mind to and don't let anybody tell you otherwise," she said now facing him. "Rasheid. You're a bless child. A gift from God. And it's not always going to be easy out there. But you got to remember, life is the employee and you're the employer. It's only going to do what you ask it to do. No more no less. If you ask for nothing then that's what you're going to get. If you ask for the best then that's what you're going to get. Everything you got going on in your life right now is what you asked for and it's going to continue to get worse until you change it. Do you hear me?"

"Yes," Rasheid said shaking his head feeling the guilt.

"Willis!" the correctional officer yelled waking Rasheid from his dream. "B&B. You made bail," he said. "I'll be back in five minutes," he walked off.

Rasheid sat up in his bunk. He realized he was tired from failing to remember when he fell asleep. The last nine days he spent in jail felt like three months. He washed his face and brushed his teeth, then sat patiently waiting for the correctional officer to return. Twenty minutes later the c.o. returned with a smirk on his face.

"You must be rich or something. I don't know too many people who can get out of jail in a hundred and fifty thousand dollar bail. I wish I could just cough up fifteen thousand dollars like it was nothing," Rasheid looked up at the correctional officer and shook his head.

"Man only if you knew," he walked off.

The officer looked at him then slammed the gate shut.

<hr>

Rasheid stepped outside for the first time in nine days and took in a deep breath of fresh air as he looked around the parking lot for Tania. He spotted her sitting in her car staring at him. He walked over to the passenger seat and got in.

"Hey," he felt a bit awkward from the tension she gave off.

"Hi," Tania started the car then drove off.

"Thanks for paying the bail."

"It's your money," her attention was still on the road.

"Look, I know you mad at me. But I promise you that I didn't kill N.O. or break into that lady house."

Tania didn't say anything but she already knew he wasn't guilty of the charges. "I got James Sterling on the case so just give me some time and promised I'ma clean this whole thing up." She acknowledged him by nodding her head.

"Baby, I know I've been messing up lately," he looked at her then grabbed her hand. "But I just need you to understand where I'm comin from."

Tania gave him an angry smile, "Rasheid, I've been trying to understand you for the past year now and I still gotten nowhere. I tried to be patient with you. I told you that I don't care about the money. I care about you. But do you listen to me. Being in the hospital wasn't a wakeup call for you so you went and got yourself a murder case," she said as the words ate through Rasheid. "But what I'm trying to understand is how can you be so intelligent but so fucking stupid at the same time!" she raised her voice.

"Who you think you're talking to like that," Rasheid gave her a look that could kill.

"I'm talking to Rasheid Willis!" she screamed looking back and forth at him and the highway. "When are you gonna see that this whole selling drugs thing is design for you to fail! You cannot win Rasheid! Your against the odds! But since you think otherwise and want to go out there like the rest of these fools and roll dice with your life, when the judge sentence you to a asshole full of time don't expect me to be there!" she parked the car in the driveway and crossed her arms over her chest looking at him.

Rasheid sat in the passenger seat looking out the window. His mind flashed back to the dream he had. His grandmother told him things were only going to get worse until he changed them.

"So what you saying Tania. You saying you leaving me. You saying you want it to be over with," he looked at her. "I mean if that's what you saying then go ahead and say it."

Tania was stuck. Her pride wouldn't let her say no but her heart wouldn't let her say yes.

"Cause I don't want you to be with me if you don't want to be with me." Tania closed her eyes and put her finger up to her temple as if she felt a migraine coming on.

"Rasheid," she said in a much calmer tone. "I see something you can't see. And I don't want to see it happen to you."

"Tania you just paranoid."

"No I'm not. Rasheid I believe in you. I believe you can overcome this. Matter of fact I know you can. I've never met nobody as intelligent as you before. I look up to you," she said as he looked over at her. "Baby you are my inspiration. But you do have danger coming in at you from a blind spot that you can't see," Tania was then interrupted by her cell phone which she didn't bother to answer so Rasheid picked it up.

"Hello. Yeah this me, what's up? I just got out. Why? What! Tell me you're bullshitting with me man! Are you fucking serious! Look, look, give me a few minutes. Just chill and I'ma be over there in a minute," Rasheid hung up the phone.

Somebody really don't like. He thought to himself as he gathered his things.

"Baby this is a life or death situation," he opened the door. "Please don't be mad at me but I gotta go," he rushed over to his car not noticing the facial expression on her face. "I'll be right back baby. This is an emergency," he hopped in his Oldsmobile and drove off.

Tania shook her head not believing what just took place.

<hr>

Rasheid drove through the projects and came to a stop when he spotted Tremaine, the Blood Brothers and a few of their lookouts standing on the corner. Rasheid parked the car and walked in their direction.

"What the hell are y'all talking about?" Rasheid said joining them.

"Man we been going back and forth with these niggas all week long. I think these niggas from Downtown," C.J. explained. "They first ran up on us at the corner we got the shooting out and shit. Nigga gone tell us to get up off the block-."

"You saw how he look," Rasheid interjected.

"Dark skin nigga wit dreads. Kind of big nigga. I seen the nigga before I just can't remember where I seen him. Anyway these niggas come through wit machine guns and shit so we got up off the block. The next day Lil Red from Trailwood got shot like three times and they saying it's the same niggas. So yesterday Black call us from Rivers Avenue talking bout some nigga trying to Debo the block. So soon as we go to roll out we get ambushed at the corner!" C.J. talked so fast he stumbled over his words. "Like it was a setup or something. Nigga just rolled up on us letting off. Ain't nobody get hurt or nothing but it's like these niggas watching our every move and we don't even know who the fuck it is. So now everybody's a suspect. The money been slow as a motherfucker. We ready to bomb on these motherfuckers we just don't know who to bomb at. Shit done got crazy as a motherfucker."

"So you mean to tell me all this shit took place since I've been locked up?" Rasheid knew things were going to get even uglier real soon.

C.J. nodded his head.

"Matter of fact I think this started the day you got arrested."

"And to top it off," L-Note added. "I got word yo boy Dee down with them niggas."

Rasheid thought long and hard. He knew he was about to take a hell of a risk with his life but he had to go through with it being that he already gave Rino his word.

"C.J. you got yo gun on you?" he asked as C.J nodded his head. "Let me get it," he took the .45 from his worker. "Hold it down for a minute. I need to go holla at some people," Rasheid held the gun by his waist, got in his car and drove off. They all just watched him as he drove down the street. Rasheid drove through the city he grew up in. The city where his grandmother died. The city that brought his aunt down to the lowest point of her life. And the city where he sold drugs at. In almost the three years he's been selling drugs, he made more money than he could ever imagine. He thought of all the money he saved up, all the jewelry and clothes that he had and some of it he haven't had the chance to wear yet and he thought about his three bedroom apartment and his cars. Then he thought about losing his aunt to the same drug that made him prosperous. His mind quickly flashed to the time when he witnessed Dre's murder. Rasheid was only seventeen and he was ready to get out the drug game. He wanted to go home to Tania and live how she wanted them to. Move away and open up a business or something then maybe he could go to school and practice law like he always wanted to. But to just leave out the game like that would have been cowardly and dangerous at the same time. He was responsible for everything that went wrong and it was his responsibility to put it all back in place. The only problem now that he didn't know where to start. As he continued to drive from street to street, he noticed a familiar face. A face that he was real close to. A face that he also looked up to and had very much respect for. It was the face of one of his mentors. Rodger. He quickly made a u turn and pulled up to the unfamiliar residence where Rodger sat comfortably in a lawn chair enjoying the outside weather. Rasheid quickly got out the car and walked up to him with a big smile on his face. Then it hit him, what if Rodger wasn't too happy to see him being that he did take over his connect. But when he saw the smile Rodger gave back to his recognition, the thought quickly left his mind.

"Rasheid, boy long time no see!" Rodger said excitedly. He stood up and embraced Rasheid with a hug.

"What's up man," Rasheid said still wearing the smile on his face. "I see you done grew up," he looked him up and down.

"Yeah man, but what's going on with you?"

"Oh I'm alright. Taking it one day at a time you know. Here take a seat," he pointed at the lawn chair then sat down with his attention on Rasheid. "So what's been going on big timer. I know it's gotta be better than what I'm hearing."

Rasheid looked at him surprised, "You've been hearing about me?"

"Boy who haven't been hearing about you. But I already know when you on top niggas gone talk shit. That's just what they do. But anyway I heard you done got yourself caught up in a lot of bullshit," he waited to hear his side of the story. So Rasheid explained everything that's been going on in his life since they last saw each other. He told him about Rookie, Tremaine, the Blood Brothers and N.O.'s murder. He told him about his crew receiving threats and all the shootings that's been going on recently. Rodger didn't say much, he just sat there and listened closely as Rasheid explained.

"You know what Rasheid, times have change since I was your age. It wasn't a lot of killing going on back then like how it is now. But as far as with this drug thing, the only thing that changed is the people. And you know, I hate to say this about my own people but niggas is greedy. A lot of black people is greedy. And one thing about greed is that there's no stopping point. The more a greedy person gets the more they want, until they end up destroying their self. But in your case, you went and got niggas who got reputations to work for you and it backed fired. As you got bigger and made more money, you got a lot more attention than you expected and that didn't turn out so good either. And to be honest with you Rasheid that's just the life of a drug dealer. But living the lifestyle that you live, you know you have to take risks. Some of them are minor and some are major but your life depends on each one."

Rasheid listened on as Rodger continued. Even though Rodger wasn't as groomed as he used to be he could see that he hasn't lost his wisdom.

"But you got a real problem on your hand. You can go shoot up his people and he can come back and shoot up your people and y'all can keep going back and forth like that or you can solve the problem from the root. Where it started at. This way you no it's no longer a threat or an issue," Rodger said as Rasheid studied him.

"You said that like you got an idea," Rasheid said.

"I got a plan," Rodger said with his eyes glowing. He knew his plan was a good one.

"So what's the plan?" Rasheid asked intrigued.

"Check it out," Rodger said detailing his plan to Rasheid.

ChApter 20

"Your Honor, I'm not sure if he want to be heard but I do," James Sterling spoke against the prosecutor, "Now these are serious charges which can't be disputed. But what could be disputed is the fact that my client Rasheid is guilty of any of these charges," Rasheid stood next to his lawyer in a two piece suit listening to every word that he said. "You heard with your own ears that Ms. Singleton nor her daughter couldn't identify not one of the people who broke into her house. Now we know that's not a good thing but who has the right to go off accusations that Rasheid commit this crime just because him and the victim's son had some differences in the past. Second degree murder is a very serious charge. But where's the malice, where's the intention. Your Honor the only witness to this case is a young woman who talked with the victim minutes before his death and the only thing she could can testify to was some people whom she couldn't identify in the area," James Sterling put some papers back in a folder and looked up at the judge already knowing he had the case beat. "Your Honor, this is the court of law. This is where we try citizens and you use your experience and your and judgment to conclude if they're guilty or innocent. Now I've appeared in front of you on many cases but not like this, where the client is charged on accusations rather than evidence. So I ask you, what proof did Mr. Raines presented that could even raise suspicion that my client Rasheid Willis could be guilty on any of these charges."

The judge looked at James Sterling then over to the prosecutor Mr. Raines. He held his head down looking through his paper work trying to find away to contradict Mr. Sterling. He felt foolish wishing he would of listened to his colleagues when they told him he was not yet experienced enough to go against James Sterling, the biggest and most talked about black lawyer in the city of Charleston. The judge looked at him getting impatient.

"Well do you want to be heard or not counselor because I would like to eat lunch sometime today," the judge snapped.

"Yes Your Honor, I would like to be heard," Mr. Raines said nervously fumbling through some paper work.

***

Tania sat on her bed looking around the bedroom. She got up and picked up the picture off the dresser of her and Rasheid. It was a picture they took together at a photo booth. It was one of the few times that they did go out. She put the picture in her suitcase, along with the rest of her things. She then looked around the bedroom and the bathroom to make sure she got everything. She then closed her suitcase and went downstairs to put it by the door. She went back upstairs and took the letter she wrote to Rasheid and placed it on the mirror where it would be easy to spot. She took one last look around the room. "He didn't even remembered I was graduating," she said before she turned off the light, grabbed her belongings then head out the door.

***

Judge Matthews looked at the prosecutor wondering how long it took him to prepare for this case. An undergraduate could do better than he did, he thought to himself.

"Well it's quite obvious that the evidence in this trial is insufficient. And being that this is the preliminary, Mr. Raines I don't believe that you presented a sturdy enough case for me to send it to the grand jury. We don't even have a probable cause that," he looked down at his desk. "Mr. Willis is it. Yes, Mr. Willis committed any of these acts. So in favor of the court I'm going to have to dismiss this case. Mr. Willis you're free to go," he looked at Rasheid. And of I was you I would stay as far away from trouble as possible. It seems to me that some people would like to see you in it. Sorry for the inconvenience but remember what I said. This court is now adjourned," he smacked the gravel as everyone stood on their feet watching him leave out. Rasheid turned around as he received smiles from his Aunt Tereesa and Eve. He smiled back as his lawyer reached over to shake his hand.

"You do need to stay out of trouble. You're a bright young man with a bright future. We don't need you behind bars," he let Rasheid's hand go and grabbed his briefcase.

"Thank you," Rasheid said to him. He walked up to his aunt as they embraced each other with a hug.

Eve walked up to him, "Damn nigga you must of paid the judge off," she whispered in his ear as she gave him a hug. "Either that or you just one lucky dude," she smiled at him.

"Thirty thousand dollars for a crime I didn't do is kind of expensive though."

"Well at least everything is dropped."

"Yeah. And thanks for coming and tell Rookie I'ma be up there to see him real soon."

"Alright. But I gotta go pick my baby up but Imma holla at you. And be safe," she walked off.

"You too. Don't forget to tell Rookie what I said.

"Okay," she walked out the door.

"Thanks for coming," Rasheid said now putting his attention on his aunt.

"What, I wasn't supposed to come or something," Tereesa stepped back claiming her right as his guardian.

"You know what I mean. Where's Tania, outside or something," he said as they walked out the courtroom.

"I don't know," Tereesa said puzzled. "I haven't seen her at all."

"Well she might be at home. She don't like coming to places like this." "I hope you learned a lesson Rasheid," they walked down the hall with Rasheid's arm around her shoulder.

"Yes I did. So tonight, we celebrating. I want you to go home and put on something nice and me, you and Tania going out to eat. We haven't been out in awhile," Tereesa looked at him smiling.

"Rasheid, I hope you really did learn a lesson. You only got a little while until you graduate. And I really want to see you walk across that stage."

"I will," he said full of confidence. "Matter of fact I don't have a choice. I gave Grandma my word that I will do it," as they continued to walk and talk until they stepped in front of Tereesa's car. Rasheid took a good look at it," Aunt Tereesa, why don't you let me buy you a new car."

She got in the car, closed the door and down the window.

"I don't need a new a car. What I need is for you to do is get your life straight," she started the ignition. "Call me when you're ready," she said driving off.

Rasheid watched his aunt drove off he saw the woman and her daughter walk out the court room. It was the first time he paid any attention to them. They walked down the steps as the mother looked over at Rasheid grabbed her daughter hand and continued to walk in the direction she was going. 'Whose going to give them justice' he thought to himself. As he got inside his car and closed the door, he picked up his cellular phone and saw that he had one unanswered message. He put the phone to his ear and listened to the message as he heard the voice say, "Problem solve." Rasheid put the phone back down as the last words that his aunt said to him ate through his conscience. He learned that the person who was responsible for the death of Dre was the one who was sending indirect shots at him. He understood through Rodger that everything and everybody had a price. And with the help of an old friend of Rodger and some cash his problem no longer existed. He just had to live the rest of his life knowing he was responsible for a few people lives. Or maybe a few people deaths. He sat in his car and closed his eyes seeing for the first time what the streets turned him into. As he drove off he figured to himself that he would spend at least a week straight with Tania. He needed it and definitely missed the affection she had to offer. When he got home he saw her car was still parked. He got out the car with a single rose and a new Jon B cd. As he opened the door he looked around his quiet apartment.

"Tania," he yelled out walking aver to his stereo system. He played his favorite single off the album, 'They Don't Know.' He turned around and caught a glimpse off himself in the mirror and liked how he looked dressed up. He figure he'll do it more often.

"Tania," he yelled the second time walking upstairs thinking she fell asleep. "Tania," he looked around the empty room. His attention quickly went to the letter that was on the mirror. He grabbed the letter with anticipation hoping nothing went wrong. He couldn't believe what he was reading as his eyes followed the words on the letter.

Dear Rasheid,

If you're reading this letter then you probably got the impression I left. It shouldn't be a mystery why but if you really don't have a clue. I was just tired. Tired of waiting up for you late nights wondering if I was going to get a phone call stating that you was dead or that you're in jail. I was tired of waiting for you to realize that you had something good. Rasheid, I know you love me and I love you too. I will always love you. I just couldn't take a risk no more with my heart. But I hope that you find whatever it is out there that's for you. And I hope you understood.

Love Always
Tania

Rasheid looked back in the mirror and placed the letter on his bed as he listened to Jon B's words soaked through his heart. 'Don't listen to/ what people say/ they don't know about bout you and me/ put it out your mind cause its jealousy/ they don't know about this love.

"Stop right here," the guard said to Rookie. He took the hand cuff off and opened the door for him to step into the visitation room. As he stepped into the room he saw Rasheid sitting on the other side of the Plexiglas. He suddenly felt ashamed and jealous at the same time. Rasheid charges was more serious than his and he wasn't even in jail for two weeks and here he was sitting in a concrete cell for months now, he thought to himself. "You got thirty minutes," the guard said as he closed the door.

"What's up," Rasheid said.

"What's up," Rookie had a slight smile on his face not giving him eye contact. Rasheid automatically sensed something was wrong.

"What's up man, you alright."

"Yeah I'm alright," Rookie looked into his eyes for the first time. "What about you. I done heard so much shit about you I probably can write a book."

Rasheid smiled at him, "Well I can tell you right now that ninety percent of it ain't true."

"Them stories came from somewhere. But I got to ask you this," he started to feel a little more comfortable. "Did you and Tania break up for real?"

He nodded his head not wanting to talk about her no time soon.

"Damn man. I'm sorry to hear that. So is you and Kiana serious or is it just a thing."

Rasheid shrugged his shoulders, "I mean I like her. It's just to early to be precise. But anyway what's up with you," he changed the subject. "How your case looking?"

Rookie broke their eye contact again.

"To be honest with you," he tried to choose the right words. "It really don't look good."

Rasheid put his face closer to the Plexiglas, "What you mean?"

"It just don't look good Rah," he let his eyes roam across the floor.

"You need some money or something?"

"Naw man, I need to get on the other side of this wall."

Rasheid sat back in his seat still looking at his best friend hoping that this case wasn't getting the best of him.

"Rasheid, I'm about to have a child. Deanna's pregnant. I can't be the type of father to my child like my daddy was to me! My daddy got locked up the day after I was born and I just don't want follow in his footsteps!"

Rasheid closed his eyes and tried to gather his thoughts before he said anything.

"I'm just trying to understand. What exactly are you saying. Matter of fact what's the people saying. How much time you looking at."

"They said I could plea out to fifteen years."

Rasheid's heart dropped to his stomach.

"If it was just me, I could ride it out. But I'm bout to have a child. I can't do no fifteen years with a child out there."

"Look man, don't even allow yourself to get into that mind state. I promise I'm going to do whatever I can to get you up out here."

"Ain't nothing you can do," he looked away from him. "Unless you friends with the judge."

Silence fell upon the two as they went into their own thoughts.

"Rasheid, I really don't know what to do man," he sounded as if he was going to breakdown.

"Rook, whatever you can do , you gotta be strong."

"Be strong," he said with a smile. "It's easy for you to tell me to be strong when you're on the outside looking in. You still got your freedom. You still getting money. You can get some pussy whenever you want to. I'm locked the fuck up!" he raised his voice. "I'm bout to have a child on the way! I'm not gonna see the streets again for another fifteen years cause I was helping you move them bricks! So how the fuck you gone tell me to be strong when you still out there living your life!"

Rasheid looked at Rookie in shock. He couldn't believe he just said what he said. He wanted to go off on him but the last thing he wanted to do was to get on his bad side.

"Rookie, I didn't make you do nothing. This was your choice. You making it sound like this is my fault," he said calmly.

Rookie then started feeling annoyed about the whole visitation, "You know what man," he shook his head. "I'm out. I'ma holla at chu," he got up and pressed the button to alert the guard his visit was over. Rasheid sat there heart broken realizing his best friend was turning his back on him. He got up and walked out the room. He knew there was a good chance Rookie could turn into a snitch, so if he wasn't careful before, he knew he had to be extremely careful now.

"Yo what's up Rah," the guy said to Rasheid like he knew him.

"Yo what's up man," he looked at the familiar guy as he slammed his locker shut and headed towards the student parking lot. He was aware of the rumors that was going around about him. People was stating that he killed N.O. and got away with it. Some hated him for it and some praised him for it but they all had much more respect for him. He stepped outside and saw Kiana standing on the side of the building waiting for him looking as beautiful as ever. She smiled at his approach looking him up and down from his all white air forces, gibaud jeans, crispy white tee shirt to his freshly low cut tempo fade.

"What's up," she walked up to him and gave him a hug.

"What's up with you," he took a quick glance at her almond brown legs down to her neatly pedicured feet. Kiana was wearing her cut off shorts with a skin tight halter top that complimented her perfectly curved D-cups that read, 'I Love Me Too.'

"Nothing. I was thinking about you today," they held hands as they walked over to Rasheid's car. A few of the other females looked on with envy in their eyes.

"Oh yeah. Was it a good thought?" he smiled at her.

"Maybe," she teased. "It all depends."

"Depends on what?"

"Depends on if you give me a ride home," they both laughed. "I'm serious," she playfully slapped him on his shoulder.

"You know I got you," he opened the door to his Cadillac as she got in on the other side.

"I like this car," she said feeling leather interior.

"Yeah," he shut the door and started the ignition. "This my favorite one too."

"Over the Benz," she looked at him shocked.

"You know the Benz aiight. That's more of luxury car. But I feel a lot more comfortable in the Lac," he drove off.

Kiana just looked at him studying his facial features. Rasheid glanced at her from the corner of his eyes.

"Yo, why you staring at me so hard for?"

"I don't know," she rested her head back in the seat. "I like the way you look," she said in a kid like voice. Rasheid looked at her and smiled.

"What!" she said excitedly. "You think I'm crazy or something." "Naw. I don't think your crazy," he said sarcastically. "Yes you do," she playfully slapped him again.

"No I don't. I like the way you look too," he said as she blushed.

"Can I ask you a question?"

"What's up."

Kiana thought long and hard before she said a word, "Do you sell drugs?" she sounded like a five year old.

Rasheid looked at her then back at the highway.

"I done lived a life that forced me to do a lot of things I didn't want to do," he paused as she listened on. "I done did some things that I'm gone have to take to the grave with me. I wouldn't say I'm a bad person. But I probably done made some bad choices," he cleared his threat. "I know you done heard a lot of things about me. And to be honest with you, I could care less what it is. All I can do is live my life for me. I'm not ashamed of who I am. I'm not ashamed of where I come from. And I'm not ashamed of how I got to where I'm at now. It's just that there's a lot of things people wouldn't understand unless they're put into that situation. And until then, I really feel like they don't have the right to stereotype or pass judgment. So to take it back to your question. Do I sell drugs?" there was a long pause between them. "I'm still alive," he said as he looked away.

Kiana always knew that he was a good person, it's just that people didn't understand him. She looked over at him again not knowing if she wanted to feel sorry for him or give him a badge.

"Oh make this left right!" she said almost forgetting about the ride home. Rasheid had to slam on breaks so that he wouldn't miss the turn.

"Sorry about that," she said agitated that it broke their vibe.

"That's aiight. Damn! This your neighborhood!" Rasheid looked at all of the two and three stories houses.

"Yeah," she said unmoved.

"I didn't know you was rich," he looked over at her.

Kiana laughed at him.

"We're not rich. Just both of my parents have good jobs."

"Oh," Rasheid wondered how it would feel to have just one of his parents in his life. He probably would have been living somewhere like this too.

"I live right there," she pointed to the two story house that sat beautifully on the curb. "So what about your parents? What do they do? That's if you don't mind me asking," she added quickly hoping she wasn't getting to noisy.

"I don't know them," he was still looking at her house. "You have a nice house. I'ma get one like this one day."

She just looked at him," Oh I'm sorry, your parents dead," she was embarrassed at how rude she could be.

Rasheid came to a stop and put the car in park," I don't know. I don't know them. But check this out?" he quickly changed the subject. "Am I going to be able to see you besides school?" he looked into her eyes. Kiana snapped back to reality.

"Yeah," she said meaning it. "You can see me whenever you want to. Matter of fact what you doing this weekend?"

"Whatever you want to do," he said as they both leaned over to share an intimate kiss. Kiana pulled back seeing her mother stepping out of the house looking directly at her and Rasheid.

"Oh boy, here comes my mother," she grabbed her bookbag wishing they would have went somewhere else. "Do me a favor and wave at her so the least she could say is that you wasn't rude."

Rasheid waved at Kiana's mother as she waved back never taking her eyes off him.

"I'ma see you tomorrow in school," she opened the door and stepped out. "Aiight. Bye."

"Bye," she walked towards her mother. Rasheid waved at them once again before he left.

"Hi Mom," she said walking into the house.

"Hey Baby," her mother said with a smile standing in front of her Mercedes Benz.

"Kiana, who was that?"

Kiana turned around and looked her mother in the eye.

"A friend," she opened the door and walked in the house. Her mother watched her then looked down the streets and shook her head.

"I hope she's not serious with him," she said not wanting no thug around her daughter as she got in her car and drove off.

ChApter 21

Senior Year

"Is the coffee hot?" Ms. Karabetso asked one of the teachers hoping it'll be exactly what she need to calm her down.

"Oh yeah, it's hot," Mr. Williams said checking her out at the same time. She was an attractive twenty-six year old straight out of college. It was her first year as a teacher and she was teaching twelfth grade english. She put the student roster down on the table and fixed her a cup of coffee. She was so nervous she almost dropped her cup spilling the coffee on the table.

"Oh my God!" she stepped back and looked at herself glad that none of the coffee spilled on her.

"Let me get that for you," Mr. Williams grabbed some paper towel and wiped off the table. "I can see you're nervous."

"It's that obvious?"

"Oh yeah," he picked up her roster and gave it to her. His eyes strolled down the name on the rosters.

"Thank you," she said.

"Rasheid Willis," he looked at the very last name on the paper. She smiled at him and poured some more coffee in her cup. "I'm surprised he made it to the twelfth grade."

She looked up at him with a smile, "Excuse me."

"Oh no, I'm just talking about one of your students, Rasheid Willis," he poured some coffee in his cup.

She looked down at the roster to spot the name then looked back up at Mr. Williams.

"He's one of the ones and I hate to say it," he said in a low tone. "But he needs to be in prison."

Ms. Karabetso wiped the smile off her face.

"He's one of the biggest drug dealers this city has," Mr. Williams went on. "But the bad thing about it is that's not where it stops. Last year, he killed a fellow student and got away with it," Ms. Karabetso now looked at him shocked. She then remembered the movie Dangerous Mind and hoped that she wasn't taking on the real life role that Michelle Phiefer played.

"He actually killed somebody," she whispered in disbelief.

"Well there are rumors going around stating that he didn't do it. But I'm willing to bet my last dollar if he didn't do it, he definitely had something to do with it."

"Well I probably can imagine what type of person he is," she felt nervous all over again.

"Actually he's more of the quiet type, you know those are the most sneakiest ones. Well I have to get to class. Look forward to chit chat with you later," he walked out of the teacher's lounge. "Oh yeah," he turned around and looked at her. "You'll do great, just hang in there," he walked out of the door.

"Thanks," she said wondering what she got herself into.

Rasheid sat in class wondering where did the summer go to. For the past few months everything has been going so easy he thought he was dreaming. Rookie's trial kept getting put off for what reason he didn't know. But he continued to keep his eyes and ears opened for anything that seemed out of place. The Blood Brothers and his workers had everything back under control for the time which meant that he was still getting money and still making Rino happy. He haven't heard nothing from Tania but spent more time with in the past few months with Kiana than he ever spent with Tania. What made their relationship even better was that there background was the complete opposite. They had an understanding for each other that no one could come between. Kiana knew that Rasheid had business to take care of in the streets so she never gave him no hassle about it though she was concern about his safety.

"Good morning class," Ms. Karabetso walked briskly through the class as the students chatter came to an end. She put her paperwork and coffee on the desk as she took a good look at the class. It was all black students. She wasn't prejudice it's just that standing in front of an all black class was something she wasn't use to so she was even more nervous. "Okay," she said as all the students looked on sensing she was a little nervous. "My name is Ms. Karabetso. And I'm going to be your English teacher."

"We can see that," one student said which made the whole class burst out in laughter. Ms. Karabetso even had to laugh.

"So we're going to start this by calling role, when I call your name can you please say here or raise your hand. Starting with Thomas Anderson."

"Here," a light skin girl said holding up her hand.

"Okay. William Brown."

"Right cha," the same student who made the comment earlier said as everyone laughed again.

She continued to call role as all the students either said here, raised their hands or made a funny comment. She was starting to get a little more at ease sensing that the students wasn't harmful. As she got to the last name she looked at the classroom. She wanted to get a good picture of him.

"Rasheid Willis."

"Here," Rasheid held his hand up. She stared at him for a second. He did stood out from the rest of his classmates. Not just by the expensive clothes he wore but his whole aura. It was like he had the confidence that he could do whatever he wanted to. Ms. Karabetso automatically didn't have a liking for him and was willing to do anything to see a loser get out of her class. She didn't want to have to tell her family and friends that she was the teacher of a drug dealer and murder.

Rasheid looked at her as if he could almost read her thoughts. They done got to her already, he thought to himself as he shook his head and took out his pen and paper.

When school was over the hallways and student parking lot was packed with students dress their best and ready to impress. The guys stood on the side checking out the girls as the girls did the same. North Charleston High was so live on the first day that people who didn't even go to school made it their business to be there at two o'clock on the dot. Just to see all the students show off whatever they had to offer. Rasheid walked out of the building accidently stealing all of the attention from the girls. He saw Kiana walking in his direction.

"What's up Boo?" he said as she gave him a peck on the lips.

"What's up," she held his hand showing all of the fast ass girls in the parking lot that he was taken. The time she spent with Rasheid, he gave her just the boost of confidence that she needed. She felt like she was queen every time she was in the presence of him. The day he took her virginity he gave her a feeling she never knew existed. Pure ecstasy. So it wasn't no doubt in her mind that she was in love. She didn't know what Tania was thinking though she's glad she left him.

"Baby, I got Mrs. Cunningham again for math. I don't know how that happened."

"Ms. Cunningham seems like she aiight," he opened the door to his Benz and got in.

"I mean she is," Kiana got in on the passenger side. "It's just that she gives out too much homework. This is my last year so all I'm trying to do is relax."

"You'll be aiight," he drove off. "So what's up with Deanna? When was the last time you heard from her."

"The other day. She'll be back in school after she have the baby. Did you and Rookie had a fall out or something?"

Rasheid looked over at her.

"Naw, why you ask?"

She shrugged her shoulders," I just asked. It seems like since we been together, she really don't have nothing to say about you and I kind of figured it had something to do with Rookie. But to me that'll be a good thing because I really don't trust Rookie. Not saying that he's a bad person or nothing, I just think he attracts trouble and you don't need to be around him like that."

Rasheid just listened to Kiana ran off her mouth. It seems lately that's all she did in his company, talked non-stop.

"So what you doing? You going to my house or yours?" he asked.

"I'm going to your house," she looked at him like that was a stupid question. "I'm trying to be away from my mother as much as possible."

"Why, your mother seems like she's cool."

"Well I wish she'll say the same about you," she leaned back in her seat rubbing the back of his head as she continued to talk about her mother's disapproval for him.

"You can't get mad at her. She's just looking out for your best interest," he pulled up in his driveway. "Look, I gotta go take care of some things. I'll only be about a couple hours."

"Okay," she grabbed her bookbag. "What do you want for dinner?"

"It don't matter," she reached over and kissed him. "As long as it ain't burnt," he said teasing her but serious.

"Shut up," she smiled at him. "And don't be all night. I have to be home at eleven," she got out the car and closed the door.

Rasheid watched her as she took out her keys entered his apartment and closed the door behind her.

"Damn she sexy as hell," he pulled out the driveway wishing he could go in with her.

Kiana stepped into the living room, dropped her bookbag on the floor went to the stereo system and played a R. Kelly cd. She then took a stroll around the apartment looking for anything out of place since her last visit but found none. Being satisfied that there was no suspicion, she then went up to his room and went through the closet she left some clothes in. "I need to buy some more clothes," she said to herself seeing nothing that she wanted to wear. She then went to the drawer Rasheid kept his under clothes in and pulled out one of his tee shirts and headed to the bathroom. Playing house was something she could get used to. She took off her shoes, pants and shirt standing in the bathroom with nothing but her underwear and bra on. As she unstrapped her bra she then imagined Rasheid walking in on her and being mesmerized by her naked body and doing it to her right there on the bathroom floor. She felt a little wetness arriving between her legs as she tried to ignore it by turning on the hot shower. She put on a shower cap and stepped in the tub letting the hot water soothe her body. When she finished her shower she dried herself and put on one of Rasheid's tee shirts and a pair of her thongs and went downstairs to figure out what she's going to cook him for dinner.

Rasheid took the bag from Tremaine and looked inside of it.

"How much money is this?"

"One hundred and sixty-two g's," Tremaine said lighting the blunt.

"Are you sure?" Rasheid looked back at him. "Positive," he inhaled the weed smoke.

Rasheid then counted out forty-eighty thousand dollars and put the money in a separate bag.

"So what's up with Rookie yo? How his case looking?" "I don't know. He act like he don't want to talk to me."

"Yo Rasheid," he inhaled the weed smoke then sat the blunt in the ashtray.

"I know that's your boy and everything but you sho this nigga ain't leaking," Rasheid continued to put the money up not looking over at him. "I mean I really don't fuck wit the nigga like that but I'm still down to put up some bread just for the simple fact he's a part of the team and the uncle of my son. But this nigga acting funny as hell. He'll call the house and when I pick up he'll just say put Eve on the phone, don't got shit to say to me. I ask the nigga if he need some loot he said he don't need nothing from me."

Rasheid zipped the bag up and faced Tremaine.

"Well Rookie do got his own money."

"Okay," Tremaine said still not understanding. "But to top it off Eve said the prosecutor keep putting off his case. Now I done had a case before and if the D.A. keep putting the case off that either means two things. One," he held up a finger. "They don't got no evidence. Or two, they're using you to build up information for another case," he had Rasheid's full attention. "Now its kind of hard for them not to have no evidence on Rookie when he got knocked off with a half of brick and the marked money," he reached for his blunt and lit it back up feeling like he made his point. "I ain't trying to start no static between y'all but that shit just don't seem right to me."

Rasheid nodded his head not wanting to look at his best friend that way but he had to be honest with the facts.

"We done came too far to go out like that," he said as Rasheid stood up with the bags of money in his hand. "I'ma check it out, you just keep doing what you do," he adjusted the gun on his waist and walked out the door. He went outside and put the bags of money in his trunk, hopped in his car and drove. Instead of going home he decided to take a trip to the projects first, just to make sure nothing was out of line. As he turned into the neighborhood he saw his lookout on the corner. He blew his horn as the kid threw his hand up happy to be noticed by him. As he got to the spot where C.J. and his crew worked out of, he parked his car and went inside of the shaggy looking house. The house reeked, carrying the scent of smoke and days old garbage as Rasheid fanned the scent from his face.

"What's up Rah," C.J. said to him coming out of one the rooms wiping sweat off his forehead.

"How the hell can y'all work in this stink ass house."

"I don't even think about it," C.J. grabbed the scale off the counter. "I just do what the fuck I do and get fuck up out of here. Ayo Black, bring me that beeper number off that dresser when you come out there!" he yelled out. "So what's up though man. How everything going?" he said while weighing the cooked up cocaine then putting it in Ziploc bags.

"I'm just making sure everything is in accordance," he looked around the house. "Yo how much money you paying them lookouts?"

"Shit, I give them little niggas like five dollars a hour."

"Bump it up to seven."

C.J. looked over at him. He was about to say something but thought against it. If he says do it then must be a good reason, he thought to himself.

"I got chu," he put his attention back to what he was doing.

"Well I'ma holla at chu," he said as his mind went back to the money in his trunk.

"It was nice of you to come down and mingle wit the common folks," C.J. teased him.

"Whatever," Rasheid smiled as he stepped out of the house. Out of all the Blood Brothers, him and C.J. were the only ones who had an open line of communication. He then got back in his car and drove home. When he pulled up in his driveway he got out of the car to retrieve the bags of money out of the trunk. As he walked up the steps with the bags in hand, he suddenly took over a bad feeling. He didn't knew exactly what it was. It just felt like something wasn't right. He adjusted the .45 on his waist as he took a good a look around him to make sure he wasn't being watch. He then inserted his key into the lock and as soon as he opened the door he heard the smoke alarm go off.

"What the hell is going on?" he ran to the kitchen where the smoke was coming from.

Kiana was at the kitchen sink running water in a pot she over cooked some food in.

"I don't know what happened baby!" she said with disappointment all over her face. "The direction said let it boil for fifteen minutes. I let it cook for the fifteen minutes while I was watching something on t.v. and when I came back the whole kitchen was smoky!" she pleaded to him as she turned the water off.

Rasheid looked over at the stove.

"Baby you got the burner on high," he said as he went over and turned it off.

Kiana held her hand over her face trying to cover up the look of humiliation she had. Rasheid walked up to her and held her waist as he lightly kissed her on the forehead.

"It's aiight," he rubbed her side.

"No it's not," she pouted to him as she buried her face in his shoulders. "It seem like I can't do nothing right."

"Well I'll feel like you wasn't right if you didn't have no type of cooking skills but then out the blue whip me up a gourmet meal with no problem. You're not perfect," he held her head up and looked into her eyes. "Nobody is. But we all can strive for perfection. And the only way you can do that is by knowing you have flaws but trying to correct them. Now if you want I can pay for you to have cooking lessons," he said rubbing his finger on her cheek. "Plus I was in the mood for some Chinese food anyway," he said as they both shared a laugh.

"How come you always find the right words to say," she said with her arms now wrapped around his waist.

"Cause I got the right girl in my life," he said as he gave her a long passionate kiss.

"I love you," she pulled back and looked into his eyes.

"I love you too," Rasheid said as he gave her another kiss then grabbing her butt and picking her up with her legs wrapped around his waist walking her up the steps to his bedroom.

ChApter 22

"Kiana you've been in that bathroom for over a hour. Now hurry up before you're late for school," her mother said from the other side of the door. Kiana rolled her eyes and looked at the door holding the curling iron in her hair.

"Mom, could I please get myself together just once without you putting pressure on me every morning. Dang," she went back to doing her hair. Mrs. Simmons looked at her watch then back at the door.

"Well are you driving your car or are you riding with that boy."

"Mom, what difference does it make, as long as I get to school!" she snapped.

"I just don't see no sense in you always riding with that boy when you have your own car. Especially after how you bothered me and your father to get it for you."

"Because Mom, that boy whose by the way named Rashcid is my boyfriend. And that's just one of the things couples do these days. Ride to school together," she unplugged the curling iron and stepped out of the bathroom. "And oh yeah," she stood in her mother's face. "When he comes over for dinner tonight, could you please try not to embarrass me," she then stormed off to her bedroom. As she finished getting dressed, she looked out the window to see Rasheid pulling up in the driveway. She grabbed her bag and hurried downstairs. Glad that her parents both left the house already, she walked outside and locked the door behind her.

"Hey Baby," she got inside his Cadillac and closed the door behind her.

"What's up," Rasheid said backing out the driveway and driving off.

"How come you don't drive your car no more?" she looked over at him thinking about what her mother said earlier.

"Because I'll rather ride with you," she looked at him hoping he didn't felt like she was smothering him, "Why you ask?"

"I was just wondering," he shrugged his shoulders. "Cause that's a nice car you got."

"You wanna drive it."

"Baby I can't drive your car."

"Why not?"

"Because your parents bought you that car."

Kiana eyes wandered from left to right, "My parents bought the car for me. Therefore it belongs to me and I could do whatever I want with it. Now we can ride in my car if you want," she said looking at him. "Do you want to?"

Rasheid looked over at her and smiled, "Girl you don't know how lucky you are. Your parents love you so much they brought you a brand new car."

"Rasheid!" she was shocked he said that. "If anybody is lucky it's you. You're still in school and you have your own house. Your own money. You drive a Mercedes Benz. You don't have a curfew. You probably don't even know what a curfew is," she laughed. "You come and go as you please and free to do whatever you want. You are the lucky one not me."

"And I'll trade it all in to have a mother and a father," he said in a serious tone.

Once again Kiana felt humiliated. She then looked out of the window not knowing what to say to him. They both rode in silence for the rest of the ride.

"Good morning class," Ms. Karabetso said entering the classroom. The students quiet down and took a seat. Rasheid took out his pen and paper as the girl who sat in the front of him, dropped a folded piece of paper on his desk and smiled at him before she took her seat. He unfolded the letter and read it.

Look, I know you got a girlfriend and everything but I noticed how you was checking me out the other day when I had on my jean

skirt. I've been wanting to get your attention ever since last year and now
since I think I finally got it I was wondering would you like to get to know
me even better. Because I'm definitely trying to see what you about. Now if
you think you can handle it holla at me after class and I' ll give you my
number and address. And don't worry I'm down
to keep it on the low. Malisha

He folded the paper back up and put it in his book. He was checking her out the other day but he didn't knew she seen him. The chances of him acting on her invitation was slim. He had girls throwing themselves at him all the time, so he wasn't really all that moved.

"I know you all are probably thinking of the weekend you have ahead of you and I'll hate to rain on your parade but today you have a pop quiz," Ms. Karabetso said.

The students started ahhing and cursing under their breath as she mocked them.

"It's not that bad," she said passing out the quizzes.

"Man I thought you was cool," one student said flopping back in his seat.

"I thought I was cool too," she said sarcastically thinking she was being funny. None of the students thought so. "Okay," she finished passing out the quizzes and stood in front of the class. She was starting to enjoy being a teacher. "Its only fifty questions. You have thirty minutes and it all startsss now!" she said as if she was the referee to a race. She walked around the class monitoring her students making sure they wasn't pulling none of the cheating stunts her classmates pulled when she was in school but most of her attention stayed on Rasheid.

"So let's get this straight, Tremaine sell drugs out of this address in West Ashley," Detective Ryans said to Rookie. Rookie exhaled the smoke and flick the ashes in the ashtray. He knew he was selling his soul. And he knew what he was doing goes against everything moral he's been taught growing up in the hood. But he felt like his back was against the wall. Either he was going to get out and raised his child or have his child go through what he's been through and probably worse. He inhaled the cigarette smoke nodded his head at the detective.

"And C.J. work at this address in Liberty Hill and Black work at this address in Macon."

Rookie looked at the two detective and nodded his head again taking another pull of the cigarette.

"Now y'all got what y'all want. So when the fuck do I get out of jail!" he snapped.

"Whoa. Slow your horses cowboy," Detective Morris took a seat in front of him on the corner of the table. "Now it doesn't work that way. You get time off once we get a conviction. See we need a strong case against these guys. Once we feel that it's strong enough to take in the court of law and you testify against them. Then we can give you a time cut.

"Hold the fuck up man," Rookie stood up. Both of the detectives quickly looked at him. "You ain't said shit about me getting on no stand and testifying against nobody!"

Detective Ryans looked at Morris then back at Rookie.

"Well I'm sorry about the misunderstanding Reginald. But that's a part of the procedure," Rookie looked at Ryans then at Morris.

"I don't know about that shit man."

"Reginald, this is the only way you can avoid doing twenty years in prison. Now if you want to get out I can help you. But you're going to have to get on the stand and testify," he said.

Rookie sat back down in his seat and buried his face in his hands then looked back up at the detectives.

"Is that it," he said ready to comply but cursing himself on the inside.

"Well not exactly," Morris said. "The person that we really, really need is Rasheid. Now I can't make any promises on these other guys but I will assure you this. If you help us build a case around him, you wouldn't see no more than thirty months in prison," he looked Rookie in the eye. Rookie buried his face back in his hands. School was over and Rasheid was putting his books away in his locker. As he slammed his locker and turned around he saw Malisha standing directly behind him.

"So what's up?" she said in a seductive voice. Rasheid looked at her trying not to stare at her thirty-six double d's. He had to admit she definitely had a body as she stood with her chest out and cleavage showing. "I thought you was going to holla at me after class," she said.

"You right. I was checking you out the other day but I got a whole lot going on in my life right now and I got a girl. So I'ma have to pass up on this one," he tried to walk off.

"Are you sure?" she stepped closer to him making sure he get an eye full of her breast.

"Yeah I'm sure," he walked off brushing his back the locker trying not to bump into her breast. "But I'ma see you around," he walked off.

The girl balled her mouth up and storm off in the opposite direction.

As Rasheid stepped outside he saw Kiana waiting for him in her usual spot.

"Hey Baby," she greeted him with a kiss.

"What's up," he said as they walked side by side to his car.

"I'm sorry for being rude this morning. I didn't realize what I said until after I said it."

"That's aiight," his mind was still on the incident that happened with Malisha.

Kiana got in on the passenger side and closed the door as Rasheid drove off.

"Would you really trade everything you have to have your parents back in your life," she asked.

"In a heartbeat," he looked at her then back at the road. "But I don't want you to feel sorry for me or nothing. I never knew my mother or father. So for me it's normal. But I'm cool though. I don't feel like it handicap me or nothing. Plus my grandmother gave me enough love to make up what I was missing. So I'm straight."

Kiana still couldn't help but to feel sorry for him.

"So," he changed the subject. "Can your mother cook better than you," he teased her.

"Yes she can," she pinched him on his thigh.

"Oww," he yelled out. "That hurt."

"Well that's what you get for hurting my feelings," she said as he pulled up in her driveway. "Now remember, six o'clock on the dot. Don't be late."

"Have you ever known me to be late," he bent over and gave her a kiss.

"We'll see," she said as she grabbed her things and stepped out of the car. Rasheid watched her as she went into her house. As he drove off he was thinking about everything Tania told him. How she use to argue with him every day. But he finally understood what she was saying. For some reason he knew if he continued to sell drugs he was either going to end up dead or in jail. He figured it was time for him to quit. To get out of the game while he was still ahead. The more he thought about it the more he felt he was right. It had to be right.

"I'm out the game," he said to himself. "It's a wrap. I'm through. I'm done. I don't want no more parts of it. I'm gone!" he down the window and yelled out of it as he drove down the streets. "I'm out the game. I'm done. Y'all can have it back. I quit! Tell Rino I quit!" He had to get it out of his system. Rasheid sat back in his seat smiling to himself while he was driving down the highway. "Soon I'll be able to live a normal life."

As he drove up to the spot where C.J. was at he walked in the house without knocking to the door. Black quickly drew his gun out aimed directly at him.

"Damn Rasheid! Man you almost got murked!"

"Well at least you on point," Rasheid continued to walk in unmoved.

"C.J. what's up. You got that."

"Yeah come on," he directed him to the back room.

When they got to the back room C.J. picked up the bag that contain seventy-two thousand dollars and gave it to him. Rasheid opened the bag and looked in it. He then looked up at C.J.

"What you doing next weekend?" he asked him.

"The same thing I do every weekend. Grind baby," he rubbed his hands together. "Unless you trying to go on another shopping spree."

"Naw," Rasheid smiled. "I'm going to the fair next weekend. Me and my girl. And I want you to go wit me. I'll feel more comfortable if I had somebody on the team with me."

"Aiight. I can do that. My baby mama always be talking bout I don't never take her nowhere. So that's what's up."

Rasheid just stared at C.J. for a moment.

"You aiight nigga," C.J. said to him.

"Yeah," Rasheid rubbed his face. "Check this out C.J. I'm getting out the game," he looked back at him. "I'm finish with it man."

C.J. looked him up and down with a frown on his face, "What you mean you through with it. We just getting started."

"You might be just getting started but I'm through with it. I'ma holla at my connect. I can't make no guarantees or nothing but I'ma try to plug you in. I feel like you'll be the best person for the job."

C.J. was at a lost for words. He literally didn't know what to say.

"I'm holla at you," Rasheid patted him on his back. "And don't let nobody else know. I'll tell 'em myself," he said as he walked out the room.

"How you doing Mrs, Simmons," Rasheid shook Kiana's mother hand and gave her a rose.

"I'm doing fine. Thank you," she smiled holding the rose. "Well it's nice to finally meet you since all my daughter do is talk about you," she laughed as Kiana walked up behind her with her hands on her waist.

"I didn't think that was funny."

"Well I did," her mother smiled at Rasheid as he smiled back. "Let me go put this in some water," she walked off.

"How come I didn't get a rose," Kiana walked up to Rasheid.

"A rose is nothing compared to what I got planned for you," she smiled as he put his arms around her. "This is a nice crib you got," he said looking around adoring her house.

"Yeah, well come on. Dinner is ready and my father and should be home any minute," she grabbed his hand and walked him in the kitchen. Rasheid sat at their dinner table as Kiana set it up.

"So y'all eat dinner on this big table everyday," he asked still amazed at her house.

"Nope, we walk pass this table everyday and go eat in the garage."

"So you got jokes," he looked up at her smiling just as her father came through the front door.

"Hi Daddy!" Kiana said excitedly. She put the plate down ran up to him and gave him a hug.

"Hey baby girl," he kissed her on the side of the cheek. "Is that's the mystery guy's car parked in my spot," he dropped his briefcase and walked in the kitchen with Kiana in his arm.

"Daddy this is Rasheid. Rasheid this is my father Leon Simmons," the two shook hands staring each other in the eye. Mr. Simmons stood about three inches taller than Rasheid, dressed in a two piece suit. He was the same complexion of his daughter with a goatee, though Kiana looked more like her mother.

"You have a sturdy handshake young man. That's a good thing because I don't want my daughter being around no punk."

"Daddy leave him alone," she said still in her father's arm.

"You're my only daughter," he looked down at her. "So I'm not going to leave alone any guy that you bring into this house. He's going to have to meet my standards before he can take you out. So you better get use to it," he said as Mrs. Simmons walked into the kitchen.

"Okay everybody have a seat. Rasheid, I hope you like steak and baked potatoes."

"Yes ma'am," he took the seat next to Kiana.

Mrs. Simmons served everybody toss salad, steak, baked potatoes, corn on the cob and strawberry cake. They all ate, talked and laugh with one another throughout the whole meal. Rasheid told them how he maintained a three point two g.p.a. throughout high school and how he plans on going to college to practice law. Mr. and Mrs. Simmons were highly impressed. Mrs. Simmons felt bad about stereotyping him at first, but now after she heard how he articulated himself he won over her stamp of approval.

"So Rasheid, what do your parents do?" Mr. Simmons took a sip from his glass. Mrs. Simmons looked up wanting to know as well. Kiana held her head down hoping that he'll choose the right words.

Rasheid closed his throat, "I don't know my mother or father sir."

"You're a foster child or something?"

"No sir, my grandmother raised me until she passed away then I moved in with my aunt."

"Oh," Mr Simmons nodded his head. "Well I'm sorry to hear about that. At least you didn't let it stagnate you. It takes a lot of courage for somebody who's been through that type of lost to keep striving in life. You have a whole lot of potential and I like that. And if there is any time I can be a guidance to you in any type of way all you have to do is say the word," he extended his hand to Rasheid.

"Thank you," Rasheid shook his hand. Kiana was so happy that she almost shed a tear.

"Well we have to go, I don't want to be late for the movie," she said standing up ready to be alone with Rasheid. She figured she shared him with her parents long enough.

"The movie don't start until 8:45 and it's almost 7:30. You got over a hour," Mrs. Simmons didn't want to break up a good evening so early.

"Mom, we haven't decide what movie we're going to watch and you know the 8:45 movie is the most crowded one of we get there early we could get some good seat. So I'll be back later on tonight," she grabbed her purse off the counter.

Rasheid said his goodbyes to Mr. and Mrs. Simmons as they walked them to the door.

"You two be safe," Mrs. Simmons smiled watching her baby girl grow up right in front of her eyes.

"Okay," they said in unison as they got into Rasheid's Cadillac.

"I didn't know you was trying to go to the movies tonight," he said as he started the ignition.

"I'm not. We're going to your house," she said in a sexy tone.

Rasheid couldn't help but to smile at her, "If your mom only knewww," he sung as she blush.

"Whatever," she said as he drove off.

ChApter 23

Mrs. Karabetso passed out the quizzes from the past week. The test scores mainly gave her an idea of which students she'll have to work with and who needs more help. She wasn't expecting nobody to ace the quiz. A few students did exceptionally well but out of all her students Rasheid didn't just score the highest, he had almost a perfect score, missing only one question. This made her very inquisitive about him.

"I wasn't to please about the scores but that's okay. We're going to work together," she stood in front of the class. "You're helping me to help you, and I'm helping you to help me. Your job is to walk across that stage at the end of the year and my job is to get you there. So if there is a question about anything you don't understand in the near future, please don't be afraid or embarrass to ask questions," she said as the bell rung. "And I will see you guys tomorrow," all the students got up and headed out of class.

Rasheid walked out of class wondering how it would feel to walk across the stage with his diploma in hand. He couldn't believe he was just months away from it.

"Rasheid," Ms. Karabetso interrupted his thoughts. He looked over at her. "May I have a word with you," she took a seat at her desk. Rasheid put his bookbag on his back and walked over to her.

"Yes."

"I just wanted to congratulate you for scoring the highest on my quiz."

"Thank you," he said ready to walk off.

"Um, I also saw that you have a pretty high g.p.a. score."

"Yes ma'am."

"But how come you keep getting into trouble?"

"Excuse me," he looked at her confused.

"From my understanding you've been in trouble with the law."

"Yeah but that all stemmed from misunderstandings."

"Would you like to talk about it sometimes?" she asked intrigued.

"No thank you. I have to get to class but I appreciate your concern. See you tomorrow," he walked off. He was mysterious and now Ms. Karabetso really wanted to pick his brain.

Rasheid sat down on his bed after he counted the money he had saved up. He was less than three hundred thousand dollars away from a million. He would of never thought that he would accumulate that much money by the time he was eighteen. He laid back on the bed thinking about the eleven kilos he had left. After he sold those he was out of the drug game and there was nothing that could bring him back. Soon he'll never have to live a stressful life. He wouldn't have to worry about dealing with a bunch of people, being in the streets all day and night and constantly carrying his gun around everywhere he went. He was young and rich and soon he'll be free. Suddenly his best friend popped up in his mind. Then he wondered what Rookie was going through.

"So how much money you got left?"

"About three hundred dollars."

"Damn Deanna! You can't be blowing money just because you got it."

"Well what do you want me to do Rookie. I had to buy some things for the baby, pay a couple of bills for my mama and I had to go shopping," she said as if her going shopping was a necessity. "I went up from a size four to a six. If I end up losing my shape over this pregnancy I'ma curse this child out when he gets older."

Rookie couldn't help but laugh, "Look, on the real stop spending this money so fast. I'm locked up and ain't no telling how much money I'ma put up when it's all over with.

"Are they still trying to get you snitch on Rasheid?"

Rookie broke their eye contact as he nodded his head.

"Well what about the Blood Brothers and Eve baby daddy. How much time they gone take off if you snitch on them?" Deanna felt bad encouraging Rookie to be a snitch. But she would rather him be labeled a snitch and be with her than to see him do twenty years in prison.

"Them niggas just pawns. Rasheid is the top dog in Charleston. You gone see a hell of a drought on the streets if something was to ever happen to him. If they get the Blood Brothers the only thing they gone do to them is what they doing to me so they can try to bring down Rasheid."

"Baby I really don't want to see Rasheid go down."

"I mean I don't either Deanna but that's the rules I gotta play by," Rookie said as he felt the guilt settling on his conscience for the umpteenth time. "That's my dog," he looked away from her. "But what the fuck am I suppose to do."

"Visitations over," the guard opened the door. Rookie looked over at him then stood up.

"I love you yo, take care of my child and be easy wit the money."

"Okay baby. I love you too," Deanna said not wanting him to go.

"I'ma call you tomorrow and don't you go running your mouth to Kiana either," he held his hand up to the Plexiglas as she did the same.

"I'm not and make sure you call before ten o'clock because I gotta go to that appointment," Rookie nodded his head at her and was escorted through the door by the guard.

C.J. looked at the bag that contain four kilos of cocaine.

"Only four," he said.

"Yup. I'm at the bottom of the barrel. After I pay my connect for these bricks it's a wrap," Rasheid said.

C.J. zipped the bag up and held it in his hand looking at Rasheid.

"Ayo, what's the problem for real Rah. You getting scared. You think you going to jail, is somebody trying to kill you or something?" C.J. said knowing it was a reason why Rasheid was getting out the game.

"It ain't no problem. It's just that my time is up. The sun has set."

"Man Rasheid you just getting started baby. If you quit right now a whole lot of shit gone be fucked up in the streets. We might have to travel to Florida to get a good connect."

"I told you I'ma put a word in with my connect to try to get you in."

"But what if it don't work out," C.J. cut him off. "What if he don't want me to work for him. Look Rah," he put the bag on the floor. "Let me do all the work. You don't have to do nothing but stay connected. I'll do everything else and still give you your cut."

"Then you'll be under paid."

"Its better than getting no pay."

"C.J. I gotta roll," he looked at his watch. "I'ma put a good word in for you with my connect but right now that's all I can promise. That and I'm getting out the game. I don't want to do this no more. I'm tired of this shit. Look at me, I'm barely eighteen years old and I can pass for twenty-four. My youth is gone. The only way I can't let this shit turn me into something I don't wanna be is by getting out of it. And I mean getting out of it before it's too late," he walked off to the door then turned around and looked at C.J. "You still rolling with us to the fair?"

C.J. nodded his head.

"Aiight then. I'm holla at you," Rasheid walked out the door.

"Your skin look like its glowing," Kiana said to Deanna as she got in on the passenger side of her car and closed the door. "That pregnancy looks like it's doing you some good," she drove off.

Deanna looked at her friend and rolled her eyes. She then pulled out her mirror looking in it and adjusting her hair.

"Girl if you only knew. It seem like since I've been pregnant my pussy stay wet. Rookie locked up so I can't get no dick and I'm tired of using my two fingers," Kiana burst out laughing. "I'm tempted to go steal that long ass dildo my mama got under her mattress."

Kiana continued to laugh.

"Shit girl I'm serious. It don't make no sense how horny I am."

"No you didn't just put your mama business out there," she said.

"She'll be okay," Deanna said still looking in the mirror adjusting her hair.

"How does it feel knowing that you're about to be a mother?" she asked.

"For real, for real," Deanna put her mirror back in her purse. "The only time it feels different is when I think about it. Then it's like a strange feeling that comes over me letting know that I'm going to be responsible for a life," she used her hands to help express how she feel. "And sometimes I wonder do I really have what it takes to be the mother of this child. The other half of this child belongs to Rookie and that makes me feel even better knowing that the person I truly love with all my heart is just as much responsible for this child as I am. And I just take in a whole different feeling, I mean it's scary but in a good way, knowing that I'ma soon have my own family," Kiana listened closely to every word she said.

"Are you ready for it?"

"No," Deanna laughed. "But I don't have no choice. It's coming."

"Damn, my girl is about to have a baby," she looked at Deanna then back at the highway. "You gone let me be the God-mother?" she asked smiling.

"If you want to," Deanna smiled back.

"So does Rookie know when he's coming home?"

Her eyes wandered off, "Not really. But hopefully it'll be soon."

"Soon like when," she looked at her.

"I don't know," she looked out the window. "Hopefully next year or the after.

"Damn. That's along time."

Deanna looked over at her, "So what's up with you and Rasheid?"

"We alright," she smiled. Deanna smiled with her. "First my mother was skeptical about him but now she can't stop calling his name ever since he came over for dinner last week."

Her smile faded away as she looked out the window.

"What's wrong?" Kiana sensed her mood shift.

"Nothing. I remember when I first tried to hook y'all two up, you wasn't trying to pay him no attention and he ended up being your fist love."

Kiana blushed.

"So what made you fall for him?"

Kiana then squint her eyes trying to remember what first turned her on about Rasheid.

"I gotta say it was his attitude. At first I thought that he was acting like he was all that but then I realized that he wasn't, he was just mature for his age. And when I started taking notice to him that's when it seemed like I was always hearing wasn't matching his personality, it just made me wanted to get to know him even more," she said as her mind continued to reminisce.

"Do you think he loves you?"

"I know he do."

"How do you know?"

"Because I can see it in his eyes. I can feel it when he kiss me, when he touches and whenever we have sex… umm," she shook her head.

Deanna looked at her friend now with a big smile on her face. She knew Kiana was in love with him and she would hate to be the reason their happiness came to an end. Her smile faded once more as she gazed out the window.

Kiana looked over at her and smile.

"It's going to be alright. Rookie's coming home soon," she patted Deanna on her thigh thinking she was jealous.

"Well soon ain't soon enough so you might not want to touch my thigh like that again," she joked as her and Kiana laughed.

Rasheid drove over to his aunt's house expecting to give her a surprise visit. He felt guilty for not coming over to see her in almost three months. As he pulled up in her driveway he saw an old beat up Lincoln parked beside her Volvo. He figured it was one of her friends. As he parked his car and walked up to the door he knocked four times before an older guy probably the same age as his aunt opened the door.

"What's up man," the guy said to him.

Rasheid peeked inside the apartment.

"Is my Aunt Tereesa here?"

The guy stepped back as Tereesa walked towards the door looking like she haven't slept in days.

"Hey Rasheid," she wiped her hair down with her hands. "Um…" she looked at her friend then back at Rasheid. "So how you been doing?"

"Alright," he looked at the two sensing something wasn't right.

"Uhh Rasheid, this is an old friend of mine. Gerald," she said as the guy extended his hand to him. "This is my big nephew I was telling you about."

"How you doin man?" the guy said.

Rasheid hesitated for a moment looking back and forth at the two. He shook his hand realizing he was being rude.

"What's up."

Tereesa then stepped outside grabbed Rasheid by his arm and walked towards the driveway.

"He's over here helping me fix my toilet," she said in a low tone Rasheid just looked at her. "The other day the toilet over flooded and mess up the whole place. Want you come back later on this evening this way I can have everything cleaned up by the time you get back," she said as they stopped at Rasheid's car.

She's high. Rasheid thought to himself. He couldn't even look at her no more. Whenever something seems to go right in his life, something else always goes wrong. He was to hurt to try and say anything to his aunt, so he got in his car without saying a word. Tereesa felt the vibes he was giving off as she stood there feeling embarrassed watching him drive off.

The look Rasheid gave to her confirmed that she was messing up. She knew she came too far to turn around, but the drug had a grip around her neck. She wanted to stop but now the fight seemed worse than ever. Her will power was too weak at the moment though for some reason she knew of she didn't stop soon this would be the death of her.

Ch A p t e r 24

"Yo, turn the volume down a little bit Rasheid," C.J said sitting in the backseat as he answered his cellular phone. Rasheid turned the radio down as he stole a peak of Kiana's thigh in her mini skirt.

"Your eyes should be on the road," she said with an attitude.

"My eyes are on the road," he pinched her cheek.

"Oh, so now you wanna play," she pushed his hands away. "Earlier you had that little stink attitude. I couldn't even touch you."

"Who attitude you calling stink," he tried to stick his finger up her nose only because he knew she hated it.

"Stop!" she screamed out trying not to laugh as she kept pushing his hand back. "Stop it Rasheid before you get into a accident. Stop it!" she laughed still pushing his hand back.

C.J. ended his phone call and laid back in his seat beside his girlfriend. They both watched Rasheid and Kiana flirt with each other. His girlfriend looked over at him seeing the trouble in his face.

"What's wrong Baby," she rubbed his thigh.

C.J. shook his head as he played with his toothpick in his mouth.

"Well why you always look like you got more problems than the president?"

"I probably do," he took the toothpick out of his mouth and looked at her. "Bill Clinton don't got half of the issues I got."

"Well I hope you getting paid for them issues, cause come Christmas we need to be riding in something like this," she admired the backseat of Rasheid's Mercedes Benz.

"Oh so what. The Acura ain't good enough for you no more!"

"No Baby, I love my Acura," she placed her hand in her chest. "But this Benz feels like we riding in a airplane. We need to be pushing something like this for the new year."

"Well you need to go buy it then," he put the toothpick back in his mouth and laid back in the seat. She sucked her teeth at him as her attention went back to Rasheid and Kiana.

"Baby, I seen this crazy Louis Vuitton suit that I want you to rock to the prom. I mean haven't seen nobody with it yet."

"Then why didn't you get it for me?" Rasheid asked.

"Cause I didn't have fourty-eight hundred dollars."

"All that money your parents make, they couldn't threw you a few grand," he joked.

Kiana gave him a sarcastic look.

"What you think we're rich or something."

"Y'all are."

"Be quiet," she picked at fingernails as he laughed at her.

When they arrived to the state fair in Columbia, South Carolina, it must have been thousands of cars in the parking lot. It took them almost twenty minutes to find a parking space. When they got out the car, they were all relieved to stretch their legs out after three hours of driving. Tiffany, C.J.'s girlfriend couldn't help but wanting to compliment Rasheid on his attire. He was wearing a burgundy velour Nautica outfit with some burgundy and white air forces and a white tee shirt that complimented his built.

"Rah, let me holla at you real quick," C.J. stepped away from the girls. Rasheid walked up to him.

"I know this probably ain't the right time to be talking bout this but you might wanna rethink a lot of shit. I got a spot for us out Savannah. My man told me the coke stepped on like a motherfucker. Rah we can make hundred grand money in no time. And it could just be me and you if you want to. I can still do all the work, all you need to do is stay plugged in, lay low and stack yo bread."

Rasheid gave C.J. a pitiful look. He then saw that selling drugs was the only thing he knew how to do. The more he looked into his eyes the more he saw that he was afraid. Rasheid could of felt his pain, he understood what he was going through.

"The same thing that's going on in Savannah is going on in Charleston and every other black hood in America. This phase of my life is finished," he held his hands out. "Now its time foe bigger and better. I'm trying to have business out there. You remember that day we went on the shopping spree and you told that lady we own a record company."

C.J. nodded his head.

"Well I'm trying to be on level like that for real. We could make it happened. The only thing that's stopping us is us. All we have to do is do it," he said walking off. Kiana and Tiffany was trying to eavesdrop on what they was saying. Kiana grabbed hold of Rasheid's hand as Tiffany held C.J.'s and the four entered the park. The fairground was crowded with people. It was as if everybody in the state of South Carolina was there. The four stayed closed to each other throughout the night. If one couple got on a ride the other couple stood until they were through and vice versa. Rasheid and Kiana was having the time of their life while Tiffany was still trying to put C.J. in a mood.

"Come on Baby, let's go on the Ferris wheel," Tiffany said pulling C.J. by his arm.

"Girl you see how long that damn line is," C.J. said not wanting to go on any more rides.

"Come on Baby," she pleaded. "This is the last ride," she said as C.J. dragged along beside her.

"You said that two rides ago," he said as they stood in the back of the line.

"Kiana I'm tired, I'm about to go sit down," Rasheid said taking a seat on the bench. Kiana took a look around the fair ground as she spotted the candy apple stand.

"Rasheid!" she said excitedly. He looked up at her.

"Baby they got a candy apple stand. I haven't had candy apple since I was in elementary."

"What you expect Kiana, this is the fair," he was trying to get comfortable on the bench.

"Ha ha. Let me get some money so I can get so me."

Rasheid pulled a rolled of money out and headed her a ten dollar bill, "Get me one too."

"Nope," she took the money and walked off. Just then Rasheid's cellular phone rang. He answered it and quickly got engage into a conversation.

Kiana walked over to the candy stand and waited patiently in line as she watched all the happy faces around her. About one hundred feet from where she stood was Q and his younger cousin.

"Q, you crazy as hell for bringing a forty ounce in here," his cousin said to him.

"Man I don't give a fuck about this shit. Fuck all these motherfuckers," Q said taking another sip another sip from his bottle. As he took the bottle from his mouth and screwed the top back on, he took a good look around. Suddenly he just paused staring long and hard, squinted his eyes then shaking his head in disbelief," I know this ain't that motherfucker," he said as he looked back up to see that it was to Rasheid. "That is that motherfucker!" he felt the anger raging through his body as his mind went back to what Rasheid did to his mother and sister. When he heard that N.O. got killed and all of his home boys were put into the hospital he fled town knowing that he would have been next. But when he found out what had happened to his mother and sister, he promised on his life that when he ever laid his eyes on Rasheid again he was going to kill him. And the time was now.

"Here's your candy apple and your change. Thank you."

"Thank you," Kiana said to the guy behind the stand as she took the candy and walked off. She looked up to see Rasheid still talking on his cellular phone with his head down. She then took another look around the fair. She wish that her girl Deanna was there with her. She would

have felt a lot more comfortable. She then saw a familiar face that was
out of place. She couldn't stop looking at the guy, probably because he
was the only one who didn't seem happy. Then she noticed something
else. He was staring at somebody. She looked to see who he was staring
at and the direction in his eyes looked as if they were directed towards
Rasheid. Suddenly something really was out of place. The guy pulled out
a gun and had it aimed directly at Rasheid. Kiana then panicked so hard
her thoughts wouldn't enter her mind fast enough. All she knew was
that someone was trying to kill her man as she dropped the candy and
ran towards him.

"RASHEID!" she yelled out. People started ducking and screaming
when they saw it was a guy brandishing his gun.

Rasheid looked up at Kiana puzzled putting the phone down. He
then heard the bullets but didn't have a clue where it was coming from.
Within seconds the fairgrounds was scattered with people running in
every direction. Kiana then jumped on top of Rasheid causing them both
to fall on the ground as two more shots were fired. C.J. then came out of
nowhere with his gun in hand aimed directly at Q. The first shot he fired
went through Q's shoulder almost causing him to fall down. Q then aimed at
his new target not even realizing he's been shot yet. He shot twice in the
direction of C.J. as C.J. was already laying on him send a shot in the
center of Q's chest but he was a split second too late. He felt the bullet
burned through his midsection causing him to fall down. Rasheid quickly
grabbed his gun and aimed in the direction the shooting was coming from.
All he heard now was a bunch of screaming and yelling. No more shots
were fired. He then felt something was wrong as he felt the blood pouring
down his body.

"Baby I think I got hit," he said pushing Kiana up as she flopped
back down on him. Rasheid looked at Kiana as his heart pumped faster
than it ever did before in his life. He then looked back down at his
midsection realizing that he wasn't shot. The blood was coming from
her. "Oh shit!" he said as his voice cracked. He quickly got up and laid
her on her back. "Kiana," he said softly as the tears felt helplessly from his
face. "Baby get up," he said holding her arms up as it felt back to the
ground. "Baby please…no..," he cried still trying to pick her up. "Get up
Kiana….I have to take you home…baby….come on baby….Kiana,"

he looked up at her again and saw that her eyes were sealed tight. Her mouth was wide open. If it wasn't for her whole body covered in blood she'll look as if she was asleep.

"Kiana," Rasheid said now picking her up. "Kiana!!!!"

⸻

Rasheid sat in the waiting room of Richland Memorial Hospital covered in blood not able to believe what just took place. Tiffany sat in the chair beside him trying to get a hold of herself. He looked over at her seeing how traumatized she looked and that confirmed that this was all real. Just hours ago him and Kiana was at the fair having the time of their life and now he was in the hospital waiting on her while she was being operated on. Just then Mr. and Mrs. Simmons bursted through the door with the look of confusion and worry written all over their face. When they spotted Rasheid they quickly walked in his direction .

"Rasheid," Mrs. Simmons said as he stood up. "What happened," she looked at all the blood on his clothes which obvious didn't belong to him. The tears then started to dwell in her eyes. "What happened Rasheid?" she said now grabbing him. "Where's my daughter?"

Rasheid opened his mouth but the words wouldn't come out. He didn't have the strength or could find the words to tell this woman her only child just got shot.

"Rasheid. What happened?" Mr. Simmons said in a tone as if he was ready to take matters in his own hands.

"We was…we was at…" he stuttered trying to get the words out as his eyes wondered everywhere but in the direction of Mr. and Mrs. Simmons. "We was at… we was at the fair….. and," the tears started to fall down his face. The doctor then came from out of the back room looking in the direction of the three. Silenced filled the room as they watched him back with anticipation.

"The parents or closes relatives of Kiana Simmons."

Mr. and Mrs. Simmons heart started beating faster when they heard their daughter name.

"We're the parents," Mr. Simmons said as they walked in his direction. The doctor eyes fell down as he looked back up at the two. No matter how many times he went through this procedure, it was just something he could never get used to.

"I'm sorry," he took a deep breath. "Your daughter didn't make it. We done everything we could."

Mrs. Simmons shook her head knowing he had the wrong person. Mr. Simmons held her tight as the tears fell down his face.

"Not my daughter!" Mrs. Simmons cried out. "You've got the wrong one! She's only seventeen! Leon!" she gave her husband a hysterical look. "He can't be talking about our baby! He's not talking about Kiana!" she cried out stealing the sympathy from the administration and everyone else in the room. "He's not talking about Kiana!" her husband held her tightly in her arms as she cried in his shoulders. "Not my baby!" The room was definitely filled with emotions. Just a little too much for Rasheid to bare as his knees gave out on him. He cried helplessly on the floor. "Rasheid!" Mrs. Simmons yelled out pushing her husband away. "Rasheid. What you done to my child," she was now walking in his direction. Rasheid didn't even look up. He was now lying on the floor face down crying his heart out. "Rasheid," she pulled at his shirt. "What you done to my baby. What you done to my baby!" she screamed out as she started kicking and punching his back. Mr. Simmons ran over to her, picked her up and took her outside as she continued to scream at the top of her lungs. "God damn you Rasheid! I hope you burn in hell! I hope you fucking burn hell!" she screamed as her husband took her outside. Rasheid still didn't move from his position on the floor. He couldn't help but to feel Mrs. Simmons was right. No matter who fired the shots he was still responsible for what happened and why it happened. He was responsible for what happened to C.J. and he was responsible for the death of Kiana.

Ch Apter 25

"Rasheid! Rasheid!" Eve yelled out pounding as hard as she could at his door. She then stepped back and looked through the windows.

"He's in here Tremaine," she said pounding to the door again.

"Let me try it," Tremaine said as she stepped to the side. "Rasheid!" he pounded even harder. "Dis Tremaine and Eve! Open the door so we could talk to you man!" he stepped back and looked at the door.

"He ain't in there," he looked at Eve ready to give up.

"He gotta be in there. All of his cars are here," she knocked to the door again. Then for the first time she turned the knob and the door opened with no problem. "Damn," she gave Tremaine a stupid look as they both entered the apartment and closed the door behind them.

"Rasheid!" Tremaine yelled out as they both headed upstairs.

"Rasheid," Eve opened his room door seeing him passed out across his bed with the same bloody clothes he had on the day of Kiana's death. "Rasheid," Eve nudged him.

Rasheid then jumped up looking dumbfounded in the face.

"Are you alright," she sat down next to him on the bed. Rasheid looked over at her then at Tremaine trying to gather his thoughts. He then shook his head and wiped his eyes as he took a second look at them. "You alright," she asked again.

"Where's Kiana?" he asked knowing when he fell asleep she was beside him.

"Rasheid," Eve whispered rubbing the back of his head. "Kiana's dead."

The words ate straight through his chest as he remembered holding her lifeless body in his arms.

"I figured since you wasn't at her wake this morning I should of at least come to see how you was doing," Eve said.

"Her wake," Rasheid looked up at Eve. "Her wake was this morning?"

"Yeah Rasheid. Are you okay?" she said now looking at him concerned.

"What's today?" he asked.

Eve looked at Tremaine then back at him.

"Rasheid today is Thursday. And her funeral is tomorrow."

"Tomorrow," he said still looking puzzled.

"Damn dog. You really are fucked up," Tremaine looked Rasheid up and down.

"You are really scaring me Rasheid. Now you need to get yourself together cause I never seen you like this before."

Rasheid looked up at Eve then down at the floor.

"Her funeral is tomorrow?" the tears fell down his face. Eve almost started crying when she seen how pitiful he looked. She then pulled his head towards her and gave him a hug holding him tightly in her arms.

"You have to pull yourself together Rasheid," she said rubbing his back. "That was messed up what happened to your girlfriend but it's not your fault," he pushed her away and stood up.

"It was my fault," he said as some spit came out of his mouth as he walked over to his dresser and looked at himself in the mirror. "Q was trying to shoot me but she jumped in the way," he looked at Eve in the mirror as the tears fell free from his face. "She fucking jumped in the way of my bullet," he said breaking down again. Eve walked up to him and grabbed his shoulder.

"Rasheid," she whispered. "What is meant to be will be. God don't make no mistakes. You can't keep blaming yourself for what happened. It was a tragic loss but you are still alive, you are still living. You think that Kiana would want to see you like this? Rasheid, you got to get yourself together. If not for you then at least do it for her," she said as he wiped the tears from his eyes.

"Ay look," he paused for a few seconds. "I'm straight. Thanks for coming by."

Eve looked in his eyes and could tell that he wasn't alright, "Are you sure. You don't need me to get you nothing."

"Nah. I'm straight," he said without looking at her. "I just need to be by myself."

Eve looked over at Tremaine as he gave her the signal it was time to leave. She then looked back at Rasheid hoping he wouldn't do nothing crazy.

"You sure you're going to be okay Rasheid?"

"Yeah," he nodded his head as he looked up at her. His eyes were blood shot red. Eve saw that he was really hurt.

"Well I'll be back to check on you," she walked out the door still looking at him. "You take it easy. I'ma see you later."

Tremaine walked out behind her," Keep your head up Rah. You gone get through this," he said as he closed the door.

Rasheid went into a daze as he looked at himself in the mirror. He sat in his Cadillac watching Kiana relatives and friends from school entered the church. He noticed there were a lot of cars that had Michigan license plates in the parking lot. He didn't get a chance to see her parents but he saw Deanna walking in looking devastated as she was accompanied with some guy he wasn't familiar with. He had doubts about entering the church. How could he face her parents when he was the reason their only child was lying in a coffin. After everyone entered the church he could have heard the music playing from the inside. He still didn't have the strength to go inside but he had to see her one last time and this was his last chance to do it. He felt the tears mustering up in his eyes again as he wiped his face with his hands then checked his reflection in the mirror. After debating back and forth with his thoughts about going inside he forced himself to open the car door and step out. He walked slowly to the door, the closer he got the louder and clearer the music became. He held his hand on the knob as he felt it turned and someone opened it from the inside. A middle aged man dressed in a suit walked out as Rasheid got a glance on the inside but he quickly shut the door behind him.

"Hey," he smiled as he got into the hearse and drove off.

Rasheid watched as the car disappeared down the street then put his attention back on trying to enter the church. He put his hand on the door knob the second time and this time he opened the door. His heart was racing as he took the first step into the church and looked around at everyone whose attention was at the front alter where the preacher stood and Kiana's body laid perfectly still in a coffin. She was beautiful as ever, dressed in a white gown with her hair coming down to her shoulders. The usher closed the door as everyone's attention went to the back of the church. Rasheid suddenly felt out of place as most of the eyes in the church rested on him. He then spotted an available seat near Deanna as he walked in her direction. Some of the people in the church watched him closely as he could of felt the few people talking under their breaths. Suddenly Mrs. Simmons turned around sensing the barely noticeable commotion in the back of the church and spotted Rasheid walking over to a seat.

"Hell no," she said in an exhausted voice tears pouring down her face as she stood up facing the back of the church. "Get the hell out!" she screamed as everyone looked on in shock. Rasheid stopped in his tracks looking at the floor then continuing on his way to his seat as he carried the pain and guilt along with him. Mr. Simmons tried to grab his wife. She pushed him away walking towards the back of the church. "You killed my daughter! You drug dealing son of a bitch killed my daughter!" her husband and a couple ushers picked her up and took her to the back, "I wish it was you who got killed! You should be laying in the casket!" she yelled trying to fight them off. Your drug dealing ass suppose to be dead!" she cried out as they finally got her in the back of the church. "Not my ba-by!" she managed to scream out before they closed the door. Everyone else was looking back and forth from Mrs. Simmons and Rasheid. They didn't know if she was over reacting or if he was really responsible for the death of Kiana. The preacher tried to pick up his sermon where he left off as Rasheid took a seat next to Deanna feeling more humiliated and pain than he ever felt before in his life. He looked at Kiana lying in the casket. He was never going to get the chance to say that he was sorry and how much she meant to him. He was never going to get the chance to move her away from Charleston or experience life in college with her. As he sat there with his elbows rested on his knees and his hands locked on front of his face staring at her body, he couldn't take it no more. He got up and ran out of the church. Everyone looked on until he ran out the door leaving it wide open. With tears racing down his eyes he got in his car and drove off with no destination in mind.

After hours of driving he somehow ended up in his driveway. He got out of the car entered his apartment and walked upstairs to his room. He then sat on the bed staring at the floor. He wished that it was somewhere he could go to pay somebody some money so that he could go back in time a week earlier. Knowing that was impossible he then turned his head as his eyes greeted his .45 on the floor by his dresser. He stared at the gun for a moment then picked it up. He examined it as he held it in his hand. He then looked in the mirror as guilt settled in his heart. He thought about his grandmother, his aunt Tereesa, Dre, Tania, Rookie and now Kiana. He couldn't understand why everybody in his life who he loved he seemed to always lose. He didn't want to go on living anymore. As he felt the cold metal barrel to his temple he closed his eyes and squeezed the trigger.

"Stop it Jarrell," the little girl yelled at her classmate. "Mrs. Davis can you tell Jarrell to stop hitting me," she wined.

"Jarrell," Ms. Davis sat behind her desk. "I already have a meeting with your mother after school. Don't make me add on to your list of behavior problems," she said as if it was rehearsed. "Damn that boy is bad as hell," she whispered to Tania who was staring at him," Get ready for it, because your patience is going to have to be long of you want to do this," she continued grading some papers still whispering to Tania. Tania smiled at her as her attention remained on the boy.

She was now working as an intern at Richneck Elementary School in Newport News, Virginia. She tried to leave every problem she had in Charleston, in Charleston. Money was tight once again but she wasn't dead broke. She got back on the dating scene, she met some interesting people but nobody who she could see a future with. Rasheid still haunted the back of her mind like a ghost from her childhood but she blocked him out every chance she got. It was time for bigger and better things to happen in her life and he was definitely not a part of it. As she took her attention from the boy and back to what Mrs. Davis was saying she noticed a middle aged light skin woman entering the classroom just as the bell rung. All the students besides Jarrell exited out the classroom.

"Mrs. Roundtree?" Mrs. Davis asked standing up changing her tone of voice as the woman approached her.

"Yes, Mrs. Davis, I'm sorry I couldn't make it down here earlier but I had some affairs with my husband," she said shaking Mrs. Davis hand.

"Oh-no. It's okay," Mrs. Davis said as they both took a seat. Tania grabbed her things and was about to leave out.

"Ms. Tania you might want to stay for this. Oh this is my assistant for today Ms. Tania Roberts. She's an intern," she said as Tania and the woman shook hands. The two then engaged into a conversation about the behavior problems of the boy as he sat next to his mother with an embarrassed look. Tania continued to look at the child as she couldn't help but feel sorry for him.

"If I may add, if you don't mind Mrs. Davis," Tania interjected the two. "Oh no. Go right ahead," Mrs. Davis wanted to hear what she had to say as the two women listened on.

"Well I think that Jarrell is very intelligent, he just need someone to not force but show him different avenues he'll end up in life so he can have a better understanding of why he should not do this or that. Instead of people telling him what not to do then punishing him afterwards," she said as the child looked at her surprised. Both women listened on. "Our children today, especially young boys already feel like the mass is against them. But if they don't have that direct relationship with their parents or teacher then they're going to feel like you to are against them as well and that's when they go look for love or understanding elsewhere. These days children are joining gangs at a very young age. Selling drugs, ending up dead or in prison. So we need to establish the line of communication with them so that they could be confident that we got their back."

Mrs. Roundtree looked down at her son and closed her eyes for a few seconds then looked up at Tania. When they finished their meeting Tania gathered her things together said bye to the two and walked out of the room. Mrs. Roundtree and her son followed her.

"Excuse me, Ms. Tania," she walked up behind her.

Tania turned around smiling, "Yes."

"That was well put ," she said as the two stood face to face. "Do you have any children?"

"No," she shook her head. "But I had a friend who use to act like he was a child sometimes and you know being with him helped me learned a whole lot about men," she laughed as Mrs. Roundtree laughed with her.

"Yeah I heard you. So you're just getting out of college?"

"Yes I went to the University of Charleston in South Carolina."

"Oh really!" she said shocked. "I'm from South Carolina. Matter of fact I'm from Charleston. North Charleston," she smiled.

"I'm from North Charleston too," Tania said as they touched each other hands.

"That's maybe why we have so much in common," Mrs. Roundtree added.

"That's where our foundation is," Tania said. "That's probably why your son caught my attention because he reminded me a lot of my boyfriend in Charleston. They look like they could almost be brothers," she said as the woman smile started to ease away. Tania didn't noticed, she continued to run off her mouth. "But I use to tell him all the time about the choices he made. He is very smart, he just made stupid choices. So now when I see children who have potential I try to correct it early on in their life," she said not even realizing the last few words she said she was talking to herself.

"So how old is your boyfriend," she said grabbing her son hand as he shot her an impatient look.

Tania eyes went to the corner of her head," he just turned eighteen in July, the woman now looked as if she seen a ghost.

"He turned eighteen in July?" Tania started to get worried about her asking questions. "It wasn't by chance July eighteenth was it?" she said hoping it wasn't.

Tania now looked at the woman shocked. Something was going on that she didn't know about.

"Yes, how did you know that?"

The woman went into her own mental zone blocking Tania out. She was now reliving that tragic chapter in her life she thought she closed forever but deep down she always knew it would come back to haunt her.

"Mom, are you alright?' the boy asked startled by his mother's behavior. She just held his hand even tighter.

"What's his name if you don't mind me asking?"

"His name is Rasheid," Tania looked at the woman like she was crazy. "Are you okay?" she asked thinking that the woman would have a nervous breakdown or something.

"You wouldn't happened to have a picture of him would you?"

Tania looked at the woman then opened her purse and took out her wallet looking for the wallet size picture of her and Rasheid took together. When she found it she pulled it out and gave it to her. The woman took the picture, after looking at it a few seconds she broke down crying holding her hand to her mouth. Tania grabbed the woman dropping her belongings on the floor.

"Are you alright?" she asked as the woman was still looking at the picture crying. "Do you know him or something?" she was still holding on to the women.

Mrs. Roundtree looked at the picture wiping the tears from her eyes.

"His name is Rasheid Willis," she looked at Tania. Born July eighteenth nineteen eighty-two," after a long pause she looked down at her child then back at Tania. "He's my son."

Epilogue

Rasheid stood up with the rest of his classmates as he blocked out everything else that was being said. His mind kept centering around Rookie. He got sentenced to sixteen years in prison at eighteen years old. When he heard the news his heart was broken. He couldn't even bring himself to visit him yet. No matter how lavish the lifestyle appears to be, at the end everyone loses. There was a lot of rumors floating around that Rookie snitched on the Blood Brothers to cut his time in half and regardless or not if that's true, as of now it doesn't even matter. It definitely wouldn't change anything. This puzzle would still be a messed up picture. Rasheid looked around at all the joyous faces around him and tried to come to grips with his own happiness. He made it all the way to where he promised his grandmother he would make it but he still felt incomplete. It was like he cheated on the way. It was by the grace of God that the day he almost committed suicide the gun was on safety or else he wouldn't be standing here right now. He kept browsing the crowd hoping that he would see his Aunt Tereesa or look up and catch Kiana not paying any attention but not seeing either of them only made him harden his heart a little more. Especially after realizing the pain he brought to her parents. He knew the only way he could get pass this was to keep moving through it. Hopefully he'll have a better understanding in the years to come. He looked ahead at the line as he watched his classmates step on stage and received their diploma. He then thought about where he would have been had his mother and father raised him. The difference his life would have been was unfathomable. Coming home from school to a mother preparing dinner right before his dad got off from work. He'll imagine himself helping his mother set up the dinner tabled as his little brother or sister was running around the house. He smiled to himself then concentrated back on the graduation. He was graduating today. The day that seem to take so long to get here is now looking him in the face. The only thing he hoped was that he made his grandmother proud. As he looked up at the podium. The principal announced the girl in front of him as he fixed his composure. Ironically he was the last to cross the stage. There was a lot of cheers for her whom he remembered seeing occasionally. Then he looked up at the stage. It was his turn.

"Rasheid Willis," the principal said as he stepped on stage. Rasheid got to center stage and to his surprise, people was really cheering for him. He took his diploma as he shook the principal's hand and looked at the audience. They was really cheering for him. He waved his diploma at the audience as he stepped off stage with the rest of his classmates as they all then looked up at the principal.

"You have in your hands a key that could be used to unlock the doors that stand before you as you unravel through the journey that awaits you. The world is your stage and I hope you do with it as you may. To the class of nineteen ninety-nine," they all through their graduation caps in the air as everyone greeted their family members. Rasheid smiled as he looked around at everyone hugging and kissing each other. He made his way around his classmates then figured he'll go home and pack his bags. He didn't know where he was going, but he knew he was leaving Charleston.

"Alright Rasheid. Take care man," a classmate said to him.

"Thank you man. You take care too," he said as he patted the guy on his back. Then as he turned around he couldn't believe his eyes. It was Tania. And she looked better than ever. Rasheid literally was at a lost for words. She was so beautiful he just wanted to scoop her off her feet. She couldn't hide how she felt as well. Her hair was cut in a new style. She had in a beige skirt that stopped right above her knees. She smiled at him as she waved. "Congratulations," she said.

He couldn't believe she was standing in front of him. He wanted to start kissing her right then and there. Instead he tried to keep his composure. "Thanks."

"You finally did it. I'm proud of you."

Rasheid just looked at her. He didn't even notice the woman standing next to her. He took this as the chance to fix their past. He knew God was giving him another chance at happiness and he wasn't going to ruin it.

"Tania I'm sorry about everything I ever done. You was right from the beginning." She held her hand at him as she shook her head. "Baby please let me explain. This is the least I owe you. That day you left I-"

"Rasheid," she stopped him. "I'm not here to talk about that."

"Baby, I'm just so sorry about what I done in the past and I made a promise to myself if I ever got the chance to explain that to you I would," Tania shook her head as she closed her eyes. Rasheid approached her as he grabbed her hand. "Baby just listen to me just this one time and then you're free to do whatever you wish but I have to get this off my chest. You was right about everything," he said as a tear came down his cheek. "I was just so caught up I couldn't see what I was turning into. You're the only thing that matter to me. You're who I want. I don't want to do this without you. I'm sorry about everything I've done and I just want the opportunity to make this up to you. And that's all I'm asking. Just don't cut me out of your life. I'm getting punished enough," he said as a tear came down her face as well. "Baby...I missed you," she wiped the tear from her face as she grabbed his hand and put them by his side. Rasheid just looked at her.

"Rasheid," she wiped the tear from her face. "I came here to introduce you to someone," she said as he just looked at her. She then turned to the woman as Rasheid looked over at the lady for the first time then back at Tania. He then looked back at the woman and noticed her eyes were teary as well. He held a confused expression as he looked back at Tania. Then something struck him as well as he looked back at the woman. He didn't know what was going on but his intuition felt strong towards her. He then looked back at Tania as he waited for her to explain.

"What's going on?"

She smiled at him as another tear came down her face.

"Rasheid," her voice cracked. "I would like to introduce you to Mrs. Jennifer Roundtree. Your mother."

Rasheid looked over at the woman as his heart raced. He tried to contain himself as he wiped the tears out of his eyes. He looked back at the woman again with his eyes full of tears. "You my mother?" he asked.

"Yes," Jennifer said as she broke down crying. "Yes. I'm your mother."

www.ingramcontent.com/pod-product-compliance
Lightning Source LLC
Chambersburg PA
CBHW032032240626
47154CB00003B/881